COCONUT

Dear Anastasia —
Sometimes your life can end up
being so much more than you
hoped for!

Maul Paull H

COCONUT

BROWN ON THE OUTSIDE, WHITE ON THE INSIDE

MANUEL PADILLA JR.

Library of Congress Control Number: 2020920505
ISBN: Hardcover   978-1-6641-3717-2
               Softcover   978-1-6641-3716-5
               eBook   978-1-6641-3715-8

Print information available on the last page.

Rev. date: 11/06/2020

To order additional copies of this book, contact:
Xlibris
844-714-8691
www.Xlibris.com
Orders@Xlibris.com
820391

CONTENTS

For Ed, Ray and Father B.

INTRODUCTION

In the mid-1980s, an interesting phenomena began in America, notably within Los Angeles. At the time, I was working as a grant-writing assistant for a non-profit mental health agency that addressed the needs of the underserved. Within a short period of time, we began to see large influxes of Central American refugees who were seeking treatment after leaving their war-torn countries. This arrival mirrored what was happening throughout the country – immigrants were coming to America in large masses.

We had several bilingual counselors and continued to add to those numbers as the caseloads of Spanish-speaking refugees grew. In my job, it was not important that I spoke Spanish as I wasn't directly involved with the clients. This was good, as at the time I barely spoke a word of Spanish, although I am Mexican-American. Strike that. After taking a DNA test a few years back, I learned I am 51% European, the majority of which is Spanish, so I have since been refocusing my lens which was always based on my understanding that my roots were firmly placed as an American of Mexican descent. It is interesting to suddenly learn that your ancestry was not what you had spent your life understanding it to be. I occasionally test myself to see if I feel any different with this knowledge. Nope, still the same person.

I was born in America in the early 1960s. At that time, speaking Spanish was frowned upon, in fact it was shunned, so my parents chose not to teach their children the language. They were born in America in the 1930s and learned Spanish from their immigrant parents.

Now, before you go labeling my parents as being unfit for not teaching their children their native tongue, understand they were behaving in the manner in which a great many Latinos raised their children at the time. Assimilation was integral to the fabric of the country, and coming just a few years after McCarthyism, any deviation from the tried and true definition of being an "American" could be viewed as being subversive. Having a Spanish accent meant being labelled as a "beaner" or worse. Plus, we looked like minorities and there was still a great deal of prejudice throughout America. My parents didn't want to put us at any additional disadvantage by choosing to teach us Spanish and perhaps burdening us with an accent that could be fodder for those looking for any excuse to discriminate. The vast majority of Latino students in my school were raised in a similar manner. Having been born and raised in Los Angeles' San Fernando Valley, my elementary and high schools were attended by every nationality. Spanish was not spoken there nor in any other schools that we knew of: it was not spoken in stores, not spoken at the Department of Motor Vehicles. Speaking Spanish just wasn't something that was done.

Getting back to my role at the counseling agency and how quickly this all changed. I remember going to a work lunch once at a Mexican restaurant. We had guacamole on the table and I asked one of the Spanish-speaking counselors who was militant about race relations to "pass the guacamole." She blew up at me (apparently she had been holding some sort of resentment). She said, "Gawd, can't you even pronounce guacccaaammollleeee right? What kind of Mexican are you? Are you ashamed of your race?" That struck deeply as I wasn't really ashamed of anything. I was raised as an American, nothing more, nothing less. Now, I found myself in the mid-1980s, working in a multicultural environment and suddenly everyone was speaking Spanish and expecting me to do the same. I began to get resentful as I recalled what it was like to live in America in the sixties, and now, suddenly what was being expected of me. It was as if my country was being taken over by people who spoke in tongues and I began to feel like an outsider in my own city.

Other things were going on in America during the same time. As more and more refugees and immigrants began coming to America – and Los Angeles specifically – I began to see familiar things change. This wasn't the America I grew up in and I didn't know who these people were. They weren't like me and they had different customs. Strangers soon began treating me like an immigrant based upon my "look." I remember registering to vote outside a department store one day. A man was parking his bicycle behind the registration table and I heard him utter, "Don't you need a green card to register to vote?" I didn't pay attention at the time as I assumed he was talking to himself or someone else. It finally hit me when I was driving home from the store – I was the only person at the registration stand at the time, so the insult was meant for me. It really made me angry as I thought we were getting past all that.

Years later, I was a newspaper real estate editor. In attending social events, I would wear a tuxedo and carry a camera to photograph the happenings. During one event, a fellow guest asked me to bring him a scotch and soda. I looked around, realizing he thought I was a waiter. My responses had gotten quicker as I had matured, so I responded, "I'm an editor not a waiter" and walked away. I bet he never made that assumption again.

I should add that the reason I was a newspaper editor was because I have a bachelor's degree in Journalism. I received my degree during a time when less than 8 percent of Latinos earned a college degree. My older brother, who got his first degree in 1979, was the first to graduate from a university in our family. He did so during a time when only 7.5 percent of Latinos graduated from college. These mentions are not meant as bragging rights. While attending college, it was pretty clear how small a number of minority students were on campus. Our attendance at college may be based upon our upbringing. My father graduated from high school and my mother left during eleventh grade to marry my father. This was common at the time. Advanced education just wasn't emphasized as a priority per se, in part because there were far greater limitations on minorities pursuing professional careers. Within our family, as youths, we were given two options upon high school graduation: 1) Continue with education, live at home and pay no rent; or, 2) Get a job, live at home and pay rent or move out. So, you can guess which path I took. Oh, and according to census statistics, 17.4 percent of Hispanics were enrolled in college in 2016, so progress is being made.

One of the themes in "Coconut" is *la familia*, the family. The family was and remains a very powerful influence within the Latino culture. For many, the family is the center of everything, and its care, cultivation and nourishment takes precedence above all else. Offspring are expected to plan their futures around the potential needs of the family, and there is rarely talk of topics such as "nursing homes" as it is expected the children will care for aging parents. As we were raised to be "Americans," the philosophy of *la familia* was not emphasized in our household. It was expected that we would be born, grow and leave the nest to fulfill our destinies whatever they may be. Growing up, I did see the *familia* mentality in many other families, and it always perplexed me that parents would limit the future of their children based upon what I perceived as an out-of-date parenting model. As I have gotten older, I have come to better appreciate the virtues of *la familia,* however that has not changed a thing in the direction of my life, nor has it stopped me from reinforcing the importance of education with my nieces and nephews.

Within "Coconut" there are uses of racist terms such as "wetback" and "beaner." It is important to understand what these terms mean to those of Latin descent. They are highly charged, derogatory expressions which can carry the same weight as the "N" word. I'd go so far as to say they are the Latinx versions of that expression and carry similar negative connotations.

Over time I have come to accept that ignorance often results in the use of these terms. I am at peace being an American of Latin descent, and now understand I can appreciate the gifts I have been given as a person with ethnic roots. As I have matured, I have come to embrace all cultures and nationalities coming to our country as I think we are a far richer nation because of it.

Within our race, perceptions of what Latinos are continues to change. When I was young, I was considered "Mexican American." In the sixties, we became "Chicanos." Now, we have a new term, "Latinx." So, you see, we continue to evolve.

Over the years I have made attempts to learn Spanish. At this point, I WANT to learn Spanish, but I understand that unless you speak any foreign language continuously, the odds are it won't stick. And, sorry yes, to me Spanish remains a "foreign" language, as it was not something that I was directly raised with. I don't blame my parents for not teaching me nor my brothers Spanish. They were doing what was expected of Americans at the time – to become one of the squares in the big quilt known as Americanness.

As time continues to show, we still have the other thing, that prejudice thing. It was bad at times when I was growing up and it continues to rear its ugly head – just when we think we are making progress. That is why "Coconut" exists.

CHAPTER 1

BEANER

"Beaner! Beaner! Beaner! Get away from here you smelly beaner!" The words etched like hot burning coals into the five-year-old mind of Aurelio Rodrigo. "Get off of this merry-go-round. You don't belong here. Go back to stinking TiAjuana."

As the pair spun round on the metal apparatus, Aurelio looked at the little girl who screamed the confusing words at him and considered the situation as only a child could.

"What's a beaner?" was his first thought. He deducted from the little blond girl's harsh manner that it wasn't a very acceptable thing. He surmised that it must be something quite bad, considering her tone and the way that blue veins were bulging in her freckled little neck. Further, he reasoned that he must perhaps be one of them and that concerned him. He looked down at his chocolate brown arms, rubbed the perspiration from the brow beneath his straw black hair and hung his head down toward his flat and wide bare feet. He thought once again, "Does this have something to do with being a beaner?"

"Am I a beaner?"

Aurelio, who most often was referred to as "Oree," began to feel light-headed, and sweat began running down his flush cheeks. In his young mind he tried to piece together why he was being called something that didn't sound very nice, in fact it sounded really bad.

He had heard the word before but he had never been called it himself, so he wondered what had changed to make him worthy of being called such a name.

He spun around on the merry-go-round trying to make sense of it all as the little girl continued to glare in anger. In considering everything, even in his young mind, he knew he had done nothing wrong, which was even more confusing. He was suddenly very hot and bubbling up through his perspiration, he felt shame and guilt, like the times his mother punished him for misbehaving. Then, he began to feel like he wanted to cry. The words had hurt him, not like getting stung by a bee or falling off his bike, but instead it hurt *from the inside.* As the little girl continued to scowl, he grew concerned that she might try to hit him, so he felt it was best to take action – and quickly.

He jumped off Brand Park's steel-gridded merry-go-round, skinned his right knee during his fall onto the sand and ran off to find his mother.

"Momma, mama, mommy, what's a beaner?" he said, crying in part because of his hurt knee, but also because of the unmistakable feeling that he had been wronged. He felt a lump of dry spit clog in the crux of his throat as his sobbing continued.

Maria Rodrigo, who was reading the *National Enquirer* on a bench under the canopy of an olive tree, looked down at her child and saw tears welling up in his dark brown eyes.

"Aye *mijo*, who called you that name?" Maria asked, spitting on a Kleenex she had pulled from her sleeve and cleaning his bloody knee with it. *Mijo*, or my son, but only dearer, was a term of endearment Maria used when her children were in need. "Now, who hurt you Oree?"

"That little girl over there," he pointed. "She made me get off the merry-go-round and I fell. She called me a beaner and said to go back to Tiajuana. Where's Tiajuana?"

Maria wiped the tears from his cheeks and began to rub his back which always seemed to calm him down when he was upset. As she rubbed, she thought carefully about her response. She had been in similar situations with her other two children, and she knew there was no easy answer.

She finally spoke as Aurelio's breath calmed. "Beaner is a bad word. One which we don't use. People use it sometimes to describe Mexicans. Only stupid people use that word, and Tijuana is pronounced as 'Tee-juana,' not Tiajuana. T.J. is part of Mexico, the place where your grandparents came from," Maria said calmly.

Looking over toward the merry-go-round, she spied upon the pink and white mound of flesh in a yellow, gingham sundress and white sandals. The glob hopped on and off the merry-go-round as two pigtails flopped up and down in the air. Maria could tell the girl was much older and bigger than Aurelio and she could easily beat him up. Given the topic and the size of the little girl, she didn't want to draw too much attention to the situation.

"Sit with me a minute, you're too hot and you know you get bloody noses when you're overheated," Maria said. "Maybe the little girl will get tired of the merry-go-round and you can have it all to yourself."

"Here, have some Kool-Aid," she said, pouring the sweet red liquid from her steel-grey Thermos into a cup. Aurelio, seemed to calm down as he took sips, the whole time his eyes remaining fixed on the little girl spinning round and round.

Maria sat back against the bench with the paper clutched in one hand and the Thermos in the other. She thought back to the time of her youth. Of wintery Saturday afternoons at the movies when the Mexican, Asian and Negro children were ushered up to cold balconies while the Anglo children sat in the heatered warmth of the main auditorium. Of standing in lines at Woolworths, where fair-skinned, little girls always seemed to get waited on before her: "No little girl, the blond one was here first. I saw. Don't your parents teach you about manners, about taking cuts?" Of school teachers who on the first day of class asked Maria if she spoke English: *Se Hablan Engles?*

She remembered her first year in middle school and how her best friend who was Anglo, suddenly didn't seem to know her when they switched from elementary to junior high schools, and how the *pachucas* from Mexico would surround her and taut her with names like "*gavacha.*" She wasn't brown enough and she wasn't white enough.

Her memories were interrupted when Aurelio let out a big belch. "Much better!" he exclaimed, handing her back the cup lid which she put back on the Thermos.

Maria looked over and saw the little girl still spinning around on the merry-go-round. She thought it best to ignore what happened and hoped that the little girl had forgotten her earlier treatment of Aurelio.

"Well, you ready to go back to the merry-go-round?" Maria asked Aurelio, whose lips were now a bright red.

"Yup, not gonna let her call me any other names," Aurelio said.

"No," Maria stopped him. "Just ignore her. We all have to learn to get along, and some times that means just turning the other cheek."

Maria understood the world of the 1960's was not a place where prejudice should be tolerated, but that sometimes it was best to just ignore things. She held out hope that things like this would continue to improve with time. After all, we had the Kennedys and there was Martin Luther King who told us that we all would overcome (she remained curious as to when that would be happening). She also knew that her son, as dark as a Hershey's bar, would have many a battle to fight over the course of his life. It was best that he learned to choose his battles wisely.

"Off you go," Maria said as Aurelio jumped off the park bench. "I'll be here if you need me, but you should just try to ignore her if she says anything else."

Aurelio skipped back to the merry-go-round and jumped onto the spinning metal apparatus, perching on the center crown as it turned. He liked to sit up there as it made him feel big; kind of like a king looking down upon his kingdom. He looked down at the little girl who lay on her back with her head hanging over the side and her blond pigtails being pulled off into the air by gravity. She was smiling until she lifted her head and spotted Aurelio.

"I thought I told you..." she began.

"Shut up and leave me alone," he yelled, a thin bead of sweat trailing down his cheek.

"This is my merry-go-round BEANER. You don't belong here," the little girl continued, her face getting red with anger.

This time Aurelio didn't stop to think. He jumped off the crown, then off the merry-go-round. The little girl pulled herself up and holding onto a pole on the merry-go-round, she opened her mouth to yell.

He grabbed a fist-full of sand and threw it at her as she spun around toward him with one of her hands outreached and forming into a fist. Her mouth filled with the gritty particles and she began squinting her eyes. Aurelio couldn't see it though. He was already running toward his mother.

Hearing the commotion, Maria turned her attention away from a story on an alienation invasion and looked up. Aurelio was running full bore and jumped onto her lap. He didn't say a word and he was breathing heavily. Not far behind him, she saw a Nordic-sized woman dragging the little blond-haired girl, who now was dramatically coughing and flailing her arms wildly, behind her.

"Hey you," the Amazon woman yelled toward Maria. "Your son just threw sand at my daughter."

Maria decided not to escalate the situation, and rather than respond, she hurriedly put Oree's shoes on and grabbed him up in her arms. She picked up the Thermos and paper with her free hand.

"You beaners are taking over everything – my daughter is American and has rights," the woman stammered as Maria got up and began walking away. "If your son does this again, I'll call the police and have you deported. You should go back to where you came from!"

Maria turned back, glaring at the woman. Inside, she was fuming and wanted to say, "We were born here *pendeja* and are probably more American than you!"

She leaned into Aurelio and whispered, "Let's go. Just ignore them." As they hurried away, she heard a string of profanity spewing forth from the oversized woman. "Close your ears, Oree."

They got in their blue station wagon and Maria angrily sped out of the parking lot. By the time they got home after picking up her 10-year-old Annie from ballet class, and 9-year-old Anthony from basketball, both had calmed down. Aurelio made his way straight to the living room, where he crunched into a ball on his favorite pillow and spent the rest of the afternoon watching black and white reruns of "The Andy Griffith Show." He sat in front of their 13-inch black and white TV and occasionally adjusted the foil rabbit ears to remove the fuzzy white dots which made the picture look like a mosaic. He was mesmerized whenever the commercial for Lincoln Log toys appeared as he wanted to make houses like that. He would have to remember to ask Santa for them for Christmas.

Maria retreated to the kitchen where she sought to calm herself by taking her butcher's knife to a block of Spam, cutting it up into slices slightly thicker than bologna. It had been a while since she had been so upset. She distractedly continued with her meal preparation. "How dare she threaten to have us deported. We are Americans," she muttered as she stirred boiling macaroni and turned the crackling Spam over in her hot cast iron skillet.

Maria wished her husband, Albert, could be home to help with situations like the one that had transpired that day, but with his two jobs – the supermarket during the day and waiting tables at night – there was so much their family needed and just not enough money. As it was, Albert's attendance at family dinners was generally reserved to once or twice a week. He didn't like to be bothered with child-rearing things.

By the time the children sat down for dinner, Maria had sufficiently calmed herself, and kept an eye on the unusually quiet Aurelio. She sat at the table spooning mounds of macaroni and cheese, Del Monte green beans and the Spam slices onto their plates. She handed a plate to Annie and then to Anthony. Aurelio, who already had his plate, toyed with the shiny yellow pasta.

"*Mijo*, are you o.k.?" she asked. "Aurelio?"

"Yeah mommy. I should 'a told that little girl she should have had chili put in her mouth like the time you did when I used that bad word," he said.

"What happened?" Anthony asked.

"This big little girl -- I mean she was gargantuan -- called me a beaner," Oree said popping a macaroni in his mouth.

"She called you a beaner? Really?" Anthony exclaimed.

"Did you punch her?" his sister Annie added. "I wouldn't have let anyone call me a beaner. I'd pop 'em."

"No, your brother did not hit her. He threw sand at her which I don't encourage as a way of solving problems. I don't want any of you kids getting in fights over race things. It's just not worth it," Maria continued, trying her best to sound like a voice of calm reason, although inside she found herself repeating, "Deportation? How dare she!"

Then, seeking to turn her attention toward another topic, Maria asked, "Annie, what did they teach you in dance today?"

Annie, whose birth name was Anita, smiled a semi-toothless grin and said somewhat sarcastically, "We learned to be pretty, pretty ballerinas, although I don't understand why they said we all could stand to lose a few pounds if we are going to get serious about it."

"You're not fat Annie, now eat that macaroni and cheese," her mother interrupted.

"Well, you don't have to worry about being pretty as that will never happen?" Anthony laughed.

"Stop it Anthony or I'll sock you," Annie said, shoveling a spoonful of macaroni into her mouth.

They returned to their meals, each turning toward their own thoughts. Aurelio, who was constructing a small mountain out of the macaroni and cheese on his plate, had already begun to forget the events of the afternoon. Maria was running a mental list of the items she needed to get for the children in anticipation of their return to school. Annie tried to make sense of her ballet teacher's comments, and Anthony, mulling over the word "beaner," took a minute to recall a term he had heard from a friend before school let out.

"Hey mom, now that we know we aren't beaners, are we Chicanos?" Anthony said as casually as he was asking for more mac and cheese.

"Where'd you hear that?" Maria said, her tone turning gruff.

"Chicanos, you know viva la raza and all that stuff," Anthony continued. "I heard about them in school and someone said I was one."

"I am going to be a Chicano when I grow up," Annie added.

"No you're not Annie. Chicano means chicken," Maria said disdainfully. "We are Mexican-Americans and don't let anyone tell you otherwise. There's a whole bunch of idiots out there trying to make us something that we're not. Remember this all of you, we're Americans and this is America. When your grandparents came here we were Mexicans, and now we're Mexican American. There is no such thing as a Chicano."

"Should I be a Chicano?" Oree asked. "It sounds better than beaner."

"Enough of the Chicano talk," Maria finished. "Now finish your dinners. Annie it is your night to help me with dishes. Anthony, you can bathe Oree."

Later that evening, after she fed Albert who usually got home from work around 10, Maria was preparing for bed and again thought of that time so long ago in Woolworths. She hoped that times had changed enough, and that education would be enough, and that her children were smart enough to maneuver around any issues related to their race. She surmised that education certainly was one way in which they would be able to create better futures for themselves.

She stood in front of her vanity, rubbing lotion into her fingers, again thinking about Oree's encounter at the park. She pondered over what she could have done differently. Should she have packed up and left at the first hint of trouble? Should she have argued with the woman? Should she have had Oree play in another part of the park? No, running away wasn't the way to handle things. Looking at Oree's response, Maria realized there was no way she could have known her son was going to quiet his offender with a fistful of sand. Although she would never admit it, she was somewhat proud of his act of defiance.

Maria was disheartened that her youngest, and most innocent child, had undergone a baptism that day, but he was starting school and would likely have other incidents, so she was somewhat encouraged to see he would be able to defend himself.

She decided it was best to put the thought and herself to bed. Tiredly turning off the bedroom light, she crawled under the covers and dozed off to the sounds of her husband's quiet snoring.

CHAPTER 2

THE RODRIGO'S AND ALIZACA'S

Long before they met, the path of Maria and Albert Rodrigo's lives was forged by their parents in small towns across Mexico, and then nourished in fields and cities within the United States. It was in these places that their parents learned of the sacrifices that are made for children, the compromises that come with hopes for a better future and the ever-present yearning for acceptance in a country that often viewed them as outsiders.

Albert absorbed most of his perceptions of being "American" from his father, Eduardo "Ed" Rodrigo, whose last name wasn't always Rodrigo.

Ed was born in 1910 in Chihuahua, Mexico, to a family which ultimately included eight children. By the time he reached 15, he had grown tired of his mother's habitual pregnancies and his parent's ongoing reminders of the need for everyone in the household to pull their own weight. When he could no longer take the burdens of his family, *la familia,* he left home and took on a multitude of jobs – picking fruit, washing cars, scrubbing dishes and the like – eventually working his way up to Mexico's northern border where he migrated to the United States in 1930.

In most of his many jobs, he heard of a wealth of work in "El Norte," and after years of barely getting by in Mexico and to listening of his co-workers constantly lament, "One day I will go to America and leave this shit hole," he decided to take action and make the trek. In making his journey to the Central Valley, he boarded a bus which took him from Calexico to Bakersfield. At the half way point, the Greyhound made a stop in Los Angeles. He peered out the bus windows in awe, having never before seen such wealth and prosperity. The stunning buildings, pristine vehicles, well dressed people, swaying palm trees and rumble of street cars all seemed very exciting and alive. At that very instant, he set a goal to one day return to the city and to make it his home. He wanted a wife and family, and he surmised they would likely have greater success living in a thriving city than being stuck in dusty produce fields.

His trek dropped him in Dinuba, California, a small farming town in the Central Valley, where Ed picked plums, nectarines and whatever else he could to help him to survive in this strange new country. He had heard there was something called "The Great Depression" taking place in America, but looking at the bounty of fruits and vegetables that spread out in front of him every day, he wondered, "How could a country with this much wealth, be depressed?" He was joined by "okies" from the Midwest who also ventured to California in efforts to leave their dustbowl existence behind.

Life in the Central Valley was difficult. Eduardo's goal was to save for the price of a bus ticket and a week's food, and then head back to the "City of Angels." When he got to Los Angeles he figured he could sleep – somewhere, anywhere – as long as he was far from the smell of pesticides and fertilizer. He found that he was often competing for jobs against the okies who came in search of the same economic freedom. Wages were bad and the influx of migrants from both within America and Mexico, further pushed down the meager wages. Eduardo constantly heard utterances of "wetback," beaner" and "mojado" when he was picked for jobs over his Anglo counterparts. At times, the okies would throw rocks at the Mexicans with the hopes of injuring them enough that they couldn't work. The ranch managers overlooked these activities and usually didn't care about the color of their worker's skin, as long as they had broad shoulders and strong backs to reap the harvests.

During the thirties, America was in the midst of a vast "repatriation" which ultimately resulted in the deportation of one million Mexicans, the majority of whom were American citizens. Ed, who was light-skinned, quickly learned to "pass," fearful that his American dream could be shattered before it had a chance to be realized. Thus, he kept a low profile when he was not working in the fields, picked up English quickly, and equally important, learned not to react when he heard the words "wetback," "spic" or "beaner."

He knew field work was not the type of life he wanted, and he spent many days concentrating on what it would be like to step onto a street car in shiny black leather shoes, taking him to a very important job that he had yet to discover.

His strong arms and back helped him land many jobs as employers cherry picked workers for a harvest or farming. A few were even generous by not overcharging for food and board which frequently created a life of indentured servitude for those who weren't smart. Eduardo wasn't like them.

He resolved that farm work was not a long-term solution to building the life he wanted in America. By then, his English had improved enough that he could consider his options. He had grown tired of breathing the air that smelled like chemical fertilizer and dirt. He had smarts and ambition, and within three years, he had enough to leave.

Sitting at the Dinuba bus stop, he felt a tightness in his lungs. He wasn't sure if it was from the pesticides or the nervousness of moving to a city which was bigger than anything he could imagine. Regardless, he was now on his way.

For Elizabeth Soto, who would one day be Eduardo's wife, things were far different. She was born in in 1915 in Pueblo, Mexico, and was sent to live with her spinster Aunt Dolores in Los Angeles when she was 5-years-old. Her parents wanted a better life for their sole daughter of five children. They knew that being a young woman in Mexico could result in many things, including unwanted pregnancy. They had heard whispered tales of *vaqueros* sweeping up young women alongside the road as they galloped by on their horses, only later to be forced into marriage as the young women's bellies began to rise.

Aunt Delores would often write to her sister in Pueblo, saying how she wished she had family with her in the vast and sometimes cold City of Angels. She had a good job working days as a waitress at the Cole's French Dip downtown, a job she was able to secure based upon the fairness of her skin and lack of accent which she worked hard to conceal. She would tell people she was Spanish which was considered "exotic" and made life in Los Angeles easier.

When young Elizabeth was sent to live with her in 1920, Delores was resolute in making something of the girl. She made sure she had new dresses which were always impeccably clean and she would bathe Elizabeth nightly. Aunt Delores scrubbed so hard that Elizabeth sometimes thought she would rub all the brown off her skin to reveal a layer of white underneath. Delores was determined that her niece would never hear derogatory terms like "wetback" or "spic."

The first few months were hard for both of them. Elizabeth cried herself to sleep every night. Her five-year-old mind could not grasp why her parents would force her to leave a home which she loved. Aunt Delores had few maternal instincts and was strict. There were no other children for Elizabeth to play with, and she learned that this new country – this new life – had a whole set of different rules that she had to assimilate to. Elizabeth quickly learned English as Aunt Dolores would only respond to her if she talked in English, or at least tried to. Thus, she did better in school than other immigrant children as she was such a fast study – Aunt Dolores wouldn't have it any other way.

By the time she was 19, Elizabeth had blossomed into a beautiful and patient young woman as Aunt Dolores often had a short temper and quick tongue. She secured a position selling train tickets at Union Station, a job she enjoyed. She also felt she played a very important role in helping people to travel from city to city – finding the destiny that would bring them happiness.

On the day she first met Eduardo Rodrigo, she hadn't a thought in her head that the person standing before her at the ticket counter would be by her side for the next five decades.

"Do you know what time the train is coming from Chicago this morning?" Eduardo asked, looking at the woman who he thought was the most beautiful person he had ever seen.

Elizabeth checked the train schedules without peering up at him.

"Uh, 10:30, but sometimes they're late," she said, looking up. She noticed that the man in front of her was smiling ear to ear with a gold capped tooth in front. His hair was carefully slicked back and he appeared to be a bit nervous.

"Uh meeting the missus," he stammered, as he began to perspire. He was afraid his attraction toward her was showing. "Not my missus, I mean my boss' missus. He owns Little Joe's, the only Italian restaurant in Chinatown, and his wife is coming home from Chicago. He asked me to pick her up."

Elizabeth was amused but couldn't let on that she understood the nervousness of his response. For she too was stammering inside. There was something strangely attractive about this "goof," she thought.

"Is there something else?" she said feeling vaguely flush and strangely giddy. This gold-toothed man was attractive, charming and seemed to be in little hurry to leave her ticket window.

"Oh nothing," Eduardo said, trying to string together his next sentence, while thinking he had never before seen a woman so poised. She was almost regal.

"*Es un dia muy bonito.* It's a pretty day," he said smiling.

"Shhhhh," Elizabeth said sharply. "I could get fired for speaking Spanish. It's not allowed here."

"Plus, I don't speak Spanish," she added, overlooking the fact that when she called Mexico once every three months to speak with her parents, she would only talk to them in Spanish.

"So sorry, I just thought. Oh never mind," Eduardo said quietly as he looked down at his shoes which were impeccably shined. Looking up he changed the subject and muttered, "Hmm, I'm wondering what I should do for the next hour."

"Well, there's a coffee stand, or you can sit on the benches and wait," Elizabeth said (she always appreciated the vastness of Union Station and the library-like sense one experienced while sitting on the hard, wooden benches).

"That would be very nice, thank you," Eduardo said. "And again, I hope I did not offend you. You are a nice lady."

Elizabeth smiled and nodded. When he left her window she watched him cautiously meander over to the coffee stand, seeming like he wanted to turn back around. To Elizabeth, it felt like he was watching her with eyes in back of his head. "It's almost my break time and he seems like a nice man, but the speaking Spanish is a big no no," she thought. Still, she was appreciative that in this vast city where no one seemed to communicate with each other, she discovered a man who seemed nice and could speak her native tongue. She would not tell Aunt Dolores about this encounter.

It was close enough to her break time. She put the wooden "Next Window Please" sign on her counter and left to meet her destiny.

In talking with him while strolling in the garden outside of the main hall, Elizabeth understood that Ed began his career at Little Joe's as a dishwasher and worked his way up to being a waiter, but that he would not be satisfied until he became a manager. She was also surprised that his name – Rodrigo – was not his birth name, that was Rodriquez. Ed's manager, who was his sponsor for citizenship, told him he should change his name when he was granted nationality. After all, "If you wanna be accepted as an American, you gotta lose that beaner name." Eduardo thought that the editing of his last name to Rodrigo sounded almost Italian, which fit perfectly for his job.

Elizabeth surmised that Ed's boss would be a perfect fit for her Aunt Dolores who was constantly hounding her to behave like an American. Everyone these days was saying how "You gotta shape up or ship out." She surmised that Ed seemed very disciplined and that he would be capable of giving her the American life she sought. Plus, she was not getting any younger.

Yes, at the tender age of 20, Elizabeth was well aware of the timeframe she had in finding a suitable husband. Aunt Delores reiterated quite frequently that every young woman had this stated "window of opportunity" and that she herself had neglected to notice that her window had shut tight long before she recognized it was closing. She did not want Elizabeth to miss her opportunity.

Elizabeth and Ed were married a year later, renting first and eventually buying a home in East Los Angeles to be near to Little Joe's, the place where Ed spent an increasing amount of time at as he worked his way up to becoming the first Latino assistant manager of the establishment. Elizabeth herself was busy herself following their nuptials: in a matter of years she bore three sons: Albert, the eldest, followed by Louis and Richard.

Long before she married Albert Rodrigo and bore his children, in her youth, Maria Alizaca was a book worm. As a child, she was always more content to sit and read books such as "Little Women" and "Treasure Island," rather than to play with her siblings Robert, Cathy and Dominic. They were all born in the Queen of Angels Hospital in Los Angeles and made their home in the City of San Fernando with their parents Bonita/"Bessie" and Jesus. Within the Alizaca household, the children were allowed to speak with their parents in Spanish, but once they stepped out the front door, they had an English only rule. As they grew and attended school, It became easier for them to converse with each other in English. Their conversations with their parents eventually followed a similar suit.

Religion was very important within the Alizaca household. Jesus took every opportunity to emphasize the importance of church and gratitude in his children – "We may just be Mexicans, but God has been very good to us." Each Sunday, they attended mass in Latin at Santa Rita Catholic Church in San Fernando. They were a typical American family – the mother always wearing a freshly pressed dress and long black mantilla veil; the father in an ill-fitting suit, which was procured from page 67 of the Sears Roebuck catalog; and the children dressed in frilly dresses, or starched shirts and slacks.

Jesus was proud of the life he provided for his family. He was born in 1912 in Zacatecas, Mexico, and immigrated in his teens to America as Mexico was still reeling from the Mexican Revolution. He had heard there was a wealth of work in the San Fernando Valley, and when he made his way there, he began by picking oranges and working at a packing house in Reseda.

As many of his fellow workers were older and had families, Jesus was somewhat lonely during the times he was not working. He spoke little English and could not read. So, he did what every God-fearing Latino did when in a time of need arose – he went to church to ask for God's help. He had heard from fellow workers that Santa Rita in San Fernando was heavily attended by Latinos, so one Sunday he took the bus there to attend mass.

After everyone filed out of the church at the end of services, Jesus kneeled quietly in prayer.

"My God, I am so alone in this country. I don't speak the language and I can't read. I don't know anyone and I have to be careful of meeting the glances of people on the street as I am afraid they will deport me. Please help me to become someone, to make something of myself," he prayed earnestly.

As he sat back into the pew to await God's response, he settled into calmness. He looked around and admired the opulence of the church. It had beautiful religious statues, dark wood pews and elaborate stained glass windows which filtered light across the vast interior. The most that he had seen in churches where he lived in Mexico were wooden crosses and dirt floors. As he continued in his thoughts, a priest in a long black robe walked down the aisle towards him. Jesus hadn't been aware that when he was praying he was speaking out loud and in Spanish. He was hopeful the priest would not turn him into *la migra*. The priest walked up to him and extended his hand as he introduced himself in Spanish as Father Sanderson. Jesus was surprised he spoke Spanish so well as he didn't look Latino. They sat in the pew and spoke for an hour. Jesus explained his situation and Father Sanderson listened silently.

When Jesus had finished, the priest smiled, "Jesus, I believe you are a good man and you are doing the right things in your life. I want to welcome you to our church."

The priest explained that on Saturday evenings the church provided free English language classes, and he would find someone who could teach Jesus to read. Tears welled up in the humble man's eyes, and in Spanish he said to the priest: "God is good and he has heard my prayers."

The priest smiled and said, "Well, Jesus, you are the one who will have to do all the work."

Beginning the next week, Jesus began attending English classes every Saturday evening. On Sundays after church, one of the better-off parishioners would sit with him, bringing him books, often their personal favorites, to read. He practiced writing in the evenings when he finished work. Within two years, Jesus learned how to speak and read in the language of the country he had made his new home. He vowed to Father Sanderson that he and his family – when he got one – would be loyal church-goers in return for all the church had given him.

"Well my friend, sometimes your life can end up being so much more than you hoped for," the priest exclaimed.

Jesus often thought long and hard about that statement, and when things got challenging, he would call upon the thought to remind him of all he had been given in his life. Over time, he was able to find work with the Los Angeles Olive Growers Association, picking olives at groves that spread out across the nearby hillside community of Sylmar, so he moved to San Fernando.

One Saturday afternoon before his class, he met his future wife Bessie Hernandez who was shopping at the San Fernando Mall. Bessie worked as a seamstress at one of the sewing factories situated along the railroad tracks that divided the City of San Fernando into two distinct regions – the north, being that of "the haves" and, south of the railroad tracks, being the "have nots".

Bessie was born in Los Angeles to immigrant parents, but when she was in the eleventh grade, her parents determined it was time for her to leave school to help support the family. She secured a position via one of her mother's *"comadres"* at the sewing factory and began her work life, taking the bus to San Fernando and back to Echo Park every day. Her birth name was "Bonita" but when she was hired at the sewing factory, her supervisor decided Bonita was too difficult to pronounce – "bunn-eeda" – so she was christened "Bessie."

As everyone at work was introduced to her as Bessie, in no time at all, she accepted the moniker. When she met her future husband Jesus Alizaca by literally bumping into him at the San Fernando Mall as she was fumbling for change in her purse, she introduced herself simply as "Bessie."

In talking with him when they first met, Bessie was impressed that this Jesus person spoke such good English considering he was undoubtedly from Mexico given his dark complexion and simple clothing. She was also impressed that he was taking English classes and was learning to read. As her family was Catholic, his interest in the church-related endeavors made her feel safe with him (unlike some of the other field workers she had met who were only interested in one thing).

In the beginning of their courtship, they would meet at the mall on Saturday afternoons, walking and discussing their week's activities. After a while, Jesus was able to buy a used truck and he would visit Bessie in Echo Park. From there, they would go to one of the many grand movie theaters on Broadway downtown or they would take long walks along Echo Park Lake and marvel at the Lotus flowers which dotted the waterscape.

Within a year, they were married in a small ceremony at Santa Rita with Father Sanderson officiating. Shortly thereafter, Jesus obtained his citizenship as he had married a United States citizen. Through parishioners at Santa Rita, he was able to secure a job with the City of Los Angeles Department of Water and Power, where he initially began work on the terminal structure and cascades that bring water into Los Angeles via Sylmar. The Alizacas bought a small bungalow in San Fernando which would be their family home throughout the course of their life together.

They felt comfort living in a neighborhood which was inhabited by many Hispanics and it was easy to navigate their "barrio." Jesus frequently reminded himself of the phrase his priest once shared with him: "Sometimes your life can end up being so much more than you hoped for."

CHAPTER 3

ALBERT AND MARIA

Elizabeth and Ed's son, Albert, was the product of a first generation family. Having been raised during the forties and fifties, he was taught the importance of hard work in maintaining a life and family. Although at times he heard stories of his family's distant roots in Mexico, his parents would always gloss over them, instead focusing on "being the 'right kind' of American," and reinforcing the importance of the here and now: "Today, the present, is what's important, not what we left behind!" It was this type of talk that his parents used to ensure their children understood that they weren't to be the ones who reinforced the stereotype of being the "lazy wetback," and that they were destined to have an easier life than their parents.

Because of perceptions such as these, although he understood and spoke Spanish, Albert was not allowed to speak a word of it outside of the family home. There would be no room for misconceptions that he came from anywhere other than America. His activities frequently reflected this philosophy.

In his youth, Albert played high school football and was often seen mirroring his clothing after the then popular teen idol, James Dean. He would wear faded Levi's with rolled up cuffs; a tight white t-shirt which accented his thin, long body; and he would smear dollops of Tres Flores into his black and wavy hair to fashion a pompadour like his idol.

Despite whatever opinions one may have assumed based upon the dark tan color of his skin, he was as American as apple pie.

As he was preparing to go out on the night where he ultimately met his future wife, Albert was having one of those evenings when he felt anything was possible. For the most part he enjoyed his job at the supermarket where he worked and he was beginning to entertain thoughts that at some point in his future, he might enjoy having a wife, and further on, even possibly children.

That same evening, enjoying herself was the furthest thing from Maria Alizaca's mind. She sat at the edge of her bed, looking down at her plaid skirt and oxford saddle shoes which were popular during the fifties. Looking at her, you would have thought she was the ideal girl next door – shoulder length brown hair, light brown eyes and a trim build which reflected her years of tomboy-hood. (The latter being the result of the fact that she always felt more comfortable playing football with her brothers than playing dolls with her sister Cathy.)

"I wish they would stop pushing me," she said to herself, patting down the pleats in her skirt while thinking of her parents Jesus and Bessie. They were forever telling her how fortunate she was to live in the great country of America and to have all the opportunity that was never afforded them. And, at least she wasn't born in Mexico where by now she would be caring for a fat, *vaquero* husband who had kidnapped and then impregnated her, thus forcing her into an unhappy marriage and a life of misery.

Maria, who had recently celebrated her eighteenth birthday, was supposed to go with Cathy and their friends to the Hollywood Palace to hear the Tito Puente Orchestra.

Tonight, like other times since her recent graduation, Maria felt a pull – she was faced with two choices, either find a husband or get a job; neither of which really appealed to her. One of the things Maria was very aware of as a result of her culture and upbringing, was that *la familia* was the underlying "glue" which held the entire universe together. This meant that the care and nurturing of that family took precedent over anything like secondary education, job success or moving out of the house until one was wed. This made "Option A: Find a Husband," much more important to her parents. She was always surprised when one of her friends was forced into a wedding following an unplanned pregnancy; it always seemed that the impacted families circled the wagons and quickly embraced the new son- or daughter-in-law, acting like the miraculous event had all been part of the deigned blueprint of the family's history.

Maria wasn't like this and was smart enough to think through the options she might have in her life, even though they might be somewhat limited given that she was a woman and also a minority.

Her mother Bessie had maintained connections within San Fernando's seamstress factories long after she stopped working, and she suggested a career in sewing to Maria. However, Bessie's children had grown accustomed to a relatively middle class lifestyle and the thought of sewing clothes for all of eternity was not very appealing to the modern thinking Maria. She had dreams of being a secretary at a high powered law firm, or perhaps even selling perfume at May Company, downtown on Broadway, now that would be an exciting job!

"Maria, will you straighten up?" her sister pleaded as she twisted her curled hair in her fingers. "The girls will be coming to pick us up and if you keep showing that sour puss, you'll act like man-repellant. And, no one likes man repellant. You gotta be nice to them if you want them to like you."

Maria thought to herself that Cathy was always trying to be nice to some boy and to making him happy rather than thinking of what she really wanted. She reasoned that this preoccupation originated with Cathy being her father's pet; she was always trying to please daddy. Maria herself, would rarely give a feather if her father or a boy liked her or not, still she thought that someday perhaps, she would find her match. Her mood turned hopeful as the Maguire Sisters' "Sincerely" came on the radio and her mind meandered as she swayed to the music: *"Cause I love you so dearly, please say you'll be mine."* She sighed, again thinking she would never find someone to love her as sincerely as in the song. She reasoned there was little possibility of her finding a boy who could keep her attention, and, she had been told by everyone from her father on down, that she was subject to "Maria moods," which was not a compliment. Still, she held out hope. After all, it was the 1950s and life in America was changing. Maria and her peers were inundated with all these images of blond haired, blue eyed girls with pretty bangs, smiling and being carefree. She wanted that too, she just wasn't sure that given her brown eyes, skin and hair that she would ever attain that state of being.

Maria put two fingers to her lips and then pressed them on the lips of her picture of James Dean which was taped on the mirror of the dresser she and Cathy shared. She sighed, pulling her hair back into a ponytail, slipped on her pink mock-angora sweater, applied a fresh coat of baby pink lipstick and went to the living room to wait with Cathy for their friends.

The Hollywood Palace was a popular place for the youth of Los Angeles to bask in the glow and excitement of Hollywood. A trip to a night club was something that was planned for weeks, and Latin groups like the Tito Puente Orchestra were often "code" that it could be an evening where those from all races could enjoy each other's company without some of the racial undercurrents which sometimes ran through the coarse veins of Los Angeles. In fact, her parents provided constant reminders that at the first hint of trouble anywhere, the girls were to immediately call them. They had remembered the Zoot Suit Riots of the forties and didn't want their daughters to be part of any such business.

Albert Rodrigo was dressed in pleated chocolate brown pants, a crisp white shirt and a narrow pink tie which he thought made him look like a Latin Marlon Brando. He and his friends stood in the back of the Palace looking over the crowd when he spotted the pink angora sweater.

"Nice peepers," he thought as he gazed upon Maria. He watched her for half an hour before mustering the courage to introduce himself. She didn't seem very interested in the crowd, in fact she looked kind of irritated. He found that perturbed look strangely attractive and decided to see what was beneath the demeanor.

"Hi, my name is Albert," he said, extending his hand. Maria looked up at him as if he had broken her trance. "How are you?"

"Oh, I'm sorry. I'm Maria. Fine," she said, suddenly aware that she was in the midst of a huge nightclub and not at home in her bedroom.

"I work down the street at the Hollywood Ranch Market on Vine," he smiled. "Have you ever been there?"

"No," Maria said, now taking notice that this man was wearing a tie the same color as her sweater. That must be a sign, she thought. Of what? She couldn't think that far in the future.

"Let me tell you, I have seen some strange things there," Albert continued. "Like these celebrities come in drunk late at night and get things like Hostess cupcakes, Cheez Whiz and potato chips. They eat worse than we do."

Maria smiled and thought: "He sure is enthusiastic about working at a supermarket." Still, she found his twinkling eyes engaging.

They ended up spending the night talking in the lobby of The Palace. She learned from Albert that he was born in 1934, served in the Korean War for two years and returned to Los Angeles where his father got him a job through the produce buyer for Little Joe's at the Los Angeles Produce Mart. He said he liked the job well enough, but when he became friends with someone who was employed at Hollywood Ranch Market, he was soon offered a job working in the market's produce area. He shared that he wanted to get married and have a big family. Maria hadn't much thought about children yet, but Albert was a few years older than she and had served in the war, so she surmised he must have had more time to consider such things.

They learned that neither had an aptitude for math in school, that both enjoyed the ocean, and that vanilla was their favorite ice cream flavor.

They immediately felt comfortable with each other and Maria was surprised that it could be so easy to talk with someone who was a perfect stranger only an hour or so ago. Eventually, Maria's sister Cathy came out to the lobby to get her.

"Maria, time to go," Cathy smiled. "And, who have we here?"

Maria introduced Cathy to Albert, and then turned toward him. "Well kiddo, I gotta go. You know the Valley shuts down for business at 11 p.m. and the Cahuenga Pass isn't the best drive this time of night."

Maria reached out her hand and pressed a piece of paper into Albert's palm. It contained her name and phone number which she had written down a half hour before in the ladies room, clutching it in her hand until the right moment to give it to Albert. Guess it was now or never.

Maria and Cathy walked away and Maria looked over her shoulder giving him a "toodles" kind of wave. He looked at the slip of paper and smiled. He raised his hand, pantomimed an "I'll call you" gesture and winked.

"What a goof," Maria thought as the four girls walked out into the cool air that set upon Sunset and Vine.

Albert and Maria began their courtship much like any other young couple. They were both born in America and in Los Angeles specifically. Their parents were also both obsessed with them being "the right kind of Americans." Maria shared that when she wanted to perm her hair, her mother said she didn't want her daughter "looking like a greasy wetback." When Albert wanted to buy a zoot suit, his father threatened to kick him out of the house for being a "pachuco." They both finished high school and Albert toyed with the idea of going to college. Those thoughts were quickly replaced by the Korean War and he was more than proud to defend "his country." Over time, they started talking about what they wanted their future to be.

As Albert had a car, he was soon spending more and more time visiting Maria in the Valley. Soon, they were going to places like the San Fernando Valley Fair, Dairy Queen and Harry's Roller Rink in Glendale. He began to entertain thoughts of marrying Maria and decided that the Valley would be a good place to settle down. With its many open spaces, the area was expansive and rapidly growing as many families bought new "tract" homes which were rapidly dotting the landscape. Albert reasoned it was close to his work, and was convenient for both families. Maria had already introduced Albert to her parents and he had already received what was akin to the Good Housekeeping™

seal of approval when her father said "That's my boy," one day. They always welcomed his visits, so Maria knew if they were to get married, they would receive her father's blessing.

Their relationship grew closer amidst the backdrop of change that was rapidly taking place within America. It began with the Civil Rights Movement and some of it was good, some was bad. There was the Brown vs. the Board of Education Act of 1954 which ended all racial segregation in schools. That same year, the United States Immigration and Naturalization Service began its "Operation Wetback" program which was designed to deport Mexicans who had entered the United States illegally. They heard that in its first year of existence, "Operation Wetback" was responsible for the deportation of over 1 million Mexicans – many who were Americans – and they did not want to be part of that mess. As a precaution, the pair took their birth certificates with them everywhere and avoided places where they suspected "*la migra*" may be waiting. Both understood that although they at times spoke to each other in Spanish privately, they were not to speak it in a public setting. They took great pains to dress as "American" as possible.

It was as if they were living in two worlds. When they were together, they felt safe, never thinking about their "Americanness," or the color of their skin. However, once they ventured out into the world to places like the movies, or malt shops, it was anybody's guess if they were to be served, or greeted with "Out wetbacks" or similarly derogatory phrases.

One night, Albert was driving Maria home after seeing a double feature at the Van Nuys Drive-in. As they drove along Van Nuys Boulevard, red lights began flashing into their car from behind. Albert looked back and saw it was a police car. They and the police cruiser pulled over.

"Good evening officer," Albert said. "Did we do anything?"

"Let me ask the questions," the police officer responded. "I need your license and registration."

Albert pulled his license out of his wallet and grabbed the registration out of the plastic sleeve on the steering wheel shaft. He handed them to the officer. The officer shined his flashlight into Albert's eyes and then across the inside of the car. Maria, who was sitting close to Albert, sat quietly and looked forward. The officer looked at both of them.

"Should you wetbacks be out this late?" the officer chuckled. "Doesn't work in the fields start early?"

"I was just driving her home from a movie. Did we do anything officer?" Albert again asked as he tried to understand why they had been pulled over.

"Is this your girlfriend? She's pretty," the officer said, shining the light across Maria's face. "I'll be back."

As he walked away from the car, Albert and Maria looked at each other and said nothing. They had heard about people getting beaten by the police for no reason other than the fact that they were brown, so they understood it was best to keep quiet. Albert began to perspire and Maria could feel her heart thumping in her chest. The officer returned to the car.

"You know I could take you in – you both look kind of young to be out this late," the officer said. "And, for all I know, you could be hiding a bunch of wetbacks somewhere in this car."

The officer then moved the beam of the flashlight again throughout the car. Still holding onto Albert's license and registration, he moved toward the front of the vehicle and shined the flashlight along the front of the hood. The light cascaded across the polished metal blinding both Albert and Maria as it moved up toward their faces. Then, the officer positioned the light downward so it cast upon Maria's breasts. He kept the light focused on her sweater as he returned to the driver's side. He could see Maria breathing heavily out of fear and Albert's face grew pale. The officer threw the license and registration into the car.

"I guess you can go beaners," he said smirking. "Although, who knows what will happen to you if I see you on this street again."

"Thank you officer," Albert said as he forced the words out of his throat which was constricted by fear.

Albert and Maria sat in the car as the officer drove off.

"Are you o.k." Albert softly said.

Maria sat quietly as tears streamed down her face. "You better get me home."

Albert held her hand tightly as they drove along side streets the remainder of the way to Maria's home.

It would be awhile before they spoke about that night, however it galvanized their relationship. They both saw each other at their most vulnerable and they were there for each other. Albert understood how much he cared for Maria, and she felt safe and protected by his presence. Eventually they both came to the realization that their future was with each other.

Over time their feelings of fear subsided every time they saw a black and white on the street. As their relationship deepened, they began talking about the future and "joked" about having children. They vowed to do everything in their power to ensure that they would never be subjected to the feeling of unease that their parents had experienced. Yes, progress was being made – Rosa Parks refused to give up her bus seat and school desegregation was slowly becoming a thing of the past – but they weren't sure if people of their color would ever be treated equally. The incident with the police officer was a painful reminder that the playing field was not equal and that their sense of security and well-being could be shattered at any moment.

A year later they were planning their marriage and one evening they went to Santa Monica Beach to watch the phosphorescent sea. They walked along Santa Monica Pier holding hands, eating corn dogs and drinking Coca Cola. Maria recorded an acapella version of "Sincerely" for Albert for 35 cents in an arcade Voice-o-graph booth. As the sun set, they worked their way down along the beach and sat and talked as the sun set over the northern cliffs. The Santa Monica Pier was a favorite spot of theirs. Maria liked the quietness of the ocean below and she was always entranced by the gentleness of the waves lapping against the shore.

As they sat on the beach that night, Maria thought it was as if everything in her life had led up to this moment. She was in love, had someone she wanted to spend the future with, and they had magic in their lives – the waves shimmered brightly blue-white as they cast to and fro upon the shore. Suddenly, Maria felt a wave of strong emotion wash over her, and as she and Albert kissed, she wanted to show him how much she loved him. It was as if all of a sudden the universe opened up, his breath was her breath and their hearts beat in unison. She thought about the blueprint of her life and how Albert was imprinted on every page. From her passion, she felt herself open up to give him the greatest gift she could offer.

A few months after the night of the phosphorescent sea, Maria found herself pregnant. As they were well along with their plans of marriage, it was more of an inconvenience rather than a spectacle, and after sharing the news with their parents, Albert and Maria moved their wedding date up by 10 months. Anita "Annie" Rodrigo was born six months later. When Anita made her arrival, it was as if the tornado in the "Wizard of Oz" had set down upon San Fernando Hospital. She came out wailing, tiny pink fingers crumpled tightly into little fists. Her long pink toes and legs kicked as if she were swimming the English channel. The nurses exclaimed that this little girl was destined to be a cheerleader "with that set of lungs!"

When baby Anthony came a year later, Maria and Albert were prepared for anything. He, however, was much calmer than Annie, which was fine for the growing family. They were rapidly outgrowing the small bungalow they rented in San Fernando, and Albert realized he needed to do something to push them past the point of being renters.

He went to his supervisor in the produce section, Mr. Yamoto, and asked if he could be promoted to a grocery clerk position. In addition to making a higher salary, his goal was to use his role stocking store shelves and managing a cash register, to learn enough for a promotion to assistant manager or even store manager.

"I'd like to help you Al," Mr. Yamoto said. "However, you know they want the front of the store to be, how do you say this, bright white. It has to do with appearances and the people who shop here. They want people who could be their gardeners to be in the back of the store, not upfront talking with them. Why do you think I'm still doing produce after all these years?"

Albert was disappointed, but not surprised. If the store wasn't in such a high profile location, he might have stood a better chance for advancement. But, you could not argue that he was working in the heart of Hollywood, which was pretty much one of the best locations in the city. His day schedule was pretty set and he at least had one Saturday or Sunday off a week so he could be with his family. He decided to get a second job.

He had spent a few summers of his teenage years working with his father at Little Joe's, so he easily got an evening job as a waiter at the Alpine Haus in San Fernando to help sustain his growing family.

Finally, after years of renting, the couple saved enough to put a down payment on a house in a new building tract in Sylmar by the Veteran's Hospital. Albert was especially proud as he recalled Maria's father telling him that at one point minorities had been forbidden from buying homes north of the railroad tracks. Their new home was well north of these railroad tracks, and served as an indicator of how much had changed in America, or at least the San Fernando Valley.

As the family settled into their new home, Maria found out she was pregnant with child number three. Like the other two children, he was born at San Fernando Hospital. He came out with dark brown eyes, a handful of thick black hair and fingers and toes the color and texture of tootsie rolls. As the nurses toweled him off, Maria, regaining her breath, thought to herself, "This one is dark – much more so than my other children. I'm surprised at how dark he his."

Maria and her husband earlier considered the name of Robert, but when they saw the new baby's skin color, there was no denying it – this baby looked one hundred percent Mexican and no Anglo name would make him any different. They decided to name him "Aurelio" after Albert's grandfather on his parent's side. Although his name was technically pronounced "aw-REE-lee-oh," he soon came to be called "ah-RAY-lee-oh," and ultimately, the name he was referred to most frequently was simply, "Oree." His name meant "golden" and to his parents, he truly was – even if his skin was a little toasted. Immediately following his birth, his parents sensed there was something different about him – there was an awareness and brightness to his eyes, and the two dabs of brown irises shown in deep contrast against the bright whites of his eyes. It was as though Aurelio could already see and he understood that the two coo-ing over him were his parents and that they were there to protect him.

Over time, everyone found their place in their new home. Albert was proud of the life he and Maria built. He had a wife whom he loved, and together they had three beautiful children that each day filled their house with laughter, tears, joy and occasional screams.

He was also proud to be an American as he began to better understand the many opportunities his father Eduardo once spoke of, as well as the sacrifices made by all those who become parents. The sacrifices were always evident, however the opportunities weren't all readily available to him just yet, but he believed they would be soon – one day.

As the years slipped by and the children began to go to school, Albert saw that country was changing – the evening news was constantly referencing the Civil Rights Movement, Martin Luther King, and lately, a Latino, Cesar Chavez, who was encouraging Mexican-Americans to use their voices by voting. He believed these were all helping to pave the way for change.

Albert worked hard to keep his American dream afloat, and at times surmised, it simply couldn't get any better than this.

CHAPTER 4

KINDER

The night before the return to school was one of those evenings when Albert was home from both of his jobs and the house felt like a complete family lived there. The children took turns bathing and preparing themselves for the next day, and then sat down to watch Ed Sullivan. Albert relaxed in his mock-leather recliner and read the Sunday paper which he had been trying to get to since the morning. Maria was busy ironing Annie and Anthony's uniforms; Oree was starting kindergarten, and kindergartners did not need uniforms as their classes only lasted three hours a day, so he would wear brown checkered pants (his favorite) and a blue shirt that he had made his mother iron a week before ("I gotta look perfect").

"Mommy, are they going to like me in school?" Oree asked, tugging at Maria's housedress.

"Of course they're going to like you. What's not to like?" Maria said.

"Annie told me that I was gonna be the brownest kid in the kindergartener class and the teacher would have to turn on a flashlight to see me," he continued, asking with concern.

"Annie, why did you say such a thing to your little brother?" Maria asked. Turning toward her husband, she spoke in Spanish *"¿Le dirás algo?/*Will you say something to her?"

Albert looked up from his paper, "Annie, what is wrong with you? Your brother is scared enough and he has to hear that nonsense from you?"

"I was just teasing him. He's such a little Oscar Meyer wiener," Annie, who was going into the fifth grade, said.

"Annie, apologize, NOW," Maria yelled at her.

"So much for a peaceful family night at home," Albert sighed as he turned over the paper and pressed it into a new fold.

"I'm sorry Oree," Annie said. "They're gonna like you. You're gonna be smarter than all the other kids, just wait and see. But, if you see those little white kids getting better treatment than you, you say something."

"Annie, you're not helping," Maria jumped in. "Ignore your sister, she's just being herself."

"If somebody gives you any crap, you tell them your big brother Tony is going to beat them up," Anthony, who was going into the 4th grade said. "I've got a slingshot and I'll pop those little farts off."

Oree was troubled by Annie's assessment of him being the darkest kid in his class. He remembered the little girl who once called him a beaner and he was concerned they would call him that name again. He looked at his siblings: Annie was tan, she wasn't really that dark; and Anthony, well he was even lighter-skinned than his sister.

He asked his mother, why he was so dark and his brother and sister weren't.

"Oree," Maria said sympathetically. "We're all different shades of brown. Look at your father, he's darker than me, and your sister changes color whenever she's in the sun for too long. I think it's our different shades that make us pretty and unique, just like you're different from your brother and he's different than you. Now, who would want to go and have everyone look alike? It would be pretty boring, no?"

"Yeah, I guess so," Oree said somewhat unconvinced.

When it came time to go to sleep, Oree lay in his bed fretting.

"I'll have to watch to see if anyone looks like they're going to call me a name. I don't want to start school off on the wrong foot. I wonder what I'm supposed to do there? I don't know what they do in kindergarten. What if the teacher is mean? What if they try to speak to me in Spanish? I don't know Spanish. What if they want me to read, I don't even know my alphabet. I hope the kids are nice. I...." he said slumbering off with trepidation, a thousand thoughts buzzing in his head like bees swarming around a beehive.

※

"Anthony, get it in gear," Maria yelled down the hall toward the bathroom. "It's your little brother's first day and I have to take all his paperwork in."

"Mom, Aurelio just threw up," Anthony said casually walking into the kitchen, speaking like talk about vomit was part of a daily conversation.

Annie ran out of her parent's bathroom and toward the kitchen. "Mom, I just hate this uniform."

Maria quit packing lunches, ignored Annie's exclamation and made her way to the bathroom. It was times like this that she was, for lack of a better term, resentful of her husband. Sure, he got up at 4 a.m. every morning to be at work at 5:30, but it would be nice to have some help now and then. Albert viewed the raising of the children as "her job," and although she could rely upon him to be the disciplinarian when needed, she sometimes felt like the artist Michelangelo, pinned on her back trying to paint the Sistine Chapel without being able to see the complete picture, which in her case was the successful raising of her children. She had no template to work from; most often she worked to try to avoid the mistakes her parents made in her upbringing, rather than setting goals for success such as "This one will be president, this one a businessperson, this one..."

Aurelio was crying and his well-ironed blue shirt had water stains on it. A wet spot marked the front of his brown, checkered pants.

"Mommy, I don't feel good. I want to stay home with you," Aurelio said.

Maria felt his forehead, no temperature.

"Did you do number two?" she said kneeling down in front of him and while grabbing his arms, she looked into his eyes to see if he looked sick.

He nodded "no" and settled down.

"O.k. We'll just change these clothes and get you off to school. You'll like it *mijo*. It will be so much fun. After a while you'll forget that you ever stayed home with me. They have all sorts of fun things to do: finger paints, clay, coloring books and monkey bars. I used to love the monkey bars."

"What if they want me to read, I haven't learned the alphabet yet?" Oree said with a look of both concern and fear.

"Silly Oree, that's why you're going to school," Maria chuckled. "Trust me, you're going to know your ABC's in no time and you'll be counting to 10 by the end of the year. I can't remember though if they teach you those in kindergarten or first grade? Either way, you'll be fine. Now, be a little man and help me clean you up."

As she spoke, Maria felt a stab of sadness. Although she had made the same first day of school speech twice before, she realized this would be the last time she extolled the virtues of tempera paint and crayons. Standing, she cleaned Aurelio up, gathered him in her arms and carried him to his room to change his clothes. His head fell softly against her shoulder and she realized with painful awareness that a part of her life had just ended. She walked past a hallway mirror with Oree still limp in her arms. Looking out of the corner of her eye, she felt a wisp of her brown hair with a few strands of gray mixed in fall across her face. She could have sworn she saw her mother peering back at her.

Aurelio sat in the basement kindergarten of Saint Mary the Merciful, eyeing the curious green, teal and brown corrugated and scalloped borders that lined the chalkboards of the classroom. Transom windows streamed shards of light which helped to brighten the dark and musty room. Looking at a brown cork board with construction paper cut in the shape of leaves, he thought it all looked quite nice. Very adult-like and very important.

The kindergarten room of Saint Mary's was separated from the other parts of the campus which included a church, classrooms, a baseball field, play grounds, a rectory where two priests lived, a parish hall and a convent for the parish's 10 nuns. The school was set in two thick, brick, two-story buildings – grades one through four in one building, and grades five through eighth in the other building. It was in essence its own little, self-contained world of piety.

The kindergarten classroom had previously been a storage area, but since the church was "evolving" as a result of Vatican II, it was decided that greater inclusion was something Saint Mary's should undertake. That inclusion included adding classrooms for little sinful heathens such as kindergartners.

The kindergarten room had long tables that were miniature sized and they contained miniature chairs for the miniature children to sit on. Almost systematically, mothers walked their children in, took their coats and hung them on hooks that lined the classroom walls, sat them down and then left. Two teacher's assistants helped the children to get settled. Overall, it was like it was all some well-planned strategy that only adults knew – they came and deposited their children in the dark basement, perhaps never to be heard from again.

"Momma are you coming back?" Oree asked as Maria sat him down.

"Yes. Remember what I taught you. When the clock's big hand is on the 12 and the little hand is on the 11, I'll be waiting outside," Maria said. "You're going to be fine Oree. You're going to like this. I promise."

And, with that Maria shuffled out of the room like the other somnolent parents.

After the last child had been deposited, Oree spied Sister Anastasia – a long, lanky woman with an ashen, hollow face; a thick, black wool habit; and fingers that resembled the crab legs they once ate at the Santa Monica pier. As she entered the room, Aurelio thought that she resembled the witch in Snow White and he began to grow fearful. Her face was pulled in and narrow, with a nose larger than any Aurelio had ever seen. Dark brown, wooden rosary beads hung down the left side of her long robe, and along the right side, a thick leather strop holding a ring of keys that swung as she walked, jingling like a prison warden. Aurelio thought her leather-soled shoes resembled something the Wicked Witch of the East would wear and they clicked hollowly each time they touched the speckly linoleum floor.

"Good morning children, I am Sister Anastasia and I'll be your kindergarten teacher," she began with barely a smile on her pale lips. "We're going to bring you closer to God this year while learning all sorts of wonderful things."

Aurelio didn't trust her. She smiled, a gold-rimmed tooth gleaming in front like his grandfather's, but her smile was nothing like the warm ones his grandfather always bestowed upon him.

"We'll be learning all sorts of new things and if you ever have to go to the bathroom, please let me know. Only babies wet, or do worse, in their seats," she continued. "Now, I'm going to read your names and as I do, please say 'present.' This is how I will know if you're here every day."

She began the alphabetical litany of names. The kindergarten class had all sorts of names Oree had never heard before: "Leslie Anderson, Chester Chan, Mary Henry, Jimmy Jones, Christine Lopez, Robert Manetti, Aurelio Rodrigo – Aurelio Rodrigo." Oree was caught up in the syncopation of titles as he thought to himself that he had never heard such a stream of long and weird-sounding names.

"Aurelio Rodrigo are you here?" her words interrupted his daydreaming and caught him off guard.

"Presente!" Oree said raising his hand straight up in the air, half in a daze and half in an effort to impress the nun with his assumed multi-language skills.

The room suddenly grew as quiet as a monastery full of monks.

"Aurelio, please come up here," the nun said pointing a crab leg up from her name registry. "Now, I know some of you may speak other languages when you're home, but not in this school and not in my class."

Aurelio slowly made his way to the front of the room.

"Aurelio, put your hands out straight, palms up. I want you to understand that Spanish is a bad, bad language and we don't use bad language in this class. You are never to use that language again," the nun said, pulling the leather strop from her rope belt. "Now, hold your hands out."

Aurelio put his hands out and felt the hot sting of the cold belt three times against his upraised palms. As Sister Anastasia whacked, she continued: "I don't ever want to hear you using that bad language again. You do understand that this is America and we only speak English here? Americans are very fortunate to live in a country where we all speak the same language and think alike, so you can see that it is unacceptable to use other languages – especially Spanish."

Aurelio wanted to cry, but he fought back tears which stung the back of his eyeballs. As he dropped his hands to his sides, his palms felt hot from the flash of the belt. He wouldn't be embarrassed in front of the class on his very first day in school. He looked up at Sister Anastasia who smiled disdainfully. For all he knew, she could keep him after class, hack him up into little pieces and dump him in a flour sack by a river, like *La Llorona*, the crying lady of Mexico who God condemned to search rivers for her children which she had chopped up. He figured he better be good and not make a stink.

"Now, go sit down Aurelio," she said putting her bony, cold hand on his shoulder. "And, for any others of you who use any bad language in class, you will receive the same lesson. Do you understand?"

"Yes sister," the class said in unison.

As he blew on his palms to cool them down, Aurelio realized a very important thing. Speaking Spanish was bad and could get you in trouble. Being Mexican had gotten him in trouble before and it happened again, only now it was made worse by the fact that he spoke Spanish – a double whammy. He knew this was not a good situation. He looked at his red hands which were throbbing and vowed to never again speak the bad language and not to behave in any manner which could be misconstrued as not being American. He looked around at the other children who were staring at him and felt that shame again – the same shame from the merry-go-round. He had felt it a few other times, like when he was in a candy store and the Italian store owner motioned the red-haired, freckled boy behind him in line to come to the register and pay first. He still didn't know why he felt the shame, but as he was getting older, he was able to recognize it better – that realization, however, did not make it hurt any less.

He wondered what other things he would have to learn in school. Here it was, his first day and he had already made a very bad mistake. Annie said everyone would like him – well, she was wrong. He thought in his head: "Avoid Sister Anastasia at all costs!"

And, thus began the education of Aurelio Rodrigo.

That afternoon, while at home eating a grilled cheese sandwich, he would tell his mother what happened at school and that the nun hit him on the hands because he said something in Spanish.

Maria's response was simple, "Well, what do you think we're paying to send you to that school for? You know you shouldn't be speaking Spanish and must always listen to the nuns."

Following his rocky start, kindergarten quickly became a bore for Aurelio. He had little interest in making clay ashtrays and marginal interest in making papier mâché banks. For his papier mâché project, Oree decided to create a pig with a curly pipe cleaner tail and nose fashioned out of an egg carton egg holder. In completing the project, he decided to cover the pig in purple tempera paint as who would ever think of creating a purple pig? He was quite pleased with how "Elmer," as he named him, turned out.

After the first semester, Oree's class was shifted from mornings to afternoons from 1 to 4 p.m., so he soon learned to take a great interest in naps. Nice stories were always played on the record player during nap time, and he marveled at tales like "Peter and the Wolf" and "Little Red Riding Hood." During nap time, he learned that he could avoid the ire of Sister Anastasia if he closed his eyes and pretended to sleep even if he wasn't tired: "Good children sleep during nap time, so I expect you to all be good children."

He quickly learned that there was a certain protocol to kindergarten. Sister Anastasia behaved one way which made the children act another.

Talking out of turn was never permitted and singing in class during quiet time (even if unintentional) could be met with a belt on the hands. He wondered why they had to do some things over and over again – like lining up before every morning class arrival, before and after every recess, again before and after every lunch, and finally when leaving school for the day – and having to look straight ahead. It was like the soldiers he had seen on a television special about the Vietnam War.

He found it curious how the children would group into little pods on the playground during recess. The school yard had a jungle gym, swings, overhand bars, several hopscotch courts and a sand box which was canopied by a large oak tree. The children were expected to make friends, but Oree didn't quite see the point. At home he had Annie and Anthony to play with; these children wouldn't be going home with him when school let out, so why the big deal to make friends? In Oree's class, there were Anglo, Mexican, Negro and Asian children. The girls only grouped with girls and the boys most often grouped into pods of bigger ones and smaller ones. Oree was small for his age, so when he played in groups, he was relegated to the smaller boy's pod.

He, like most of the other children, didn't seem to notice the difference in their skin colors, although one time, a red-haired little girl who came from Texas and had an accent different than any he had heard in the past, chased him around the playground at lunch screaming: "Come here chickee baby, I wanna give you a big kiss on those big dark lips. We have lots of messicans in Texas and I LOVE them all!" She kind of scared Aurelio, so he made it a point to stay as far away from her as possible.

He was still quite confused over the difference between being a "Mexican" and an "American." His mother was continually reminding him and his siblings that they were American, but he had heard something on the TV about some Mexican named Cesar Chavez and farm workers who had started something called a boycott. On the television news, he saw people that looked as dark as him. As a matter of fact, he thought this Cesar Chavez might be his father, if of course, he didn't already have one. He wondered if all Mexicans started boycotts, and if so, did he need to start one?

In the end, all he was able to understand from the whole boycott situation was that when they went to the supermarket his mother said they couldn't buy grapes and then months later, lettuce. He was resentful as he liked grapes better than carrots and celery – even with peanut butter.

One day Oree had an upset stomach, so he asked if he could stay in the classroom during lunch. One of the teacher's aides volunteered to stay behind with him and grade papers. They had been working on a project in class where the children made fans out of popsicle sticks, so there were buckets of popsicle sticks and tubs of school glue on the tables. Oree looked at the glue and wooden sticks and had an idea…

It was during the annual tamale making party, one of the few Mexican traditions which the Alizaca women took part in, that Maria and her sister Cathy had an opportunity to share uninterrupted time together. Making tamales each year for Christmas was a significant event which took a lot of planning and work. First, there was the preparation. Maria was in charge of getting the masa, so early one morning on the first Saturday of December, she stood outside Cabreras' in San Fernando, a big metal pot in hand, to get the masa needed for the tamales. Cathy had been in charge of preparing the meat, so she arrived at the Rodrigo house with a big pot in the back of her station wagon. She came with her four children – Lupita, Raymond Jr., Cynthia and Narciso. Grandmother Bessie had been diagnosed with arthritis earlier in the year and her hands had been giving her problems, so she was to arrive later to help ensure her daughters were not deviating too far from the traditional recipes.

All the children had unique "assignments." Anthony and Raymond Jr. were in charge of spreading the masa on water soaked corn husks; Cynthia, Anita and Lupita were in charge of filling the tamales: either roasted green chili and monterey jack cheese, beef with chili colorado, or beef with raisins (no one liked those much except for Lupita); and Aurelio and Narciso were to put olives in some of the tamales. It was always a great treat to find a black olive in a tamale, so the two youngsters made sure to make good use of the cans of olives they were given. Maria and Cathy closed up the husks, or tied some with strings depending on the type of tamale.

The children were set to work on a table in the dining room, and when they would fill a foiled baking sheet with the prepped tamales, they would take turns carrying the tray into the kitchen to Maria and Cathy who sat at the breakfast nook. When the sisters finalized each tamale, they would carefully place them in the General Electric steamer for cooking. As they diligently worked, they spoke freely.

"So, Sister Anastasia calls me into class when I picked up Oree to show me something he did," Maria said to Cathy, as she looked across the table into the dining room to see that her youngest son had placed black olives on each of his tiny finger tips and had begun counting them. "Oree, don't play with the olives," she yelled into the other room.

"What did that little fart do now?" Cathy said, tying up a tamale like it was a Christmas present.

"Sister Anastasia leads me to her desk and sitting on top is this little cabin made out of popsicle sticks. It had four walls, a roof and the opening for a door. She said Oree made it," Maria continued. "It was all very meticulous and very well made. Each stick was glued neatly on top of the next one, and the back had this framework that would probably support a real house, if it were made of popsicle sticks that is. The weird thing is the nun said he made it in like a half an hour while the class was at lunch. She said he said he had seen it on a Lincoln Log commercial and since he didn't have Lincoln Logs, he used the popsicle sticks. Then, she said I had to pay for all the sticks he used to make his house, as they had been planned for use with another project.

"The nun said she thought Oree might be gifted or something, but it was too early to tell," Maria finished.

Cathy thought to herself that none of the public school teachers who taught her children ever mentioned anything about any of them being possibly gifted. The best she ever got was that Lupita appeared to be "militant," whatever that meant.

"Well, what are you going to do?" Cathy asked, counting tamales at bottom of the steamer. From the dining room, they heard the children animatedly engaged in a conversation about some new TV show called the "Brady Bunch" and who was Marcia, Jan or one of the other children featured on the show. She heard Anita say, "I'm Marcia, she's the groovy one. Cynthia you look like a Jan, the needy one."

"I dunno. We don't have money to send him to any special school, Saint Mary's is expensive enough," Maria continued. "Plus, even if he's gifted, what makes him different than the other two? Albert and I decided a long time ago that all our children would have the same opportunities, so I can't treat him any different than the others."

"Well, Raymond Jr. can be Greg as he's the oldest," she heard Anita continue. Maria looked over at Cathy who appeared to be a thousand miles away.

"What do you think, Cathy? I mean we try to treat all the kids the same, right?" Maria finished. "Are you o.k.?"

"Yeah," Cathy piped back into the conversation. "Raymond's been working a lot and he has been a pain to deal with. When he gets home, he's always tired and irritated, and the first thing he does is run to the fridge to pop open a beer. Then, he gets all upset if the kids are too noisy, screaming 'Shut your kids up' like I made them on my own."

"Well, your husband has always been kinda hot-headed. If you need to drop them off here any time, it's no problem at all," Maria said. "You know the kids love to see their cousins."

"Thanks Mare," Cathy said, as they heard from the other room: "Lupita can be Alice as she's the oldest, and with her looks, she'll be lucky if she gets to be a maid when she grows up." They heard all the children giggling at Anita's last comment.

Maria smiled. Anita was always the most quick-witted of all her children. She dreamt that her daughter would be the first of her children to graduate from college – something that had not been done by any member of either the Rodrigo or Alizaca families. Things were changing rapidly in America, and women were increasingly finding their place in colleges across the country. People like Gloria Steinem and those from the Women's Liberation Movement were helping to see to that.

Maria was also excited by the nun's comment that Aurelio might be gifted, but still it was the sixties and Albert was working hard enough to keep a roof over their head, food on the table and the children in private school. There wouldn't be any room in their tight budget to pay for anything related to being gifted. Plus, she had little idea what the term "gifted" meant and further how it could help her son to become anything different than what he was, a simple Mexican-American from a humble family.

When Maria spoke with the nun about Oree's activity, she asked Sister Anastasia if she could keep his log cabin. The nun obliged once Maria said she would replenish the popsicle stick fund.

While she continued with the tamale assembly, she looked up at the miniature house on top of the refrigerator. She had strategically placed it there so she could look at it every day and keep it away from the kids at the same time. Seeing it made her feel happy inside that she was doing something with her life, that her kids would become something.

She pulled her attention away from the top of the refrigerator as one of the children brought in another tray of tamales. At the same time, she heard her mother Bessie walk in the front door and the kids stopped their tamale-making to say hello. In response Maria heard from the living room, "Don't get any masa on me, this is a clean dress." Bessie walked into the kitchen, kissed each of her daughters on the cheek and asked if any of the tamales were ready to sample. Maria laughed, "It's not that late in the day mother. We just put them in the steamer."

"O.k.," Bessie said as she poured herself a cup of coffee, sat down and joined her daughters in conversation. "Cathy, you look tired. Are you sleeping?"

As he soon learned that the alphabet wasn't part of instruction until the first grade, in the second semester of kindergarten, Oree worked secretly with one of the teacher's aides at recess, to learn the squiggly letters. By the end of the school term, he had mastered the entire alphabet.

When spring and kindergarten graduation arrived, Oree felt he was an old pro at kindergarten, and he was looking forward to the first grade. He was especially pleased that he would be out from under the reign of Sister Anastasia, she with those cold, boney fingers and ever-ready shaving strop.

For graduation, the children made hats out of construction paper, and Oree was excited that the kindergarten class got to parade around the big school yard. On graduation day, he wore the outfit his mother bought him for Easter – a pair of brown corduroy big bell bottom pants and a green shirt with extra wide lapels. The young woman who sold them the outfit at the Sears Outlet said he would look "boss." He didn't know what "boss" meant exactly, but he sure liked the sound of it.

CHAPTER 5

VACATION

The summer before Oree was to enter first grade was the first time his family ever took a real vacation (outside of an occasional day trip to Disneyland). His parents had been setting aside money for months to take their family to San Diego for four days where they were to visit the San Diego Zoo and Sea World, home of Shamu the killer whale. They also planned a side trip to Tijuana. Maria made a special visit to the beauty shop to get a fix on her bouffant which lately resembled more of an underinflated bicycle tire, and by the morning they were leaving, you could feel electricity in the air as the family packed up their sea blue Buick station wagon.

Albert also loaded a box of old clothes in the back jump seat of the wagon which was already filled with their luggage which had been borrowed from Albert's parents.

"What are you doing daddy?" Oree asked.

"Oh, you'll see. It's just a little surprise," his father replied.

Maria made bologna sandwiches for the trip, filled a Thermos full of Kool-Aid and packed a big bag of Lays potato chips which she kept up front to prevent food fights. They loaded everyone into the car and made their way to the San Diego/405 Freeway. As the freeway had only been completed a few years back, traffic wasn't an issue, so if they made good time, Albert said they could stop for lunch at the Mission San Juan Capistrano, a place known for its annual migration of swallows.

Within an hour, the children forgot they were in the car and could have been headed anywhere. Anthony was reading a book on Sherlock Holmes and sat quietly. Annie was looking at the freeway signs whiz by as she toyed with her split ends and chewed on her nails. Occasionally, she poured over a *Tiger Beat* magazine which featured her current heart throb, David Cassidy. Oree, who perched with an Etch A Sketch in his hands, sat shotgun and popped up behind the center of the front seat every few minutes with one question or another.

"Do we have to be afraid of the killer whale? What if he gets out? Will he kill us?" Oree asked.

"Are you kidding me?" Annie smirked. "You dork, whales need to be in the water to live. It's not like he's going to climb out and bite your head off or anything."

"Don't call your brother a dork," Maria yelled over the back seat. If Annie had been sitting next to her, she would have seen that both she and Albert were trying their best not to smile – as they both knew, Aurelio could indeed be a bit of a dork.

"Oree is such a little douchebag," added Anthony, "always asking those lame questions."

"That's it. Say one more thing and I'm going to take off my *chancla* and start using it," Maria said. "And, you're all within reach over this seat. Now, calm down. We'll stop and have lunch at the Mission San Juan."

To make her threat more real, Maria reached down toward her leg like she was going to take off her shoe which made the children sit back into their seats. As she was bending down, she didn't see Anthony poke Oree in the ribs and under his breath call him a "dumb ass."

Maria sat back up and reminded herself to enjoy their vacation. The kids were growing so fast. This was the first time that her husband had set aside time to take them anywhere of this magnitude, and she wanted to encourage him to take part in the kid's lives.

Plus, there had been "an incident" the year before which made Maria aware that she had to work hard to keep her marriage strong.

One night, her husband came home late from his job at the market and he smelled faintly of a sweet perfume. She thought it odd that the first thing he did was jump in the shower when he got home, and she waited until the children went to bed to discuss it with him. In asking if there was anything they needed to talk about and that she noticed the scent of perfume when he walked in the door, Albert said that it was a joke – that one of the deli section ladies sprayed him with perfume when he tried to grab a few cold cuts they were assembling on a party platter. Albert's explanation didn't make sense to Maria, but she thought hard before reacting. She considered Cathy's marriage and what a nasty jerk her husband Raymond was. Albert wasn't like that at all. He never mistreated her and he had never come home smelling like perfume before. He was a good father to the children and he gave their family whatever they needed. Maria told him she didn't really believe him but she wasn't willing to make a big deal over it.

"Albert, you need to consider your family," she told him. "If you are doing things you shouldn't be doing, you will lose a lot. And, don't think I wouldn't ask for a divorce. I see my sister's marriage and I won't tolerate any of that nonsense. I want you to be very clear on that."

Maria was surprised at the firmness of her voice as she put her husband on notice. Albert didn't really respond, he only nodded quietly which made Maria even more resolute that he had indeed cheated on her. She remembered the advice her mother once gave as part of her instructions on family and marriage.

"Remember girls, we're Catholics and nothing is more important than *la familia*. When you get married, it is important that you do whatever you need to make your marriages work, because it is a sin to get divorced. If you ever have trouble in your marriage it is your responsibility to work things out. Men have a habit of behaving like little boys, and when they do, sometimes you have no choice but to tolerate it. It's one of those things a good wife has to endure," Bessie had once said as she proffered marital advice to her daughters. She was good at making complicated things like extramarital affairs sound as matter-of-fact as a peanut butter and jam sandwich. Another favorite of hers was, "You get pregnant, you marry him. So you decide how good that will feel when you're getting those urges."

Following the incident, it took several months for Maria to again begin trusting her husband. He did the usual "make up" things like buying chocolates and flowers, but she retreated into herself further when he did these things. It was like he was acknowledging his mistake every time he gave her a gift. She very rarely bought records, but it soon became a joke of the children who would croon Ben E. King's "Stand by Me," outside the kitchen window at the times Maria would play the 45 rpm when she thought they weren't within earshot. On a few occasions, the children thought they could hear crying coming from the kitchen and when they tried to enter the house to ascertain its source, they were greeted by one word – "Out!"

Maria stuffed the bad memories back into a little box, and turned her attention back toward the road. She looked over at her husband who was focused on driving, and she remembered what her mother said about things having to be "endured." She hoped that she didn't have to tolerate many more episodes like the one they had been through.

The family stopped at Mission San Juan Capistrano for lunch and couldn't find a swallow in sight. They made a quick stop at the church to pray and popped back into the station wagon, heading farther south to San Diego. Finally, after what seemed to be an eternity, they saw the bay. Within five minutes of checking in at the Mission Bay Holiday Inn, the kids were in their swim suits and headed for the pool.

"Annie and Anthony, watch out for Oree. I'll come and get you when it's time for dinner," Maria said as she began unpacking their clothes and putting them in drawers. Albert was still unpacking the car as the children rushed by him. If he had been any lighter, they would have knocked him over as they made their way to the pool.

"I'll be down there shortly, so try not to drown 'til I get there," he yelled at the blur of beach towels flying by. "Maybe Maria and I can lock the door for a few minutes," he quietly thought to himself as their relationship was still on the mend.

The day the family went to Sea World, the children were excited to see all the aquatic life. Annie loved the sea horses as she was amazed at how they floated so lightly and had such beautiful, curving tails. Anthony liked the dolphins, they reminded him of his favorite TV show, "Flipper." When it came time for the Shamu Show, Oree was both excited and nervous. The family got to the viewing stands early to make sure they got good seats, after all, Shamu was the first whale ever captured to survive in captivity.

"How about these?" Albert said pointing to the fourth row.

"Tooooo close," Oree exclaimed. "How about up there?" he said pointing to the mid-section of the bleachers.

"You wiener. I told you he won't bite your head off," Annie said.

"It's o.k. Oree, we'll compromise," Albert said, "Row 10."

"What's compromise?" Oree asked.

"It means we don't get to sit close enough to get wet," Annie smirked.

When the show began, the bleachers were full and the family was amazed at the tricks the killer whale could execute. They liked when the trainers hoisted a fish on a long pole high in the air for Shamu to shoot out of the water to swallow his treat. Oree sat there cautiously. He didn't seem to "oohhh" and "aahhhh" like the rest of the crowd, it was more like he was observing a science experiment. He was pensive and seemed more concerned with the crowd's reactions and behavior rather than what was going on in the water. At the end of the show, everyone laughed and applauded – especially those in the first eight rows who got splashed with water during one of Shamu's high flips.

When they got back to the hotel that evening, after dinner they all went down to sit by the pool. Albert, Annie and Anthony jumped in and Maria sat in a chair watching them (she didn't want to mess up her bouffant, so compromises had to be made). She was surprised when Oree crawled up on her and rolled himself into a ball on her lap. He nuzzled his nose into her armpit with his face turned away from the pool.

As everyone else was in the pool, she sat him up and could see his eyes were filling with tears: his thick, long black eyelashes glistening and clumping together with moisture.

"What is it *mijo*?" she asked.

"Do you think Shamu's sad?" Oree remarked. "I mean the trainers said he was the first killer whale they captured on purpose and he is stuck in the same pool every day. He lived in the ocean which is very big and he's very big. It's like they took out of him out of his home and put him in a place that isn't his home and where he really can't be himself. He's had to learn all these tricks just so he can fit in. It's doesn't seem very nice to me."

"Oree, where do you come up with these things?" Maria asked, somewhat amazed at the sensitivity of her child. "It's o.k. I'm sure Shamu is fine. He gets fed every day and he gets to learn all these neat tricks. People love him. If he were in the ocean, he would probably get eaten by a big whale or something, you just never know. I'm sure he's happy in the world he lives in."

"I suppose, but if I were him, being stuck someplace I didn't want to be and having to behave certain ways to get fed, I would want to get out. I would be very sad," Oree said still teary-eyed.

Maria put a Kleenex to his nose. "Blow. Don't worry about Shamu, he's just fine. Now, why don't you go play in the pool with your father, Anthony and Annie?"

Oree climbed off her and as she saw him waddle to the pool, she felt sadness. She didn't like to see her children in pain and she again felt that sense that Aurelio was different than the other kids – he seemed to see things in things that 6-year-olds generally didn't think about. Could he possibly be "gifted" as his kindergarten teacher suggested? He was always so sensitive, and he got far more bloody noses and headaches than the other two children. That made her a little nervous. He did seem to perseverate about everything and the other two children were nothing like him at that age. What if he went crazy or had a split personality or grew up to be psychotic or something? What would she do then?

The children were ecstatic the morning the blue Buick crossed over the border into Tijuana. The streets were festooned with hanging, brightly colored paper doilies and they could hear the sounds of firecrackers popping in the background. When the children rolled down the windows they could tell it was hot and the air smelled like car exhaust, burnt chicharrons and petroleum.

"This looks groovy. Are we going to stop here?" Anthony asked.

"We'll be back, but first we have to make a side stop," his father said as they drove away from the busy streets and made their way to a hillside on the outskirts of town. The children, who had been chirping and excitedly talking a few minutes earlier, began to quiet down as they peered out onto the hillsides. In the distance, and as they approached closer, they saw – cardboard.

This just wasn't a few pieces of cardboard. These were masses of cardboard that had been fashioned into makeshift housing. The houses lined the foothills and stretched down into a gulley. The configurations of cardboard resembled a makeshift housing tract, and each house was constructed with multiple large sheets of the corrugated material. They had roofs and some even had doors, or at least expanses of wood that resembled doors. There was a sense of structure to it all, like each had been carefully erected not to intrude upon the others.

"What is this?" Annie asked.

"This is where people live Annie," Albert said quietly.

"Whaaa, how, how is this possible?" Annie said incredulously.

"We are very fortunate to have been born Americans and to live in America," Albert, who had obviously prepared the speech well in advance, began to say. "Not everyone in this world is as lucky as we are, and a lot of people in lots of places in the world have to live like this. We should never take for granted the many good things we have been fortunate enough to have. You children should never take for granted your house, or your clothes or the food your mother puts on the table for you, because this could have just as easily been our life."

The children looked out over the sea of cardboard. Occasionally, they saw a shadow move in or out of the boxes; they saw people walking with buckets of water and dogs eating scraps of food along a slight trail of water that could have been a stream at some point. Trash was littered everywhere. A few shadows looked toward the car. Albert stopped the engine and opened the door gate in the rear of the car.

"Stay inside kids," he called as he began to pull the big box out of the back.

Within seconds and out of nowhere, the car was enveloped with people swarming around the box and ripping out clothes. The children locked the back doors as more and more people approached the station wagon. It was like an attack of locusts, and the noise of people speaking in Spanish began to rise to a high pitch. Albert finally threw the box out of the car and shut the door. The mass of locust people continued to swarm. They descended upon the clothes and were picking at them like they were remnants of flesh left on a chicken bone. An old man with brown leathery skin, a few strands of oily grey hair and no teeth knocked on the side window and smiled inside at Oree who, perspiring heavily, began screaming.

"Aurelio, settle down. They're just people," his mother yelled over the back seat, although she was also a bit overwhelmed and made nervous by the picture that was unfolding around them.

Albert slowly got back into the car as hands pulled at him. He started the engine, and as they slowly drove away, through the rear view mirror he could see people pulling at the clothes, until everything, including the cardboard box, had disappeared in the plumes of dust left by his car tires.

By the time their Tijuana excursion had ended, the children had for the most part forgotten the sight of the cardboard city. As they drove back to Sylmar that evening, they sat in the back of the car pouring over their treasures from the day: Anthony snagged a wooden slingshot which shot bb pellets, Oree got a patron saint of the Mexican Cinema, Cantinflas, string puppet, and Annie bought a Mexican peasant blouse and huarache sandals. They had experienced their first taste of Mexican ice cream ("nasty"), had their picture taken with funny sombreros on the back of a striped donkey and learned a new word – "pocho" – which a clerk called their father in a souvenir shop. Maria didn't take too kindly to the euphemism which was a Spanish term for a Mexican who behaved like a white person. She shouted back something to the shop owners in Spanish which her husband had to ask her the meaning of;

he thought it had something to do with their mothers being donkeys or something.

As things quieted on the way back home, Oree fell asleep and Anthony looked vacantly out the side window as a stream of highway lamps cascaded by.

"It doesn't make sense to me," Annie said as she ran her fingers over the delicate embroidery on her peasant blouse. "How can those people live like that? Why doesn't someone help them?"

"*Mija*, the Mexican government is corrupt, that's why your grandparents came to America," Albert said. "It was a long time ago and the United States wasn't so strict on letting foreigners in – your grandparents also made every effort possible to become American and that is why we are so firm about you kids appreciating what you have in this country. Mexico has always had problems and I wanted you kids to see how some people have to live to survive. We take a lot of granted at home."

"When I was your age, my dad was very strict with me – I was not allowed to speak Spanish outside of the house and we always had to look presentable whenever we went anywhere. When your mother and I were dating, the government started sending Mexicans back to Mexico – regardless if they were U.S. citizens or not. We had to be very careful to avoid *la migra*, even though we were born in the States," he continued. "That's why we haven't taught you kids Spanish – if you had accents in school or dressed like you just got here, people would think of you in a certain way, which we don't want. Look at that time your little brother got called beaner – he wasn't even speaking Spanish. You are Americans, plain and simple."

"That's why we don't call ourselves Chicanos," he finished. "Being a Mexican American is something to be proud of – calling us by another name makes us feel like there is something wrong with who we are, and that there needs to be a special name to identify us. When your grandparents got here this country only had names for us like 'wetback,' 'beaner' or 'greaser.' To be identified as an American who is of Mexican descent is an honor to me. Being called a Chicano doesn't sounds very honorable to me."

"I don't understand why people are treated differently because of the color of their skin or because they speak another language, or because they call themselves Chicano or Mexican American," Annie continued.

"It's just the way it is *mija*," her father said. "Things are much better for us than they were for my parents who almost always lived in fear because they weren't born in this country – even after they became citizens."

"Is that why we always have to eat white people food?" she added. "Macaroni and cheese, Spam, hot dogs and SpaghettiOs gets sooooo old."

"Annie, when am I supposed to find time to make you beans and tortillas by hand?" Maria laughed. "Cooking Mexican food takes a lot of time which I don't have. When I was growing up my mom started making us gringo stuff, so it only made sense for me to cook for you what I was brought up on. Plus, you kids are picky. You see how your brother acts when I make *menudo* – 'No way. I'm not eating cow guts!'"

Maria, Albert and Annie laughed as they made their way home.

A few weeks following their return, Albert was relieved that his family had taken their vacation when they did. In August, Los Angeles was beset by the Watt's Riots. As the smoke from South Central permeated the air all the way up to the Valley, Albert asked Maria to keep the children close by. People were being beaten and dying, and properties were being destroyed. Albert listened to his transistor radio continuously at work – he vowed to Maria he would head home at the slightest sign of trouble. Fortunately, the riots never got close to their home, but Albert borrowed a gun from his father just in case.

CHAPTER 6

SCHOOL

First grade turned out to be a better fit for Oree than kindergarten. He liked the fact that school lasted all day and that it was broken up into two separate parts – morning session and afternoon session.

He preferred mornings as that was when the real learning was done. The first semester, the class concentrated on their ABCs with a special emphasis on penmanship and block letter writing. As he already knew his alphabet and had been practicing it over summer, Oree played along like he didn't know. He didn't want to risk being a know-it-all with his teacher Mrs. Schultz. For all he knew she could be related to Sister Anastasia, and he didn't want to get on her bad side.

He did slip once during the lesson on "S", which for some reason the children couldn't master. He was especially bored during this tedious endeavor which seemed to go on forever ("How difficult is it to draw two opposite curves?" Oree reasoned). In his boredom, he spied upon the two perfect, waist-length, braided pigtails sported by Sandra Lopez who sat directly in front of him. As they hung casually over her seat, he quietly grabbed each and tied them in a nice knot over the back rung of her chair. He sat there pondering his work and the possible need to disassemble it while he eyed the hands on the clock indicating that recess was coming soon. It was warm in the classroom and he began to doze, slipping off while thoughts of "S" curves floated by in his mind.

He was quickly awakened by the peel of the recess bell and the scream of Sandra Lopez whose head was pulled back when she tried to get out of her seat.

"Aurelio Rodrigo, did you do this?" the teacher, Mrs. Schultz, yelled as she comforted Sandra who was sobbing and rubbing her scalp.

His antics cost him a spanking by the teacher, a trip to the office, a call to his mother and a rare paddling by his father.

For the most part, Aurelio's efforts in the first grade were by and large unextraordinary. His favorite part of the day was reading, and when the time came, he easily mastered everything they put in front of him. His favorite books were "Jack and Janet" – they always had great adventures and he excitedly poured over each and every book. He liked that the perfectly American children found in the pages of the books had toys like fire trucks, red wagons and nice clothes. His family did not have money for things like fire trucks and new clothes – most of his shirts and pants were hand me downs from either his brother or cousins, and quite often the patches on the knees of his pants had patches put over them. His mother was always saying how poor they were, as was evidenced by the inability to afford a fire truck, new pants or even a red wagon. Oree didn't mind that his family was poor, as once he learned how to sign for his library card, he was able to immerse himself in books which created a far richer existence than any he had discovered in his hometown of Sylmar. He quickly devoured all the Dr. Seuss books, and found another book that would become his all-time favorite – "Where the Wild Things Are." He especially liked "Wild Things" as he likened himself to Max, the little boy who goes to where the wild things live and becomes the king of their kingdom.

Afternoons were activity times in the first grade, and toward the end of the school year, the class was to learn a piece to perform at their year-end school pageant – "Sing a Song of Sixpence."

> *Sing a song of sixpence*
> *A pocket full of rye*
> *Four and twenty blackbirds*
> *Baked in a pie*

When the pie was opened
The birds began to sing
Wasn't that a dainty dish
To set before the king…

Everyone in the class was to participate in the performance. There would be need for a king, queen, a maid, a baker and blackbirds. Aurelio was excited as he wanted to be the lead blackbird – "the most important" as he deemed it. He knew he had a good shot at it as he was one of the smallest children in the class – and definitely one of the darkest. When it came time to assign roles, Aurelio wasted no time in making his wishes known.

"Mrs. Schultz, I want to be the most important blackbird," Oree said tugging at the teacher's skirt.

"And, why is it that we should make you the most important blackbird Aurelio?" the teacher asked looking down past her thick black-framed glasses and bulbous nose.

"I'm the smallest boy, every boy is bigger than me. And, I can chirp like a bird. Look," he said and began chirping. "Most important of all, is that the song is about four and twenty blackbirds. Well, outside of the negroes in our class, I am the blackest."

Mrs. Schultz looked down with an incredulous stare. She wasn't sure if she should laugh, but in the end she smiled, "Well, Aurelio you make a very compelling case and I will think about your proposal."

Oree wasn't sure what a "compelling case" or "proposal" was, but when it came time to announce the roles for the pageant, he was announced as the "lead blackbird" for which he got to occupy the center of the pie (a brown bed sheet cut in a circular shape which was held up as a pie crust by a few of the children). The four blackbirds stood in the center of the "pie crust" and were covered by a white sheet with black spots which was to resemble the top part of the crust and the fork holes poked in it. When it came time for the pie to open, they threw off the sheet and began chirping and flapping their arms like birds. They then danced around the outside of the pie crust, and Oree got to act like he was pecking off the nose of the maid which was part of the song's lyrics:

The maid was in the garden,
Hanging out the clothes,
When down came a blackbird
And pecked off her nose.

Their performance went off flawlessly, and at the end of the song, Aurelio was especially proud of the important role he played in making the presentation a success.

When they weren't in school, Oree spent time with his siblings. Anita was heavily into Diana Ross and the Supremes at the time, and he would spend afternoons lying on the bed in her room listening to "Baby Love," while she did homework. Or, she would have him help her paint picket posters for whatever cause she was into at the time. She would often lead upper grade "sit ins" for things like longer lunch periods, or for a more ethnic representation of food at the cafeteria (the hot dogs and burgers were pretty nasty, an occasional bean burrito would help).

Aurelio preferred the time he spent with his brother Anthony. They would often play basketball in the driveway or re-enact roller derby bouts with other children on the block, based upon what they had seen at the Olympic Auditorium's Roller Games.

One Saturday morning, Anthony had the idea of playing Evel Knievel and they would have "Evel" (Anthony) fly over his assistant (Aurelio) with his Schwinn bicycle. They created ascension and landing ramps out of egg crates and plywood on the street fronting their house. They rallied all the children on the block and charged a dime to see Anthony "take air" over his brother Aurelio, who would lay between the two ramps. Oree had his mother make popcorn which he sold for a nickel a bag (of course Oree didn't explain to her what it was for).

There was a sense of excitement in the air as 10 children, including two non-paying customers who threatened to tell their parents if they didn't let them watch, stood along the sides of the ramps. Anthony motioned for Oree to lay between the ramps: "My assistant will now lay between the ramps as he mentally prepares himself to see the bottoms of my bicycle tires. Now, I must have absolute silence in the audience, as you can imagine how dangerous this is."

Oree waved to the audience, who stood quietly, and laid down, positioning himself so his chest would rest between the two ramps (to avoid any potential damage to his head – they weren't that stupid).

"Now, I will go back approximately half a block to gain the speed necessary to successfully fly over my assistant," Anthony proudly explained, as he rode away from the crowd.

Oree lay between the two ramps and was beginning to perspire a bit, but he preoccupied his thoughts with the results of the ticket and popcorn sales which were strong enough to warrant a trip to the candy store. Oree reasoned the reward outsized any potential danger.

Anthony yelled "Give me a count of three!" to the crowd. As they did, his bike sped forward toward the ramps. His front tire touched plywood and he began to pull himself back to take flight over Oree when suddenly the plywood bowed and then broke. Instead of flying over Oree, his front tire landed squarely on Oree's chest as the back tire got stuck on the ramp and crate. Suddenly, Oree opened his mouth like he was going to scream and his eyes grew wide. He got up and started flapping his arms like a chicken and grabbing at his throat like he was choking. His face began to turn red and tears began to form first, then stream out of his eyes as he ran around in circles.

"You winded him Anthony," one of the kids yelled. "Punch him between the shoulder blades."

Anthony dropped the bike to the ground and began chasing Oree who was running around in front of him, although Oree was faster at first. "Oree, stop," Anthony yelled. When Oree slowed, Anthony grabbed the belt loop on the back of his pants, and then, "bam" he punched him on the back between the shoulder blades. Oree let lose a wail like it was the first breath he had taken at birth. He began breathing forcefully and stopped running. He leaned over grabbing his knees, first crying and then laughing. The other children applauded. The day would go down in infamy as the day that Anthony nearly killed his brother. None of the children asked for a refund as the opportunity to view a near-death experience far exceeded any thrill created by watching a flying bicycle trick.

"Do you accept the body of Christ?" the priest said, looking down at Oree as he took his first communion during his second grade year.

"Amen," Oree said sticking his tongue out as far as he could. The nuns had earlier warned them, "Don't make it hard for Father to give you communion, we all know you are capable of sticking those tongues out and it's a sin to let the communion host fall on the floor."

Oree was especially excited about receiving his first communion. His class had spent a great part of the second grade religion classes preparing for their first confession and then first communion. So, there they all lined up in front of the priest with their frilly white dresses, black pants and white shirts with white ties.

For Oree, who had gone to mass since as far back as he could remember, the church was a place of great majesty and mystery. He was always entranced by the holiday masses which were at times accompanied by the smell of burning frankincense or myrrh. When he would get bored during the regular masses, he would take naps in the pews or marvel at the Stations of the Cross which lined the walls of the church's interior. Or, he would piece together images out of the intricate strained glass mosaics which lined the windows. At times, he would become fixated upon the cross at the front of the church and become sad. Jesus had given up his life for him and when you added up the tableaus of the imagery on the Stations of the Cross and throughout the church's interior, it indeed proved what a great sacrifice this person had made.

Having understood this as only a child could, his first communion was an exciting day for Oree as it was the least he could do in return for all of Jesus's suffering. It made him feel very mature as for years he had seen fellow parishioners line up at communion time to receive the body and blood of Christ. Before his first communion, he always felt left out when he was forced to stay kneeling in the church pew while the rest of his family went up for communion. He would now be able to join them in the ritual.

Oree understood that in order to receive his first communion, he had to be sin-free, and the only way to obtain this purity was for him to confess all his sins. The thought of having to kneel in a dark room while someone spoke to you through a dark screen and dole out prayers for sins was a little frightening for him, but the class practiced going in and out of the confessional with the lights on. That helped to alleviate his concerns.

In learning the rules of confession, Oree remained a bit confused over what constituted a "venial" sin and what specifically was a "mortal" one. Not wanting to have to execute a lengthy penance (he heard of one child who had to pray for one hour straight), he decided to go light on the sins he decided to share with the priest. Yes, he had disobeyed his parents and might have used a swear word here or there, but he absolutely did not kill anyone or covet anyone's wife – whatever that meant. As part of the celebration, each child was given a scapular to wear, which was a sort of necklace with two bands of cloth bearing religious images and text. They were held together by two shoelace style bands and worn underneath clothing. It was all very exciting and Oree felt it was good luck to wear his new religious keepsake.

The best part of his first communion was that the family got to eat breakfast at Pancake Heaven, where Oree's favorite was pigs in a blanket, which were sausages rolled up in pancakes. As Oree sat feasting in a pig blanket heaven, Anita brought up a topic she had heard about in school.

"Did you hear about the Chicano student walk out last week at Garfield High School, and all the other East L.A. school walk outs? It was a bummer," Anita said picking over her scrambled eggs and hash browns. "I heard they were fed up with being treated like second class citizens and were not going to be put down by the fascist, white administration that blocked them from being free to earn a college degree."

These were very big words to hear from the 12-year-old's mouth, however since their trip to Tijuana, Anita had developed an obsession over the equality of brown people. True, the Negroes had Martin Luther King, and Latinos had Cesar Chavez, but in her young mind, she was beginning to see how civil rights was designed to mean equality for everyone – and she wanted to be part of it.

"Anita, quiet down, someone might hear you," Maria said looking at her daughter and wondering where she was picking up these thoughts. "Those kids are lucky they're getting an education, and I think it's disrespectful for them to go against their teachers."

"That's exactly why they're going against their teachers. They're the ones trying to keep the people down – and the people united, will never be divided," Anita said puffing up like a peacock. "If anyone tries to stop me from pursuing my education, I'll call the American Civil Liberties Union!"

"Anita that's enough," her father stepped in. Inside he was upset as he was trying to raise his children to be loving, tolerant and respectful. He wasn't quite sure what the ACLU did, but he had been trying to learn more about the Chicano Rights movement, without bringing it up to his wife, to determine if it would have any impact on his family. He wasn't sure how much was the fanciful wishes of a young generation versus what the reality of the situation was. He also wasn't sure if anything would come of "The Movement," but he was an adult and had a family to support. He worried a bit that his daughter, although young, could become enamored enough by The Movement to want to do anything stupid.

Finally, he surmised that he could not endorse any group that could potentially cause him to lose his job. Sure, we all wanted equality, but Albert had been passed over for enough promotions and jobs based upon the color of his skin to know better. "Eat your food children," he said, reasoning that perhaps, some things could possibly get better by people speaking up for brown rights. That would best be left up to his children's generation.

CHAPTER 7

FIESTAS & PARTIES

The air surrounding St. Mary the Merciful's school grounds was rich with the smell of sweet roses and excitement as the children prepared for their spring Virgin de Guadalupe procession and fiesta. From within the classrooms, children's eyes spied out upon the school yard as they saw the plywood booths being set up for the weekend event. Their excitement escalated with the assembly of a Ferris wheel, merry-go-round and scrambler.

It was Thursday, April 4, 1968, and the students were in their classrooms receiving final instructions for the festivities. Friday morning they were to assemble in church promptly at 8:30 a.m. for a mass celebrating the Virgin de Guadalupe. Their families were invited to attend. From there, they would begin a procession outside of church and into the street which would lead them back onto the school grounds. Leading the procession would be four eighth graders who would carry the statue of the Virgin securely fastened to a wooden litter similar to those used by ancient royalty. The children were all taught the processional song, *De Colores*, which they were to sing in Spanish in unison:

> *De colores, de colores se visten los campos en la primavera*
> *De colores, de colores son los pajaritos que vienen de afuera*

De colores, de colores es el arco iris que vemos lucir
Y por eso los grandes amores de muchos colores me gustan a mí
Y por eso los grandes amores de muchos colores me gustan a mí

Aurelio didn't understand what the lyrics meant, but he was mesmerized by the traditional folk song's beautiful, melodic flow. When the children arrived on the school yard, the principal, Mrs. White, was to give them a formal school address from a makeshift stage which would later serve as the space for the fiesta entertainment such as mariachis and 50s-style bands. One of the eighth grade girls would be crowned as "La Virgen" with a special crown woven together with roses. She was then to place a bouquet of flowers at the statue's feet and say a special prayer. The other children would then place bouquets of roses that they were encouraged to bring from home at the feet of the Virgin statue. The assembly would end and regular school activities were to resume. This student program would be followed up with the public fiesta which would run from Friday night until Sunday afternoon.

When Oree got home from his second grade class that Thursday, he was especially excited. He went to the back yard and carefully snipped a few of the roses he had been surveying in the days leading up to the activities. He knew the children would be requested to bring roses, and following on the heels of his first communion, he was excited to again partake in God's family and activities. He would make a special request to the Virgin, asking her to encourage Anthony to play with him more often and to make Annie less cross. He brought the roses into the house, broke off as many thorns as he could, wet a napkin, wrapped the flowers in the soaked paper and then again bound them in foil. He put the bouquet in a jar and went to read (their television had gone on the fritz a few days earlier and the repairman was waiting for a transistor tube).

Friday morning, Oree woke up early and didn't take any prompting to get ready for school. He was up before the alarm rang, got dressed, ate and headed for the car with his bouquet of roses. Instead of dropping the children off as she usually did, Maria parked the car and they all went into the church for mass. In year's passed, there seemed to be more joy and excitement during the mass, but Maria sensed a quietness and wasn't sure why.

Mass ended and the children took their roles in participating in the procession. Oree was enveloped by the sweet smell of roses and the chords of "*De Colores*," which he sang along with the other students. He felt very important parading in the street with all the children, and the air was crisp with the promise that a fresh spring morning brings. When they had all assembled in the school yard, the principal got up to a podium to speak.

"Good morning children and parents. We are pleased to have you join us today as part of our Virgin de Guadalupe celebration," Mrs. White began. "Before we begin our activities, I wasn't sure if you were all aware, but Martin Luther King Jr. was assassinated last evening in Memphis, Tennessee, so if we could all please have a moment of silence to honor this great man's life before we begin."

Suddenly, the school yard filled with an overwhelming silence, a few gasps and quiet whispers of conversation. It was as though all the air had been sucked from the sky leaving behind a suffocating and stilted breeze that carried an overwhelming feeling of sadness. Oree wasn't entirely sure who Martin Luther King was, but he surmised he must have been someone very important when he saw Mrs. White dabbing her eyes at the podium as she fumbled with her notes of paper. He looked around and saw some parents and a few older children quietly crying. A few of the African American mothers quietly hugged their children closely and sobbed. He also noticed his sister Annie wailing and running off into the girl's bathroom. He again thought, "This Martin Luther King must have been a very great man, whoever he was."

Mrs. White slowly continued with her speech and when she finished, the children kissed their parents good bye and went to their classrooms quietly for the start of classes.

Despite the sadness of the Friday morning announcement, the school fiesta went off without a hitch. Maria and Albert brought their family to the event on Saturday afternoon. Anthony and Annie quickly disappeared with their friends, and the two parents walked the grounds with Oree, who had been saving his allowance quarters for months so he could take full advantage of all the activities.

He took part in the cake walk and won a white coconut cake for his mother with his dime investment. He played ring toss and won a gold fish which was already floating belly up by the time he got it to the car. He bought confetti eggs which he cracked on his parent's heads, and he ate two fried tacos, topped by cotton candy for dessert. He got on the Ferris wheel with his father and was amazed how high it reached into the sky – he could almost see their house from the highest point.

In the end, his favorite game at the fiesta was "Fishing," where you paid a dime and "fished," putting a fishing rod above a wall made of plywood which had been painted to look like a cartoon sea, complete with scalloped waves, painted sea weed, fishes and a cross-eyed, smiling octopus. When you put your fishing pole into the "ocean," you could "catch" any number of prizes that had been donated by local businesses.

His second grade teacher Ms. Toyota, (not Miss Toyota – she had recently requested the principal make the change in use of title from "Miss" as was what was being requested by Women's Liberation leaders such as Gloria Steinem) was in charge of the booth and recognized her favorite student. Although teachers never say they have favorites, the curiously minded Oree truly was hers. She had christened him "The Boy With A Thousand Questions."

"Hello Oree. Are you ready for summer?" she said welcoming him.

"Yes, Ms. Toyota," he sheepishly replied not wanting his parents to know that he kind of had a crush on her.

"Your son is quite the student, Mr. and Mrs. Rodrigo," the teacher said smiling at his parents. "He certainly keeps us on our toes."

"Very well mister Aurelio, you know the rules. Put your pole into the water and see if you get any bites," Ms. Toyota said, handing him the fishing pole and winking at Maria.

Maria said, "*Mijo*, raise your fishing pole high and put it over into the ocean," to which Oree complied. She saw Ms. Toyota make a motion behind the ocean seemingly pointing at something on the other side.

"Momma I feel something, I got something and it's heavy," Oree said pulling the rod high above the ocean line.

His mother helped him retrieve the rod and there was a brown paper bag-wrapped package tied in twine attached to the plastic fish hook. Oree excitedly pulled at the wrapping and discovered a book – "The Diary of a Young Girl – Anne Frank."

"What did you get Oree?" Ms. Toyota asked.

"It's a book. It's a book," he said excitedly.

Oree curiously eyed the book. He wasn't sure who Anne Frank was, but in looking at her picture on the cover she looked like a nice girl. He liked how her face looked peaceful and vowed to read the book over the summer.

"I love it," he said turning toward his mother. "I will read it this summer."

"I don't know if you're old enough to understand it, but it is a good book," Maria said. "I read it in school. Say thank you to Ms. Toyota."

"Thank you Ms. Toyota," Oree said, gathering the book and walking away from the booth.

"You're welcome Aurelio. Have a good summer," said Ms. Toyota. "Oh, and Mrs. Rodrigo, I wouldn't be surprised if Aurelio reads that whole book this summer – his reading level is many grades ahead of where it should be, which we would have shared had you been able to make his parent/teacher conference."

Maria offered a confused and embarrassed smile. As they walked away, Oree asked looking down at the book again, "What's it about momma?"

"Well, it's about a little girl whose family has to live in an attic because they're Jewish and are trying to avoid being caught by bad people."

"What's Jewish and who are the bad people?" Oree asked.

"Well, they're a group of people, just like Mexicans, Chinese people, you know different kinds of people," Maria said. "The bad people? Well, read the book and then ask me questions."

"Oh o.k.," Oree said looking again at the picture of Anne Frank on the book cover. This Anne Frank didn't have brown skin or slanted eyes, but he surmised there were probably all kinds of different groups of important people, why not a little girl with black hair? He couldn't wait to begin reading the book as he was curious if this Anne Frank person was treated as he sometimes was – like when he was in Thrifty and asked for ice cream at the ice cream counter and the sandy-haired clerk kept cleaning the counter until he walked away, or when he heard a lady working in a toy store look at his dark skin and say: "I know you Mexicans are all alike, lazy and thieves. We don't sell beans here." He didn't tell his mother the second story as he was fearful that she would make him go back to the store and call the lady a "stupid white lady." Or, worse yet, she would go and tell the lady herself.

As the sun was setting, Oree began to tire, so he sat with his parents on a bench and listened to music of The Bel Airs, a 1950's style band. The quartet was led by a female singer, who along with the band, sang a decent rendition of "Sincerely." Maria looked at her son who had fallen asleep on her lap and then looked to her husband and grabbed his hand. She petted her son's thick straw hair and thought back to a time long ago when she would look in the mirror and sing with the Maguire Sisters. It seemed like so long ago, and so much was changing so quickly these days. She suddenly craved the simplicity of her life then, sighed and gathered her son and husband to go find their other children and head home.

"Mom, I wanna wear my Mexican blouse to my graduation party," Annie said in preparing for her eighth grade graduation party. She held the somewhat faded cotton fabric and, looking in her bedroom mirror, liked that it appeared faded and worn. It was kind of like how all the hippies were dressing these days, holey jeans and cotton shirts. She, however, imagined what it would be like to be a true Mexican peasant, perhaps toiling in the fields of Michoacán or some exotic place like that. She had lately been reading about the Aztecs and fantasized that she was perhaps the descendent of some proud warrior deigned so by the god Quetzalcoatl. On her bedroom stereo played "Dancing in the Streets" by Martha and the Vandellas, and above her bed hung a velvet, black light peace sign poster.

The morning of Annie's graduation, the family loaded into the station wagon and headed to St. Mary's. The class was to celebrate with a mass (of course). Annie and her classmates streamed into the church in a paired procession, while "Ave Maria" was sung by the school choir. It was too expensive to expect the children to rent graduation gowns and mortarboards, so they were told to wear their best dress clothes. The boys wore pants, shirts and ties, but the girls, who were rapidly blossoming with puberty, wore outfits ranging from virginal, white spring dresses to tight, bosom-fitting polyester wrap dresses, platform shoes and silk flowers festooned in their mini-bouffants.

Following mass, the activities moved to the parish hall where Mrs. White led the graduation activities. There was yet another procession of the graduates and the customary valedictorian speech made by Louise Smith who referenced Robert F. Kennedy when she began her speech: "Only those who dare to fail can ever achieve greatly…" Little did they all know, a little more than a month following Louise's speech, that Kennedy would be assassinated nearby in Los Angeles. After all the speeches and reading of graduate names, punch and cookies were served in the back of the hall by the school's Women's League.

By early afternoon, the Rodrigo household was busy with activity. Albert and Anthony set up tables and chairs that the elder had borrowed from his place of work. Maria, Oree and Annie followed by putting down colored, paper tablecloths and then setting Styrofoam cups of chips and salsa that they got from Smart and Final on the tables. Albert hung a piñata in the shape of a star from a tree limb in the back yard. He then took Oree with him to get Annie's graduation cake from Viking Bakery.

The smell of *birria* permeated the back yard. Albert had hired a local woman, who was known as "*the asador de cabra*" (the goat roaster), to cook the barbecued meat and make rice and beans for the guests. Albert and Anthony had spent the weekend before digging a hole in the back yard to serve as the barbecue pit where the goat was to be cooked. While digging, Anthony asked why they had to cook the goat in the ground and not on the stove, as it seemed "kinda barbaric." Following its roasting, the goat would then be chopped up into a stew using ancho and guajillo peppers, as well as roasted tomatoes and other ingredients. It was a delicacy only served on very special occasions.

At 4 p.m., the guests began arriving. In addition to family friends, they included both Maria and Albert's parents, as well as Albert's brother Richard, his wife Irene and their two children. His brother Louis and his family could not attend. Maria's side of the family included Cathy, her husband Raymond and their children. Maria's recently divorced brother Robert, came with a date named Angela, who resembled a poor man's version of Rita Moreno. Finally, her other brother Dominic, attended with his date and her children – Serena was an unwed woman from Mexico with three children, ages 6 through 9, who didn't speak much English.

Albert had rented a keg of Budweiser beer, and there was also lemonade, Kool-Aid and coffee for guests to drink. Music from the radio station KHJ Boss Radio with DJ Charlie Tuna played through speakers propped up in the kitchen window. As songs like "Grazing in the Grass" and "Summer Breeze" played in the background, the adults sat in the back yard around tables, drinking and laughing. When it was dinner time, everyone enjoyed the tasty, moist *birria*, and some even had seconds.

The children for the most part sat on their own table, but occasionally intermingled with their parents and grandparents as they hoped they would be chosen to be the first to swing at the piñata. Oree was Maria's father Jesus' favorite grandchild, so Oree knew if he was nice enough to him, he might be able to wrangle a quarter out of the old man.

"Hi grandpa," Oree said shimming up to Jesus' side. "How is many favorite grandpa?"

"Oreecito," Jesus smiled. "Did you come to say hello, or just to get a quarter?"

"No grandpa. I mean it. You're my favorite grandpa 'cuz we have the same color skin, look," he said holding his dark brown arm against his grandfather's.

"Yes, I see Oreecito. You're right, and we're very lucky to have such beautiful color to our skin," his grandfather continued. Then, he reached behind Oree's ear and pulled back with a quarter in his fingers. "*Qué es esto?* What's this?"

"Gee, thanks grandpa," Oree said, grabbing the coin, kissing him on the cheek and knowing that his charm had once again worked.

"There you go, my son," Jesus said, mussing up Oree's hair. "Always remember, Sometimes your life can end up being so much more than you hoped for."

Oree loved when his grandfather would tell him the phrase as it always made him feel happy. He also knew he could never let on that he and his grandfather shared their unique bond – lest the other siblings line up to beg for quarters too.

Shortly thereafter, someone remarked that it was 6 p.m. Cathy's husband Raymond had already polished off four, 16 ounce cups of beer, and Albert decided he should propose a toast to his daughter, less Raymond start to act up, which had been known to happen.

"Thank you all for coming to support my family," Albert began. "I am very proud of my daughter Annie, who has shown she has a fighter's spirit. Annie, I want you to continue with your education as I know you are destined to be a lawyer or a doctor or something smart like that. Don't get too big for your pants though. People will follow a leader who has humility far closer than the one who yells the loudest."

Anita, who lately had felt the full on blows of puberty coursing through her body and emotions, thought to herself, "You had to get a dig in, didn't you dad," but outwardly she thanked him and all her family for coming.

Following Albert's speech, everyone got up to break the piñata. As it was Annie's party, she got to take the first swing. Ultimately Anthony, with his swift batter's swing, was the one to break the star open, sending candy cascading in all directions. The children gathered as much as they could, leaving some of the ground for the adults. Eventually, they dispersed throughout the house. Annie and her cousins Cynthia and Lupita holed up in her room listening to Art Laboe's oldies but goodies radio. Anthony, Oree and cousins Raymond Jr. and Narciso played yard darts on the front grass. The children from Mexico sat in the house and spoke Spanish to each other.

"You should'a seen some of the girls at Annie's graduation today," Anthony said to his cousin Raymond. "They were wearing these tight old dresses that showed off their tee-tas. They were total foxes!"

"What's a tee-ta?" Oree asked.

"There you go again Oree, asking dumb-assed questions. Never mind what a tee-ta is or we won't let you play," Anthony continued.

"Were they wearing bras?" Raymond asked, as fantasies began to play out in the mind of the pre-pubescent boys.

"I dunno, but some of these girls were dressed like they were wanting it bad," Anthony continued.

"What did they want?" Oree asked.

Bam! Anthony smacked Oree on the back of the head and then he said, "If you open your mouth one more time, I'm gonna make you go in the house and sit with those wetbacks."

"Wait, I have an idea and it's something Oree's gonna do," Anthony continued.

When he learned of the plan, Oree said he didn't want anything to do with it, but with Anthony threatening to serve him a knuckle sandwich, he didn't really have much of a choice. Raymond Jr. and Narciso laughed, the younger one saying he'd help Oree if he wanted. They quickly reviewed the plan once more and then it was put in action.

Within minutes, the children from Mexico ran from the back door of the Rodrigo house screaming and crying. They ran right to their mother, speaking very excitedly in Spanish.

"What is this about?" Dominic asked his girlfriend.

What she told him did not sit well with anyone.

"Anthony, Aurelio, get back here now," yelled Albert toward the front yard.

"Raymundo, Narciso!" screamed Raymond Sr. who was slightly slurring his words and only used the children's Spanish names when he was either upset or drunk, which was frequently the case over recent months.

The children ran around the house to the back yard. Hearing the commotion, Annie, Cynthia and Lupita ran to the back yard as well.

"Did you tell those kids: *'aqui viene la migra,'* here comes the immigration?" Albert said to the four boys as his ears turned red.

"Goddamn it Raymond Jr. and Narciso," Raymond Sr. slurred.

"It's o.k. Raymond, Albert is handling it," Cathy said, understanding that her husband had been drinking – actually since 2 p.m. in the afternoon, before they came to the party.

"Answer me," Albert said.

"They made me and Narciso do it," Oree said. "Anthony and Raymond came up with it."

"Na ah," Raymond Jr. said.

"Anthony, we'll deal with you later," his father said. "Now all of you apologize to these kids."

The children looked sheepishly down as they quietly breathed "sorries" akin to the murmured "great game" that losers say to winners at the end of a ball game. The mother took the children inside to clean them up in the bathroom.

Oree knew he shouldn't have listened to Anthony, but the fear of getting a black eye or Indian burn on his arm made him submit to the half-brained idea. He didn't know much about *la migra*, but he knew they were bad and that they took people away to Mexico. As the Mexican children had gotten so upset, he reasoned they probably thought about *la migra* – a lot.

"Dammit Raymondo," Raymond Sr. yelled again as he smacked Raymond Jr. hard against the back of his head causing him to stumble.

"Raymond stop," Cathy cried.

"Don't tell me what to do with my son," Raymond continued. "If you disciplined these damn kids every now and then, they wouldn't behave like little assholes."

Jesus and Bessie quietly looked down wanting to help their daughter but understanding that what took place between their children and their spouses was not something to be interfered with. Still, they were ashamed that their daughter was being subjected to the public display of embarrassment. Ed and Elizabeth also sat quietly, although they both were thinking how thankful they were that no son of theirs was a drunk like Cathy's husband, Raymond.

"It's o.k. Raymond," Maria said, "Cathy is a good mother."

"Butt out Maria, you're always defending your sister," Raymond slurred. He was obviously looking for any excuse to get a roll on and let them all have it – Albert and Maria so perfect with their little white picket fence family.

"Hey, hey that's my wife and my sister in law," Albert said jumping in to defend the women.

"Albert, please, he's drunk," Cathy said. "You can't win when he's like this. It's o.k., he'll be fine once he sleeps it off."

"Get the damn kids, Cathy, we're going home," Raymond yelled. "Dammit, I can't get a break. I work like an idiot all week and I have to come home to a bunch of misbehaving kids and a wife that ignores their shit."

Cathy, who had been in this situation before, looked over at Maria and saw that she had tears in her eyes. Maria wanted to grab her and say, "Stay here with the kids until he sobers up," but she knew that anything she said would just incite Raymond more.

"I'm sorry everyone, we have to leave," Cathy said with embarrassment. "Dominic, please tell your girlfriend we're really sorry."

"Are you coming cuz I'm leaving now!" Raymond yelled as he stumbled down the driveway.

Cathy quickly gathered the children and left, not taking time to say good byes for fear of hearing the whispered advice of others amongst the farewell hugs – "If he's like this all the time, perhaps you should leave."

CHAPTER 8

GIFTED

Third grade was an exciting time for Aurelio. He was pleased with the progress of his cursive writing skills (handwriting was so much more efficient than manuscript) and he was reading a book a week outside of his class work.

It seemed that he always found time to find his way into a new book, although his report cards often stated that it would be best if he were to slow down a bit as his penmanship was beginning to resemble that of a doctor's.

In course work, the class was beginning to learn multiplication and division. Oree didn't care much for math. It was all too cut, dry – and boring. He couldn't use his imagination with math, it was simply skinny, scraggly numbers which did not harbor any sort of excitement nor bolster any enthusiasm in him.

One day, his teacher Mrs. Melon, announced that they would be conducting an important test – The Wechsler Intelligence Scale for Children. It was explained that the test would help give the school a better picture of how all the students fit together.

Oree asked Mrs. Melon how he should prepare for the test or what he should study to help improve his chances of obtaining a good score.

She smiled and said that no preparation was needed. All the class needed to do was to make sure everyone had a good night's sleep and that they "had their Wheaties" the morning of the test.

The week before the test at the supermarket, Oree asked his mother if they could purchase Wheaties for their cereal of the week. She asked why.

"The teacher said we needed to have our Wheaties before the test and I want to do my best," was Oree's response.

His mother smiled.

The night before the test, Oree found himself in knots. It was as though he couldn't focus and he had a bad headache. Maria asked him if he was getting sick, to which he responded, "No way. It's just this test is making me nervous. I asked the librarian about it and she said it was a test which would help determine the intelligence of the students, as well as if any of us were gifted, whatever that means."

There was that word again – "gifted," Maria thought. She recalled the incident with the popsicle sticks and she wondered if the term did indeed apply to Oree. He could always be found with a book in his hand and she sensed that he was different than the other children. He had little interest in football and could care less about baseball. She brushed the thought off. Didn't make much difference if he was gifted, there was nothing that could be done with that (as far as she was concerned).

The morning of the test, the classroom was unusually hot, to the point of almost stifling. It was one of those Indian Summer heatwaves that were usually followed by a bout with the Santa Ana winds, but Oree was excited about the test. He thought to himself, "If anyone is going to be gifted, it's me! It has to be me."

The testing began at 9 a.m. and the teacher opened all the windows to help keep the classroom as cool as possible. Oree began to pour over the questions.

"Do you see the figures inside these boxes? They form a pattern. Choose the figure in the answer row below that continues the pattern," read one with a series of box formations.

"Easy peezzee," Oree thought as he quickly checked the box.

He continued and the questions began to get more difficult. By the time he was three-quarters of the way through the test, his little head began to throb.

"Head stop hurting," he said to himself. "You're interfering with me understanding this test."

The throbbing continued and only seemed to get worse. By the time he had a page of questions remaining, he could barely focus on the text. He looked down at a question and suddenly it was blotted with a red dot. His nose had begun to bleed. He quickly wiped it with his sleeve and pulling his head back, he raised his arm in the air, "I have a nose bleed. I need to finish the test."

The teacher brought a Kleenex and held it to his nose, "Keep your head back until it stops. Class continue with the test please."

"But I have to finish. I have to finish," Oree said almost frantically.

"It's o.k. I'll give you extra time," the teacher responded. "It's ok., now hold the tissue there until the bleeding stops."

Oree's parents generally didn't have time for parent/teacher conferences, but when they received the invitation for the first quarter conference, there was a personalized note from Mrs. Melon.

"Please be sure to come to the conference, I have something important to share," the handwritten note said.

The night of the parent/teacher conference, Albert called in sick from his restaurant job. He and Maria sat on the tops of the third grade desks and waited for Mrs. Mellon.

"You don't think he's a problem child? You know how Annie was at that age," Albert said.

"Of course he's nothing like Annie," Maria said. "He told me he got a bloody nose during the test, so I hope he didn't blow it. He gets so nervous about these sorts of things."

Mrs. Melon walked in the classroom and introduced herself. She thanked them for coming in. She then proceeded to review the test results with Albert and Maria. The pair easily understood the terms when she began, explaining that his verbal comprehension and vocabulary were at an eighth grade level, but by the time Mrs. Melon began explaining block design and picture completion, they were at a loss.

"The bottom line, is the test seems to indicate that Aurelio, Oree, is gifted," Mrs. Melon said. "There are a number of things we can do to help him achieve his potential..."

Following the conference, Maria and Albert drove home in a quandary.

"Those things the teacher said," Maria began, "we could never afford them. I mean I want him to do good in school, but, what, I mean, what do they expect us to do with this? I could get a job, maybe?"

Albert was equally surprised. He wanted the best for his son, but he was already working two jobs. There weren't enough hours in the day for him to work at another position. The teacher had mentioned sending Oree to a special school – a very expensive one. Sending all the children to a Catholic school was pricey enough, and Annie had just started high school which added even more bills to the pile. Concessions had to be made, and compromises must be forged. There was simply no way they could entertain the thought of sending Oree to a school for the gifted.

"Maria, we are doing our best for our children," Albert responded. "I won't have you working. The children need you at home taking care of them. We will do the best with what we have and Oree will just have to do the best he can with what he has."

Maria looked out the passenger side window. It had begun to drizzle and drops of water trickled down the car window. She was proud that perhaps in some way, she had contributed to the gift Oree had been given. She also wished that times were different. Everyone she knew was poor and that likely wouldn't be changing. She knew their family was better off than many, but that didn't make her feel any better. She wondered what it would be like if her family could have all the best – a nicer home, new clothes, steaks once a week. Would it make any difference?

And, what would Oree do with this gifted thing? How could that make any difference in his life? Would that help him get a better job? His complexion was so dark, and in America that was frowned upon.

Maria knew no amount of gifted would rub the color off of that. She wanted the best for her family, but she understood how difficult it could be for people like them. Could there be a possibility that this "gift" thing were truly that? That it could somehow make a difference in Oree's life?

She felt a moist, cool drop fall upon her cheek. She wasn't sure if it was a drip of rain seeping in the window, or a tear falling from her eye.

CHAPTER 9

QUAKES

By the time Oree entered 4th grade, man had walked on the moon, America had survived Woodstock and he was reading at a 9th grade level. He had amazed all his teachers with his quench for literature. He was like a literary sponge and read everything they put in front of him – classics such as "A Tale of Two Cities," pulp fiction like "The Poseidon Adventure" and his personal favorite which he had read three times, "To Kill a Mockingbird." At parent/teacher nights, his educators continued to encourage his parents to look at other options for his studies.

Through it all, Albert and Maria remained steadfast that all of their children were to be treated equally and that Aurelio would be educated in the same manner as the others. Although Albert and Maria really didn't understand what being "gifted" meant per se, they didn't make much of an effort to learn more about it as they were both too busy with day-to-day life to think about such things. Maria had enough to do with the raising of children and Albert worked incessantly to pay for their middle class lifestyle. They made it a point to not draw too much attention to Oree's grades as they didn't want their child to get "big headed" or "uppity."

Together, they didn't really see the point of Oree being treated any differently as they knew he was a Mexican and despite any special education or treatment, he would eventually get to the point when someone put him in his place – "You're a beaner and this is as far as you're going to get in life." They wanted to believe differently, but a lifetime of experience seeing "over the wall" but getting firmly smacked with it when they tried to climb over it, left them realistically grounded in the fact that things would not change significantly in their lifetime.

As Aurelio excelled in his studies, his siblings had their own scholastic struggles. Annie was in high school and was the president of the Spanish Club, although the other students were threatening to impeach her for using the club as a soapbox for her growing political views. Anthony excelled at sports, however his grades were barely passing. When Aurelio spied Anthony's report card and saw all the Cs, Ds and the F, he was surprised – school just wasn't that difficult. He knew of classmates who got spanked, grounded or worse when they went home with poor grades. He was happy his parents were not that way, even though with his high grades he would never be at risk of grade-related punishment.

To make matters worse, Aurelio, in an effort to glean any bit of information about the likelihood for his future success, read each report card from front to back. When he noticed the fine print on the back of all report cards – *"Parents, remember if your child does not receive high grades, encourage him/her with praise to do better, rather than punishing him/her for any deficiencies"* – he made a point to read this fine print to Anthony during one of their quibbles after he heard his parents praising him for his barely passing grades.

"Mom and dad have to say things like 'You're not stupid, you just have to work harder,' because the report card says they have to do that," Oree fumed, showing Anthony the back of the report card. "They can't flat out tell you you're dumb."

For that, Oree received a bruised shoulder when Anthony punched him. Oree didn't care though, he had the best grades of all his siblings, but he never got praised or received any special treatment. He knew he was smarter and the realization that no one else saw it hurt more than any punch could. He always took great pride in his reading and writing abilities, as well as his good grades.

This pride was something the church warned against, which in turn made Oree feel another important pilaster of his faith – guilt. To help him combat his feelings of being prideful, he turned toward the mysteries of faith and asked God how he could overcome this sure-to-be sinful feeling. He decided to become a servant of God, otherwise known as an altar boy.

Since his first communion, Oree had always enjoyed going to church, particularly when it came time to sing. One Sunday, a woman sitting in the pew in back of his family remarked to him at the end of mass, "Surely, God heard the beauty of your voice today. I'm sure it reached all the way to heaven." He got a punch in his ribs from Anthony after that comment as it meant his brother was exceptionally loud this particular Sunday.

So, it was a natural fit that Oree would become an altar boy. The vestments the altar boys wore always intrigued him as he couldn't understand why boys had to wear white, frilly dresses. He reasoned that they must be an important part of the ceremony which he was not privy to. The accessories for the mass, such as the altar bell, the cruets used for water and wine, and the large cross on a pole which they walked in procession into church each Sunday, made him feel like an important part of the ceremony. He was carrying out God's work on earth and that helped to alleviate his feelings of guilt and pride.

Being an altar boy gave Oree special privileges. Each Sunday he got to sit up on the altar and look out at his heathen, fellow parishioners. He was amazed at how many of them dozed off during the mass. Once, a man in the front pew actually started snoring and Oree "accidently" rang the altar bell which roused him from his slumber with a chortle. Plus, if there was a funeral during the school week, he would often get a pass from school to participate in the mass. He especially liked weddings and baptisms as they often came with "tips" that were granted to the priests, who then in turn shared them with the altar boys.

He liked the part of the mass where he helped to put the water and wine in the chalice for the priest. One of the priests, who was known to be a bit boozy, would always motion Oree to go heavy on the wine which went into the chalice. Oree thought this rather odd as none of the other priests did so. At least it seemed to make the last part of mass more enjoyable as the priest most joyously offered overly enthusiastic words of benediction for a blessed week.

In school itself, Aurelio wasn't the picture of popularity, however he had a few friends, including Chester, a black child, and Jimmy, an Asian. Oree liked to call them the United Nations of St. Mary's the Merciless.

The trio appreciated the fact that they weren't like the other children in school. They frequently stayed to themselves, frying ants on the baseball field with magnifying glasses, bruising their arms and other body parts with acrylic "klick klacks" which when banging into each other created a mesmerizing sound, or stealing tarty Now or Later candies at the nearby 7/11.

In addition to these activities, they often traded comic books, played marbles or tetherball, or occasionally, joined the other boys in games of "pachuco," a handball game which they played against the brick walls of their school. In the game, players would take turns hitting a tennis ball against the wall with their hands – if they missed the ball, the other players could throw punches at them until they touched the wall with their hand. Oree wasn't the best at the game, so he only played when other equally deficient boys played.

April 1 was a day all minority boys looked forward to. It was monikered "Paddy Day," and no it wasn't popular because of erin go bragh, McDonald's shamrock shakes or the ability to pinch someone 'til they bruised for not wearing green. Paddy Day was the day that all the Anglo boys knew they were subject to getting beaten up by the minority boys. Since St. Mary's was in a primarily Latino and African American neighborhood, it had more than its fair share of minorities. Some of the white boys stayed home sick that day, some remained in the classroom as long as possible at recess and lunch (volunteers for eraser clapping were easily found on that day), and some tried to make themselves as invisible as possible on the school yard by hiding behind trees during break times.

Aurelio thought it was a stupid tradition and he didn't like how some of the Mexican boys tried to emulate their older siblings by acting like wanna-be gang members as they bullied the scrawniest of white boys. He didn't really fit in with these boys as they were always bigger than him, tougher than him and were "blind followers of stupidity," as he put it. It was for this reason that he saw the United Nations of St. Mary's as an important entity in maintaining the sovereignty of the school grounds.

During recess, he was in the boy's restroom urinating when he heard a commotion coming from outside.

"Why are you doing this to me? I am your friend. I didn't do anything to you," he heard the yelling getting closer.

"Why do you want to hurt me?" he heard as the voice came running into the bathroom. He heard the door lock "click," followed by pounding on the door.

"It's time you honkies got what you deserved," one of the boys outside yelled. "You better come out and get more of it or you're gonna get it worse later."

The voice crumpled down along the wall sobbing and mumbling something about "bullying." He wasn't aware Aurelio was in the bathroom listening to it all, until he looked up. Oree was washing his hands at the sink.

"It's o.k., they'll leave you alone now. They just have to get it out of their systems," Oree said like the gang outside of the door suffered from some kind of medical condition.

"I don't know why they have this stupid tradition. What did white people ever do to them?" the voice pleaded.

Oree wet a paper towel and threw it down to the person.

"Here, wipe your face. My mom always does that to calm me down when I cry," Oree said.

Aurelio knew the student to be Shawn O'Reilly. He was a sandy haired, blue-eyed boy who was generally known as a "lady's man," as far as 4th graders went.

"It's o.k. Shawn, I'll make them back off if they start anything," Oree said. He was surprised he was being so brave – he could possibly be subjecting himself to a beating for defending the boy, but he didn't like seeing people upset about things like their race. Oree knew what it was like to be prejudiced against for being the wrong color. "What's the phrase?" he thought, "Two wrongs don't make a right."

"You read a lot. I always see you with a book," Shawn said, wiping his face.

"Yes, I like to read – a lot," Oree replied.

"I like to read too, but I don't tell people because then they'd think I was a wimp," Shawn continued.

Oree knew the ridicule Shawn spoke of. He had been called "bookworm," "nerd boy" and "teacher's pet," but he didn't really care. At times, the bigger boys would punch him in the hallways or knock books out of his hands if he was reading while walking. Oree would mutter words he learned from books under his breath which he knew they would never understand – "neanderthals" or "atavists." The ability to understand and use words like these always made him feel better. He understood that these overgrown boys had likely reached the high points of their lives and that by the end of high school, their reigns would all be over as they continued in their decline with positions held at tire stores or perhaps Midas Mufflers. Thus, the enjoyment Oree derived from his reading adventures more than compensated for any name calling or bruising he would endure. He knew he didn't really fit in with the other children in the school and it was a fact he had reconciled with a long time before. School was something you got through, not something that got to you.

"What kind of books do you read?" Oree asked.

From there, the conversation continued as the two boys exchanged book titles and plots like they were trading baseball cards. They began laughing and forgot about the earlier rumpus outside. They continued talking until the recess bell chimed, and from that point forward became inseparable friends. Oree made his other friends welcome Shawn into the United Nations of St. Mary's, as after all, the United Nations is all about the inclusion of all sovereignties and nationalities.

In 1971, Oree was in the 5th grade. Their teacher for the year was Sister Mary Diane. Based upon her long-standing reputation, the class had designated a special nickname for her – "Sister Mary Diane, Our Lady of Perpetual Drink." (It was common knowledge on the school grounds that the nun was known to sneak into the church's wine cabinet in the sacristy during lunch time.) On more than a few afternoons she would stroll into the classroom a little glossy-eyed and smelling strangely similar to the priests after communion on Sunday morning. The children wondered if she had a flask sewn into her vestments.

One fall morning at recess, Oree was on the baseball field bent over tying a loosened shoelace when he felt someone shove him face down into the ground. He rolled onto his back to see he was surrounded by a group of various-sized, seventh and eighth grade boys who had formed a circle.

"You little bitch, we heard you stuck up for a honky on Paddy Day," one of them yelled at him. "When a Mexican turns on his own *gente*, we like to teach them a lesson."

"You're a frickin' coconut," another one touted. "Brown on the outside, white on the inside, you honky lover. We need to teach the bitch a lesson."

"Whaaa," Oree began asking incredulously, but it was too late.

Within seconds, he felt arms punching and legs kicking him. He tried to get up, but was pushed back down as one of the seventh graders straddled him, pinned his shoulders down with his knees and began punching him in the face. He felt pain burn his sides, legs, face and stomach. Dust was beginning to form around the group as he tried to push the bigger boy off of him. He wished his brother Anthony had been around to help, but he was already in high school and lately was either consumed by sports or girls – and at times both at the same time. In the confusion he thought to himself, "I can't believe I'm getting beat up by the people who say they're *mi gente*, my people. My ass." He felt blood begin to form in his mouth and he rolled around in the dirt as much as he could to avoid the pummeling. He heard a whistle in the distance and then the crowd scattered.

Mr. Wilson, the children's physical education teacher came out onto the playing field and helped Oree stand up.

"Are you alright? Did they hurt you?" asked Mr. Wilson. "Who was involved?"

Quickly deducing this was one of those moments in which if Oree made the wrong decision he would condemn himself to further additional, possibly worse, punishment by the gang of boys, he bit the inside of his lip which was already bleeding and kept his mouth closed.

When it finally opened, he said, "It's fine," responding to the teacher. "We were just kidding around and it got out of hand."

February 9, 1971, could have been any other day, however at 6 a.m., a 6.6 magnitude earthquake struck the San Fernando Valley, throwing everyone out of their beds and wreaking havoc throughout the area. Freeways, buildings and homes collapsed, the Olive View Hospital crumpled like an accordion, roads were destroyed like someone split them open to see the inside black asphalt, gas pipes ruptured spewing flames into the air and 64 people died. Although Sylmar was the epicenter of the quake, Albert and Maria's home did not suffer significant damage as a result of bedrock which lay beneath it. Other structures in Sylmar did not fare as well.

When the quake struck, Albert and Maria at first didn't know what the shaking was, but within minutes of being thrown from their bed, they gathered their children and ran outside to sit in their station wagon. It was as though their entire house had become one of those fun house door ways – shaking and throwing them right to left – only this ride wasn't fun. It was violent and seemed to go on for what felt like hours. They heard loud noises, yells, explosions, wood splitting and then a deafening silence. After sitting in their car for half an hour after the shaking stopped, Maria ran inside to call her parents. When she picked up the receiver, by some miracle, she heard – a ring tone.

She dialed her mother and when she heard the receiver pick up, she started speaking in Spanish excitedly. The children were walking around the house which resembled their home, but somehow was disheveled in a manner in which it was unrecognizable. They heard their mother's voice grow louder and then pleading, *"Esta muerto? Esta muerto?"* They then heard their mother screaming.

"Maria, Maria," Albert cried as he grabbed Maria who was crumpling to the floor, the phone receiver still in her hand.

"He's dead Albert, he's dead," she sobbed.

"Who's dead?" Albert stopped.

"My father," Maria sobbed. "My mom said when the shaking started he started grabbing at his chest and then he couldn't breathe and then his face turned white. We have to get to my mother's."

The children all started crying and Anita was so hysterical her father had to slap her. They put on their clothes and pulled the station wagon out of their driveway. They saw their neighbors mulling around their homes like they were somnambulistic. Some of their neighbors' homes looked intact, other houses had moved off their foundations and some had parts that had crumpled or fallen over. They drove slowly along Foothill Boulevard, being mindful of the cracked asphalt, fallen power lines and debris. They made their way down Hubbard Street toward Maria's parents' home. What they saw along the way was surrealistic, it was still like the San Fernando Valley they called home, but it all looked different somehow. Things that were familiar landmarks had seemingly disappeared, things they had never noticed before became prominent along the landscape.

As they drove, Oree sat quietly in the car and thought of the many times he and his grandfather had played the game where Jesus would pull a quarter out from behind his ear and give it to the boy. He also thought of their favorite phrase, and he softly said to himself: "This isn't one of those times where your life is so much more than what you hoped for."

When they got to the Alizaca household, Cathy and her family were already there. Driving up, they could tell the house was intact and Raymond sat out on the front stoop smoking a cigarette.

"The old guy kicked over. Here my house is cracking at the seams and we have to come here," Raymond slurred to Albert and Maria with his head in one hand, a bota bag flask in the other. Albert thought to himself that it was amazing that Raymond could be drunk so quickly following the quake. It had been an hour since the shaking stopped and here was his brother-in-law already blottoed and sipping who knows what from that leather bladder.

He reasoned he didn't have time to deal with him and he rushed with his family inside.

The family went in the house which seemed reasonably put together given the magnitude of the quake. The children joined their dazed cousins on couches. They could hear loud sobbing in the back bedroom and Maria and Albert went to the back of the house to be with Cathy, Maria's mother and her deceased father.

The recovery from the earthquake was slow, but the children didn't mind, their schools were closed for repairs for three months – they would have to make up the lost class time during summer. They also didn't mind that their cousins came to live with them for a month while repairs were made to Raymond and Cathy's house. Sleeping quarters were tight with the addition of four children, but Annie was especially pleased with the extended sleep over as Lupita was her favorite cousin and she enjoyed spending time with her.

"I'm so glad you're staying with us," Annie told Lupita while they lay talking in their beds in Annie's room one night. "These people don't get me. It's like they make believe everything is o.k. and we're all American and such, but they don't see how white people treat us. I'm so sick of being told 'America is this way, America is that way.' The only thing I see about America is that white is right."

"That's pretty heavy. Cuz, you are so right on," Lupita, who was a year older, said. "I have joined the movement. I am tired of 'the man' putting us down."

"What movement?" Annie asked.

"I have joined the Chicano Civil Rights Liberation Party – they're committed to *El Movimiento*," Lupita said. "My parents don't know as they wouldn't get it. Plus, my dad is such a lazy drunk he's always plastered out of his mind, so he wouldn't even know."

"I'm sorry about that. Parents can be so embarrassing," Annie replied, not understanding the extent of Raymond's alcoholism.

"Anyway, the Chicano Liberation Party is all about equality for our people, you know Chicano Power. The white man doesn't want us to be educated, get good jobs or live in houses next to theirs. They want us all to be farmworkers, live in shitty flop houses and make below minimum wage. They only see us as dish washers, gardeners and farm workers. The Liberation Party is going to change all that – we got to fight the man and all his oppressive behaviors," Lupita continued. "Cesar Chavez has done a lot for *La Raza*, but we have to do more. Equality has got to be more than in the fields, we deserve to have office jobs, nice cars and pretty homes – in communities where we choose to live, not barrios like we're forced to now."

Annie, who was now a sophomore in high school, didn't quite understand all of Lupita's references. Her family didn't live in a barrio, their house was in a middle class, mixed neighborhood, and her dad was wasn't a dish washer. His position at the Hollywood Ranch Market was one many a man would be proud to hold. Her family may have not had everything they wanted, but they were always well-fed and had clean clothes. In fact, they just got a color television and were on the list to get cable TV when the lines were laid in their neighborhood. Still, the feeling that she wasn't getting all she was entitled to because of the color of her skin gnawed at her. She believed her mother was brainwashed into the "white" way of thinking, but Annie was not her mother's daughter – she was going to fight for the rights of her people.

She thought back to the time her family visited Tijuana. She saw the sadness, fear and ignorance in the faces of the poor people who lived in boxes. She vowed to herself that if there was any way to help people like that, she would. In school, Annie sharpened her perceptions, justified or not, that the white children were treated better than the minorities. She was able to rationalize all the "wrongs" she had experienced in her short life on the actions of those who sought to oppress her people. She knew she was smart, however she often didn't see the need for good grades; they just weren't a priority for her and she doubted good grades would make little difference in her future success. Listening to Lupita, things made sense. She could finally find a forum for people like her – those who were tired of the injustices and were willing to take action to correct them.

"Hey Lupita, how do you get involved in a group like the Chicano Civil Rights Liberation Party?" Annie asked.

"Right on cuz," Lupita said. "I'll take you to a meeting."

And with that, Annie took her first steps toward becoming the activist she knew she was always destined to be.

A few weekends later, Cathy pulled up in front of the Rodrigo house and honked the horn for her children to come out. They had been spending their weekends back at their home cleaning up things the construction workers had fixed and trying to get things back to normal.

Maria looked out the living room window and called "Kids, your mom's here to pick you up."

In looking out, she could see Cathy behind the steering wheel. She had big dark sunglasses on, her hair was pulled up under a blue gingham bandana and she was puffing on a cigarette. Maria thought this to be odd as she had never seen her sister smoke. The kids were still gathering their things, so she walked out front and knocked on the passenger side window. She motioned for Cathy to roll down the window.

"What's up Cathy?" Maria asked as Cathy moved to turn the knob to roll down the window. She sat back up and looked out toward the driver's side mirror which again Maria thought was odd.

"Cathy, how are you?" Maria again asked.

"Oh nothing," Cathy responded as if she was in a daze and didn't really hear the question. "Just got a lot to do today."

Maria looked across the front seat and could see what appeared to be a bruise in the driver's side mirror. She walked around to the driver's side window and Cathy tried to shield her face. It was pancaked with powder, but through it Maria could make out the roundness of a black eye.

"Cathy, what happened to your face," Maria said, and seeing the children coming out of the house, yelled back, "Kids go in the house for a minute, I'm talking to your mother."

"It's nothing really Maria," Cathy said. "I was cleaning the house and I fell down over some boxes."

"Well, then the bruise should be on your arm, not your face," Maria said. "Did he hit you?"

"No," Cathy stumbled over her unconvincing response. "We're just going through some stuff and Raymond's been under a lot of pressure trying to get the house back in order. It will pass."

"Do you want to stay with us? You can come here whenever you want to. And, if you want Albert to go talk to Raymond, I can have him do so," Cathy said.

"No, don't Maria. Please," Cathy said softly. "It will make things worse. You remember what Ma always told us. You gotta make your marriages work – no matter what you go through. I've been with Raymond too long and the kids need their father. Once the house is fixed things will get back to normal. I'm fine really."

Maria wasn't sure what she should say next. She thought of her father, Jesus, and recalled the conversations he and Bessie had with their children: "Marriage is sanctioned in the eyes of God and the church. It is something not to be broken. The church condemns divorce so when you get married, you better make sure it is something that you know will last. That is your family, *la familia*, and it is something that should be protected and always be your priority."

She remembered how during conversations related to the church, it always appeared that her father was looking more firmly at she and Cathy and not so much at her brothers. Yes, she reasoned, divorce is a sin, but so is beating your wife. She also understood that *la familia* was a tie that bound a group together from birth until death, and that it could always be trusted and relied upon in times of need.

She cried inside knowing that Cathy also had heard the voice of her father and that she continued to listen to him and respect the words he had instilled in his family, even if they made little sense. She vowed to be there for Cathy, regardless of any situation her life may present.

CHAPTER 10

DIRTY, LITTLE BEANER

The summer before seventh grade was an exciting and confusing time for Aurelio.

He spent the summer doing what he loved best – reading – but his body was also beginning to change which created a distraction from his usual activities. He grew four inches in what felt like a matter of weeks, and he started thinking about girls. Actually, he was confused about the topic of girls as he had previously never thought of any difference between boys or girls, but he suddenly became fixated on the difference in their bodies and their behaviors. Girls laughed more than boys, whispered more than boys, had more secrets than boys and cried more than boys. His mother said his newfound curiosity had something to do with his hormones, and he made regular checks of his body to see where these hormones might be manifesting themselves. He had heard about breast cancer being a rampant disease and when he conducted a breast self-examination like he had seen on PBS, he was convinced he had developed breast cancer. A quick trip to the doctor confirmed that his "hormones" had created the fatty tissue behind his breasts which hadn't been there in the past.

A month before school began, he and members of the United Nations of St. Mary's went to see "American Graffiti" at the Americana Theater in Panorama City. He was enamored by the movie and bought a pair of penny loafers, which he complimented with rolled jeans and a white t-shirt. His mother was pleased as the alternative dress of boys his age was quickly becoming the "cholo look" – Pendleton shirts, wife beater t-shirts, and creased and cuffed Levi's with black felt shoes. His mother smiled as she recalled that Aurelio's dress closely mirrored what his father used to wear during their courtship.

Aurelio became obsessed with the film. He thought it represented the key to his future. If he could – or rather was – the personification of the American youth, people would have to see beyond the color of his skin. He felt like Ron Howard's character "Steve" on the inside, but when he looked in the mirror, he saw Manuel Padilla Jr.'s character "Carlos." He started to mimic the vernacular of the film and suddenly everything became "cool," "far out" and "bitchin'" (his mother was not so much enamored with the last term). On weekends, the United Nations of St. Mary's often spent their Saturdays at the Northridge Roller Rink, and Oree would dress in his finest American Graffiti attire. He always took to the rink floor when Danny & the Juniors' "At the Hop" came blaring over the loudspeakers as America itself was in the midst of a fifties revival. Curiously missing from most of these activities, lately, was Shawn who had been on vacation somewhere. Upon his return, he hadn't quite gotten back into the activities of the group. America was changing a lot in the seventies – we had free love, bio-rhythms, pet rocks and even some new type of music called disco. Countering this, was a deepening sense of nostalgia which provided a sense of comfort amidst the change. At times it felt like Oree was living the life of "American Graffiti," and he thought this was how all American youths should live. Everything was cool and fit together. There wasn't any prejudice and even the ugly guy got a hot babe.

At home, Annie was just short of her fifteenth birthday, and a few of her friends had been planning or had already completed the rite of passage known as a *quinceañera*, where a 15-year-old girl is welcomed into womanhood with the help of a mass and a big party of course. Thus, Annie raised the topic of being the beneficiary of one of those, or perhaps having a Sweet 16 party. In discussing the options with her parents, her mother had to admit: "Frankly, I wouldn't know how to do a *quinceañera*. When we were growing up we didn't have money for those sorts of things, and they frowned upon them as being a 'Mexican thing,' so I didn't even think about it." Her father added that they hadn't really set aside money for any special birthday party or activity, so perhaps a dinner at Bob's Big Boy might suffice? Annie of course took this immediately as an affront as it was yet another example of her parents denying her the rights she had as a person of Mexican ancestry. Lately, she was always complaining about the fact that her parents weren't "Mexican enough."

That summer, another phenomena exploded which caught everyone by surprise. It was a little novel about demons, faith and the existence of God – William Peter Blatty's "The Exorcist." To impressionable, young Roman Catholics like Oree, the book quickly became the source of anxiety and fear, and it didn't help that the media was promoting a wave of possession paranoia across the country. Oree had patiently waited on the library's reserve list for weeks. At the turn of the first page, he was immediately enmeshed in the world of Pazuzu and possession. However, when his mother found out he was reading a book considered "blasphemy" by the Catholic Church, she made him take it back to the library, which he promised he would. He had already finished more than a quarter of the book, and as he was dying to see what became of the tormented, young Regan, he read the book by flashlight under his bed covers. He finished the novel in three marathon late-night readings to avoid the attention of his mother.

He soon began to think he might be possessed. He was the same age as Regan, the little girl who got possessed, he was disobeying his parents more frequently, and he even lied to the priest during confession, "No father, I did not disrespect my parents." As a result of the book and film, the topic of evil became so pronounced across America, that one Sunday the priest devoted his entire sermon to the devil, how we all must resist his temptations, and that we were all at risk of being taken over by his deceptive ways. This only helped to deepen Aurelio's paranoia surrounding demonic possession. He heard of exorcisms taking place in San Francisco and other places. As he knew it was only a matter of time before the devil made his way to Los Angeles, he began to pray more frequently, and in addition to the scapular he wore around his neck, he began wearing a silver cross, which he never took off.

He prayed each day: "God, please don't let me get possessed," but never let his parents in on his fears. He was to have his confirmation in the 7th grade, and he promised God that if he didn't let the devil possess him by that time, he would make an extra committed confirmation vow. At times he would break out in a cold sweat of fear, and he began to count the days until his confirmation in the hopes that he would then be forever free of the devil's grasp.

When he returned to school, things had changed as well. The nuns had new habits – in place of the long heavy robes were ankle length skirts; winged cornettes were replaced with wash and wear veils. They looked much cooler and the nuns seemed pleased. A few said they were among the changes resulting from Vatican II which was an examination the church conducted of its doctrines.

Returning to the seventh grade, he saw that the other children had been undergoing similar transitions such as his own. Some girls had full blown breasts and some of his male classmates had pimples and even a few chin hairs. Many had grown taller than him, but the most surprising change was that some of their personalities had changed (possession perhaps?) and it was as though they were different people.

He was able to ascertain this when time came to convene the first gathering of the United Nations of St. Mary the Merciless, Shawn was nowhere to be found. His other friends didn't seem to mind as they were busy trading notes on vacation trips – one had camped in the Sequoias and the other had spent the week with an Aunt at a vacation home near the beach in Ventura. At recess, Oree finally spotted his friend – Shawn was talking with a group of jocks who together resembled the Beach Boys. They had all grown and Shawn had too. His shoulders had filled out and he was taller, but it was more a change in his demeanor. Oree observed that his friend seemed like he fit right in with them, and based upon how comfortable he seemed, he surmised that Shawn had probably been spending a lot of time with them. This change in behavior would likely explain why he hadn't returned Oree's phone calls over the summer.

The school bell rang and by the time he got into his seventh grade classroom, he had forgotten the incident as his new teacher, Sister Judith, introduced herself.

Sister Judith had a plain face with clear, blue eyes, and a large white wart graced her left cheek. Under the coif of her habit, Oree was trying to decipher if her hair was grey or a light blond. There was something different about this nun, she didn't carry herself like some of the other old battle axes he had grown accustomed to as being his educators.

"Good morning class and welcome to the seventh grade," Sister Judith began. "First things first. Now, you see our nun outfits have changed. This is the result of Vatican II, and from now on, you won't have starchy, old nuns teaching you. We've entered a new era of wash and wear. I don't know about you, but I feel much lighter now."

"Now, I know you're all getting ready to enter or are already in puberty, but I am going to make every effort to keep you focused this year in order to prepare you for your eighth grade year and graduation," she continued. "You will also be making your confirmation this year, so we'll be doing lots of work to get ready for that as well. I know for some of you that means new clothes, new shoes and maybe a new prayer book, but there is a lot to this sacrament and I want to be sure you're all prepared. Oh, and the slap does not, I repeat, does not hurt – contrary to what others may have told you."

The class all broke out in laughter, but the nun had dispelled an urban legend that had been stewing in the back of Oree's mind – and likely other students as well – all summer long. His brother and sister both told him when the bishop slapped them, he hit hard and he waited until you were relaxed, so the pain would be doubly intense. The laughter continued, until Sister Judith spoke.

"O.k., settle down now," she said pausing and taking her hand in her chin. "I was going to ask you to pull out your *'Confirmation for Catholics'* books, but you know what? We're going to do something new to start the school year. How many of you have heard of meditation?"

Not one hand was raised.

"O.k. then, today you're in for a treat. I am going to teach you how to meditate!" she exclaimed, grasping her hands behind her back and tilting her neck right and left until it made a cracking sound. "This isn't the touchy feely stuff you may be thinking of, and it's not the stuff that you think the Hare Krishna's do. This form of meditation will help you to concentrate and you can use it throughout your life – whether you're happy or sad, stressed to the max, or want to get closer to God."

"Yes, I said closer to God. When some of you tell your parents I am teaching you to meditate, some of them might think I'm channeling the devil, but I'm not. I learned this technique at an ecclesiastical retreat in Santa Barbara and it has helped me in my life tremendously," Sister Judith smiled. "Now, close your eyes and take a deep breath….."

"Do you feel different?" Oree asked Jimmy and Chester as they lay across the bleachers at recess as they waved their fingers above them like they were under the influence of some hallucinogenic. "Do you think she hypnotized us?"

Both agreed that yes, they felt different but they weren't sure what it was.

"I feel drugged. This must be how it feels like to be high," Oree continued. "My mom said if anyone tries to give you a drug to run. I'm wondering if Sister Judith is brainwashing us so that we all want to become priests or something? That part where she said 'Feel your body being enveloped by a bright, warm white light,' was really intense. It was like I could feel all the light in my body."

"That's it," Chester chimed in. "That woman is the devil and that wart on her face proves she's a witch."

All three boys sat there quietly thinking over what had transpired in their classroom and trying to interpret just what Sister Judith may have been teaching them. They sat there and in the distance they saw Shawn and the jocks walking by.

"Hey there's Shawn, let's go see what's up?" Oree said.

"Naw, he's a jock now," said Jimmy. "He doesn't want to be part of our group anymore."

"We shall see," Oree said as he jumped off the bleachers and ran off to the group.

The other two boys sat up and watched as Oree poked Shawn's back shoulder. Shawn spun around as the jocks all turned and looked down at the much smaller Aurelio, laughing like he was an alien from another planet. Then, Oree's friends saw Shawn's face turn bright red as he yelled in the distance: "Why do you give a shit what I did this summer? Why don't you just buzz off. I don't want to be your friend anymore you dirty, little beaner. I hate you!"

They saw the other children on the school yard stop and turn their attention toward the yelling. The school yard grew quiet as all the children within ear's shot turned their attention to the group hoping to see a school yard fight. Then, they saw Oree put his right forearm across his face and eyes like he was suddenly blinded by harsh sunlight. He bowed his head down and ran off into the distant school building. The jocks started patting Shawn on the shoulders and continued with their cackling. One grabbed him in a headlock, gave an "atta boy" and began rubbing a knuckle in his head. They then saw Shawn pull back, stand straight up and look toward Chester and Jimmy who were both glad it was Oree who was singled out and not them. From what they could make out, as he looked at them, Shawn's eyes looked a little glossy, like they were tearing up.

Following this event which was the talk of the school yard gossip for weeks – "I heard the jocks were gonna beat him up..." "Serves him right for thinking he could ever hang with the jocks" – things changed for Oree. They would remain different for the remainder of his seventh grade year. As the trauma of losing his best friend and the embarrassment of it becoming a public spectacle were so pronounced, he withdrew into himself deeply and avoided human interaction whenever possible. Even Sister Judith commented that at first he had done so well with his meditation practice, but lately he couldn't concentrate for as long as a flea.

At lunch time and recess, he would sit by himself, often in the bleachers or places where the other students didn't congregate. He would go home after school and retreat in his books, silently reading in his room until dinner time. His mother attributed his lack of appetite to "growing pains," and both Annie and Anthony were so involved in their own school activities that they didn't notice that their brother might be suffering.

It was like all those other times in his childhood that Oree had been mistreated because of the color of his skin came to the surface again and all at once. He experienced the feelings he had previously felt as a result of things tied to the color of his skin – the shame, the embarrassment, the feelings of self-loathing – however, this time it was much more pronounced as he fully understood what these feelings meant. Thus, they hurt a lot more than when he was a child. It was as though they were old, bad friends that returned again and again during the roughest parts of his life. At his worst point, he wondered what it would feel like to not exist – the thought scared him so much that he batted it away and took up reading mysteries which helped him to focus on story plots rather than the burdens of his life.

He avoided the United Nations of St. Mary's for several weeks. Finally, Chester and Jimmy cajoled him into returning to the group's activities with the promise that they would never mention the first day of seventh grade, but Oree didn't share the same enthusiasm as before. It was as though he was somehow detached from everything – school, his friends, his family. Even books provided little solace from these feelings of detachment. Many times he felt only numbness. He began to look forward to going to high school as it seemed to provide an opportunity for a fresh start. He wouldn't be plagued by the memory of what happened on the school yard, and there would be kids coming from other schools who didn't know he was the "dirty, little beaner."

Oree's confirmation in October was non-eventful as he continued to battle against the feelings caused by the incident. The one notable confirmation-related activity he was upset by was that as a result of Vatican II, he was not allowed to choose a confirmation name (this action was later reversed). He had planned on using the name "Frank."

Since he had read "The Diary of Anne Frank" in the summer following second grade, he wanted to use her name in tribute to the girl who lost her life because she was a Jew, because she was persecuted. Following his confirmation, he decided he no longer needed to be an altar boy as he had matured to the point of wanting more than to spend his Sundays kneeling in front of a congregation.

In late-November, his grandmother Bessie passed away. His mother took the news quite heavily, having lost both of her parents within a matter of a few years.

The day of the funeral was a crisp fall morning, and brown, yellow and red leaves fluttered across the church's court yard which was suspended by a limp, dry breeze. The Rodrigo family entered the church where Bessie's casket lay. It was tradition to have the casket placed in the church early the morning of services, in case any family or friends wanted to give a last, final farewell. Surrounding the dark, walnut casket were four ladies dressed in black. They had long black veils and took turns sobbing unconsolably. Their wails overpowered the silence and it was as though their cries were for the loss of some great profound being, it couldn't be just for his grandmother. The sights and sounds of them made Annie begin to cry uncontrollably. Her mother took her by the shoulder and led her to the front pew where they both sat and wept.

Anthony stood by his father and Oree. They were to be pall bearers. For the third time since they arrived at church that morning, Anthony went to the bathroom to comb his hair. (Now a teenager, personal grooming and preening in the mirror had become Anthony's favorite past-time, followed closely by girl watching.)

"Who are those ladies and why are they crying?" Oree asked his father.

"They are professional mourners," his father replied. "Your mother asked me to hire them, and they are supposed to cry so that God can hear their voices and welcome the person who died into heaven."

The loud and pained sobs of the women seemed to overpower the coolness of the church interior, giving it an eerie, almost surreal texture. Oree thought to himself that this was indeed what pure, unadulterated suffering sounded like – it was the sound of his pain personified. He wondered if he could sustain a career as a professional mourner. After all, in the weeks following the incident, he had done more than his fair share of crying – in private.

As the funeral mass began, his thoughts continued to distract him. He could not understand how someone who had been his best friend for so long had turned on him. He was the one who had befriended the boy in his worst time of need, and this was how he repaid him? He even got beat up as a result of their friendship. How could Shawn of all people, call Oree a beaner? He knew that word was the foulest, most cruel utterance imaginable, and here he used it on his friend – or ex-friend.

Over the following weeks, questions like these would continue to plague Oree. But, as with all things, as time passed, the hurt began to dissipate. Every now and then, the memories would resurface and Oree would again fall back on his old feelings from the past – that being brown was wrong and now despicable. That it was something that created shame and now despair. That it was the cause of all of his problems and pain. That it was something he would be reminded of throughout his life, and it was something he absolutely did not want to be.

He reasoned, if only he could change the color of his skin things would be different.

CHAPTER 11

GROWING PAINS

"So, is she pregnant or not?" Maria yelled at her son.

Anthony, who was now a senior at St. Francis the Abbey High School, looked sheepishly down at his dirty Adidas tennis shoes. He fumbled with his hands and played with the crease in his jeans like he was sharpening a knife. He was numb.

"Anthony, answer your mother. Is the girl pregnant or not?" Albert said both in resentment and also fear that his eldest son's life had just taken a detour which would lead him far away from any possible football scholarship, college education or future that he had envisioned.

"Well, she said she's pregnant and her mom took her to the doctor, who said, yeah she is," Anthony, who was never big on words, sputtered out.

"How could you let this happen?" his father continued. "You know when your mother and I gave you the talk, we said, 'You get a girl pregnant, you marry her.'"

Anthony almost smirked at his father's comment. The "talk" which he spoke of consisted of a few sentences strewn together to the effect of "You're going to start getting these urges and you need to stop them at all costs. You are under no circumstance to touch girls down there as, yes, they can get pregnant on the first time." His parents seemed so embarrassed by having to explain sex to him that the topic was better left guessed at. At that conversation, they surmised Anthony had already heard about sex talk from his peers, and that he could fill in the blanks on the conversation they were having. They hoped that their children were smarter than their cousins – after all, it was just a few years earlier that cousin Lupita had gotten herself into trouble with a 28-year-old married man which resulted in her move to Albuquerque, New Mexico, to live with a distant family member.

Prior to what they were now calling "the incident," Anthony, who had been getting "the urges" since seventh grade, figured that his sex education would be something he could perhaps ask one of the lay teachers about – a priest would not be a good candidate to explain reproduction. St. Francis was a Catholic high school and thus the only references to sexual reproduction were veiled statements about "growing pains" that were thrown into hygiene education classes. His younger brother gave him a better explanation than his parents when he read from a medical book that he had borrowed from the public library.

"The man places his penis in the woman's vagina and ejaculates," Oree said plainly reading from the medical journal to Anthony, and then interjecting, "That sounds pretty gross to me. Who would want to make a mess like that?" As a result of his voracious reading hobby, Oree was much more of an expert on birth control, pregnancy and the like than was the unread Anthony. He had learned about love, passion and unwanted pregnancies from more than a few of his novels.

All advice aside, Anthony thought to himself, "Now, it is too late, and I should have paid more attention. My life is finished.'" He reckoned that probably no amount of lectures, sex education or preparation would have mattered as every time Luz was around he could barely control himself. Nothing could prevent him from the desire of wanting to play hand puppets with her every time she came into view.

"So, what is her name? Is she in your grade? Does she go to St Francis? How far along is she?" Now, the questions were coming fast and furious from his mother.

"Luz is in eleventh grade and is a cheerleader," Anthony said, realizing how cliché his soon-to-be wife sounded. She wasn't even in a book club. "Yes, she goes to St. Francis. It happened a few months ago."

"A few months ago. A few months ago," Maria said sputtering in disbelief. "Anthony, you know what you have to do. You have to do the honorable thing. I can't believe I'm saying this – you have to marry the girl."

"The girl is probably as ashamed as you are Anthony," his father said calming down into the idea. "Your mother, you and I will go meet with her family, and we'll figure this mess out. You only have a few months to graduation, so you can get a job to support your family when you graduate. We'll talk to my parents. Maybe you and Luz can go live with them. Their house is so big and they are getting older, so they might welcome having you there. Plus, they have that guest house in the back which is sitting empty."

Albert couldn't believe he was putting his son's future together so quickly and with so much precision. He recalled a memory that he hadn't considered in years – that he and his wife had an unplanned pregnancy before they were married, so he understood how his son felt. As Anthony had not yet found the direction he sought his life, his father had often wondered what his son's future might look, until now. He was not good at school. He was good with his hands. He didn't seem to have a clue if he should work or try to get into a community college, and yet he continuously spoke of this Luz person over the past eight months that they had been dating. Now, he was going to get married and father a child. Maybe he loved her enough, and maybe they would be o.k. Perhaps. Maybe. O.k.

As the father and son spoke, Maria strung thoughts together in her own mind, remembering a time back to her youth. "*La familia* is the most important thing in life and we have been very blessed with our children. For whatever reason, God is giving Anthony this path to follow, and he must save the dignity of this family and that of the girl. I can't believe a baby is coming into our lives. I wanted so much for Anthony's life, and now I'm going to be grandmother! How can I be a grandma when I still have a son in eighth grade? I always thought Annie would be the one to do something stupid like this. That girl is always on the verge of something dumb. Now, my son is going to be a father.

What if he becomes like my sister's husband – a drunk who's full of anger and hate? No, that could never be my *hijo*. He, they, will be o.k."

Maria recalled the experience from her own youth. "I can't very well condemn them as I was once in their situation. Still, I finished school and Albert and I were engaged at the time, so we were already planning to be a family. This situation is different."

Her thoughts were cut short by Albert's statement: "Anthony, give me the phone number of this girl. I will give her father a call to set up a meeting to discuss this mess."

"You know, she could always have an abortion. Roe vs. Wade gave us women the right to do with our bodies as we choose," Annie, who was now 19 and in junior college, said to her mother. "That's another possibility."

"I should have known that you would come up with something stupid like that," Maria said in chiding her daughter. "How would I ask a 17-year-old if she wants to get an abortion? Plus, is it against the teachings of the church."

"The church. The church. When all else fails, let's fall back on the teachings of the church, because we all know what a moral compass that place is," Anita said starting to fume. "No divorce, no homosexuals, no right to choose. You know if the church didn't have all these damn rules, Aunt Cathy would have divorced that drunk of a husband years ago. Instead she stays in a crappy marriage and her kids are a mess."

"Plus, if our people had greater equality, Aunt Cathy could get a job and make her own choices and not have to rely on that drunk of a husband," Annie continued. "That's why I'm fighting for Chicano rights."

"How did this conversation turn into something about your Aunt Cathy and this Chicano nonsense," Maria continued incredulously. "Your brother's going to have to marry the girl and we're going to have to welcome her into our family."

"I'm just saying mom, we should have different choices. Joaquin says...."

Once Maria heard the name, her mind went blank with anger. Joaquin was Annie's boyfriend of the past six months. He fashioned himself to be some sort of ultra-liberal, revolutionary Latino leader, kind of like Che Guevara, Emiliano Zapata and a male version of Eva Peron all rolled into one. When Annie first introduced him to her family, Maria's impression was that he saw himself as being some sort of modern day Christ. He was skinny and wore leather sandals, torn jeans, a linen Nehru shirt and long straggly hair pulled into a braided ponytail. The last accoutrement had the signs of Annie's handiwork all over it. Hair pulled tight into a restrictive, overly done ponytail.

Joaquin was on the council of the Chicano Liberation Party, which Anita had been secretly hiding her involvement with until it surfaced during one of the many fights she had lately with her parents. "That's why I'm affiliated with the Chicano Liberation Party – to ensure that the stifled bourgeois, middle class doesn't get lulled into a sense of complacency, while big brother continues to raid their pockets for whatever scraps they have!"

Needless to say when that "affiliation" was announced, Anita was almost booted out of the family residence. It took several days of Albert coaxing Maria with statements like, "At least while she's under our roof, we can keep an eye on her and hope she grows out of this phase." Maria remained unconvinced. Annie had been in "this phase" since she was a child. At this point, she knew it was doubtful that Anita would ever become the facile, respectful young woman destined to move up in some sort of business – real estate perhaps – that she envisioned.

In some ways, Maria admired her child. She always seemed to know what she wanted, and she was always willing to fight for it. She wasn't interested in titles, appearances or the like. Maria admired her daughter's strength in that way. But, she also understood that so much of what Annie believed in was counter-productive.

As she got older, Maria had come to realize that the only way to effect change was to do so within the system, not by some radical pounding on the door which Annie was so proficient at. She had seen her husband finally be promoted from being a produce hawker to an assistant manager over the course of his career at Hollywood Ranch

Market. She saw that people appreciated his work ethic despite the color of his skin and lack of a college education. He was accepted as a respectable, hard worker – people didn't necessarily see the color of his skin as a definition of who he was which was very important to the Rodrigos. She told these things to Anita on numerous occasions, but she may as well have been talking to a person without ears as Annie continuously dismissed her mother's attempts to reason with her.

"Mom, are you listening to me?" Annie said snapping her fingers.

"Don't snap your fingers at your mother!" Maria retorted. "Yes, I'm listening, and no, abortion isn't going to be a suggested alternative to this situation."

The day of Anthony and Luz's wedding, the Rodrigos, with the exception of Annie, who was somewhere in the Central Valley picketing a produce factory with Joaquin, everyone loaded into the family station wagon like they were going on a family trip. It was all very calm and organized. They made a quick stop at the San Fernando Valley Cemetery flower shop to purchase a corsage for Luz. Aurelio, who had lately been reading "War and Peace," thought it ironic and humorous that that the book title was soon to become his brother and his new wife's wedded life.

After weeks of discussions, it was decided that Luz, who was very petite and had not yet begun to show, would stay in school so she could finish eleventh grade. She would keep the pregnancy a secret by wearing winter coats until the end of the school term -- even if it would be spring approaching summer. Anthony, who was graduating from St. Francis that year, would stay with his family until the school year ended in two months. Albert had arranged for his son to get a job at a grocery store in East Los Angeles following graduation. He and Luz would move in with Albert's parents. The elders had accepted the proposition to have their grandson and his new wife move into the guest house – provided they did not expect child care duties, and that the newlyweds would assist the Rodrigos with shopping and errand-running. Depending on how things were going with the baby, it could later be determined if Luz was to go back to finish high school. Finally, both families agreed that following the wedding ceremony, none of this would be discussed further until school let out for summer.

The two families joined on the steps of L.A. City Hall. As she was not yet 18, Luz's parents had to sign for her marriage certificate. The families greeted each other and went into the Registrar's Office. They resurfaced an hour later with Mr. and Mrs. Anthony Rodrigo. The two families celebrated with breakfast at Denny's.

Aurelio, who remained in the background during all the hullabaloo, was glad to see it end. It had been distracting from all that he had going on – it was his eighth grade year and he was graduating to go into high school. His year started off with a clean slate. He had for the most part recovered from the pain of what had happened in the seventh grade – and he avoided the jocks and Shawn like the plague. The United Nations of St. Mary the Merciless was as tight as ever, but would likely disband following graduation. Jimmy was going to another Catholic High School, and Chester would be attending a public school.

The summer leading into the eighth grade, Aurelio decided he liked movies more than reading. It was easier to view a story on a wide screen rather than have to put it together in your mind – everything you needed to know was right in front of your eyes. He saw "Jaws" three times, and during the opening of the film, he experienced his first adult erection. He wondered why the sight of a naked woman who was about to become chowder for a killer fish would arouse him so, but it happened. It was within weeks following this momentous event that he would have his first experience with that white, gooey stuff known as ejaculate. He was convinced that he would have to spend the entire eighth grade with his books being held strategically in front of his pants since things kept popping up at the worst possible moments (like when he was reciting an essay in class).

His mother, who in spying one of these unplanned moments following the whole Albert pregnancy situation told him, "You better stop thinking of those dirty thoughts or you'll end up like your brother."

In any case, a new group of students formed at the school – they were mostly boys and they smoked pot. Oree had been afraid to try it as his mother warned that it would make him go crazy and that his hair would fall out. Still, when he heard a group of boys had planted marijuana seeds in the garden of the nun's rectory amidst the roses, he, Chester and Jimmy had to go see it. One time at lunch, they crept their way into the nun's convent garden. Sure thing, amidst the roses lay a solitary marijuana plant striving to find sunlight amidst the thorny bushes. They were promised by the stoners that there would be enough for them to smoke at the eighth grade picnic, if they didn't divulge the whereabouts of the plant to any adult.

Although he did not favor mind altering substances, there was one characteristic of the stoner group that Oree did identify with. Following the popularity of the song, "Hush," he quickly became a fan of Deep Purple, followed by Jethro Tull and Alice Cooper. The stoners all seemed to like this type of music. Oree had gotten a stereo for his twelfth birthday so his mother was continually telling him to "lower that crap" in response to the blaring of heavy metal music. This was soon followed by "You better not be smoking in there" when Oree began burning patchouli incense. His other guilty pleasure was "Mad Magazine," a satirical comic book which featured Alfred E. Neuman, a red-haired, pie-faced anti-hero with a wide gap between his front teeth. The magazine was often infused with drug and fart references and the like – a perfect literary choice for any adolescent boy.

In addition to his prurient interests with heavy metal and subversive comics, Oree also liked soul music, especially Marvin Gaye. His favorite song was "Got To Give It Up" as the lyrics echoed what he wanted to happen in his life as he prepared for high school.

"…No more standin' upside the walls
Now I've got myself together, baby
And I'm havin' a ball."

If there was ever a song to mirror what was going on in a 12-year-old's mind, it was that one. Oree would lie for days on his back on the cool floor of his bedroom playing Parts I and II, and thinking: "Yeah that's right, not gonna get beat up anymore, not gonna be a beaner. Not gonna be afraid. I just gotta give it up." At times, he was surprised by his increasingly frequent bursts of self-confidence. Prior to the seventh grade event, Oree had always been sure of himself, so this reemergence of the old Oree was welcomed. He was physically growing like a string-bean and when he looked in the mirror, he summed himself up to be a "fine looking homey." For his birthday, his father gave him a 45 RPM single, "It's Hard to Be Humble" by Mac Davis.

Another thing that gave him confidence was his school studies. He would be graduating from the eighth grade with a 4.0 GPA and was to be awarded a special writing certificate at the graduation breakfast. Oree's intelligence and aptitude for learning were also no longer secrets his parents could ignore. In preparing for high school, he scored unusually high on the Stanford Achievement Test and the California Achievement Test. The results of the tests were published during the time of the Anthony pregnancy discussions. The pregnancy of course took precedent over any awareness that at least one of the Rodrigo children was destined for more than a shot gun wedding or an arrest at a public protest. Oree was to be reassessed in his high school freshmen year to see how soon he would be a candidate for advanced placement classes in high school.

Prior to graduation, there was one last project each student had to undertake – they had to sign up for a "Saturday of Service" activity which included projects such as picking up trash by the freeway, visiting a nursing home and spending the afternoon with seniors, or cleaning the house of a family in need. Oree chose the last option, and he and five other eighth graders showed up with one of the nuns one Saturday morning at a dilapidated house in Pacoima. From the outside, he saw weeds overflowing throughout the yard, the windows and house siding were filthy and looked off kilter. What fencing they had surrounding the house, was half fallen. Oree thought to himself that someone should have called the city on this property a long time ago. The nun asked for a few students to work in the yard and the others to join her in cleaning the house.

She asked the students to be respectful of the people's home – these were members of their parish who had fallen on hard times. The father had been deported to Mexico, leaving behind a wife and three children. The mother had lately been visiting the church asking for assistance in "getting through these tough times" as her husband had promised to return by spring. The Women's League had been bringing the family food, but they decided it might make a good project for the eighth graders to help clean up the home. They knocked on the front door and a 4-year-old boy in a dirty striped t-shirt, underpants and socks with holes in them opened the door. "Mama, *es la monja*, it's the nun." He motioned the group in, grabbing the nun's hand. The mother was sitting on the couch with a smoldering cigarette in her right hand, dangling it over a teal aluminum ash tray, as she looked vacantly at the group. Two other young children sat cross-legged on the floor watching H.R. Pufnstuf on an old black and white TV with a missing channel knob.

The house smelled like moth balls, cigarettes and rotten pork. Oree and the other youths wanted to wretch, but the nun quickly motioned them to the kitchen where they found a box with cleaning supplies and rags which the Women's League had dropped off. On the stove was a battered aluminum pot with something coagulated in it. Next to the stove was an open can of menudo which looked like it had been sitting there for a while. "Get to it," the nun said, as she sat down and began speaking in Spanish to the woman. One girl grabbed her nose by her hand, grabbed the pot and can of rotten menudo and threw it down the sink. She quickly opened a kitchen window.

None of the young people wanted to clean the bathroom, so Oree was awarded the task. He opened the bathroom door and looked down into the toilet. It was pink and had brown rust and other stains. It smelled and looked like it hadn't been cleaned in years. The same with the pink sink and bath tub. He began cleaning by throwing Ajax on every surface he could. He heard gentle crying coming from the living room. Opening the door, he peered down the hallway and saw the nun holding the woman's head against her shoulder and petting her hair gently as her children gathered around her, also in tears. The woman looked so somber as though all the life had been drained from her soul. He wondered what could have happened to the woman that was so bad that she didn't have the strength to clean her children or her house. His parents had always told him that their family was poor, but seeing this house, Oree better understood what real poverty looked like. Compared with this house, his family was rich.

He and the other youths spent the remaining hours cleaning silently. Oree reasoned that cleaning this mess of a house was far worse than any penance he had ever received, but he also used the time to think about how much his family truly had. His father had not been deported to Mexico and their house was well kept and in a nice neighborhood. His mother kept the house and family cleaned and well fed. She didn't sit on the couch all day, smoking and crying.

It was that afternoon when something transformed in Oree. He realized that he had to use his intelligence for something beneficial. When he grew up, he had to think of a way to help people. It didn't matter if they were white or brown, rich or poor – if they were suffering, someone with a brain like his had to help them to improve their lives. He didn't know what type of job he could take that would address this situation, but he knew he would figure it out in time. After his years of religious training and schooling, he reasoned that it was not only the Catholic thing to do, but also the right thing to do.

On the last day of school, it was tradition that all the eighth grade graduates would skip the afternoon session and leave for an unsanctioned picnic. A few of the parents and some of the graduate's older siblings volunteered to drive the youths to El Cariso Park in Sylmar. Oree was excited. He had heard the picnics turned into big party events and he was curious to have his first taste of pot or beer or maybe feel the kiss of Sandra Lopez, the girl from the first grade pigtail incident. Over the years, Oree had secretly developed a crush on her and she had grown into a beautiful young woman who had long forgotten Oree's prank.

She now considered him to be "funny" and "nice." One of the kids brought a boom box radio which played 8-track tapes, so everyone was encouraged to bring their favorite tapes from home.

About 20 graduates took their places on tables and on blankets under the trees of the park. It was a warm afternoon and felt like summer was fast-approaching. A few of the kids smoked cigarettes and everything suddenly felt awkward. At St. Mary's, the young people knew how to behave and what was expected of them. Now, their grade school was a thing of the past and there was no one there to tell them what to do or how to behave. They looked at each other for clues, a few went to play football and others lay on their backs talking about what a crappy school year it had been. They felt a sense of freedom, but also a bit of trepidation. Some had heard stories of high school freshmen getting jumped by seniors as part of their initiation. Oree vowed that if anyone tried to jump him he would punch first and ask questions later. He was not going to live through another four years of people bullying or hitting him. A few of the girls started dancing when Earth, Wind and Fire's "Shining Star" came on over the boom box.

To everyone's surprise, the group of the stoners made a surprise visit. They drove up in a 1964 primered, Chevy Nova with Jethro Tull blaring out of the windows. The driver, who was someone from high school, opened the trunk of his car and pulled a Styrofoam ice chest from the back. "Come and get it kiddies, it's Miller time for a buck a piece," the stoner laughed.

Jimmy looked at Oree, "Are you gonna get a beer?" Before he could answer, Oree was ripping a $1 bill out of his pocket for beer. He went back to his friends, Chester got a beer, Jimmy did not.

Oree popped the top off the Coors beer and sipped from the can. His first thoughts were that beer tasted nasty. Once he warmed up to this new, different taste, be began to enjoy the saltiness and carbonation. It made him belch immediately and he felt very mature.

The stoners pulled a blanket out of the Nova's trunk and joined the group under the trees. Within minutes, a 12" glass bong with hand painted marijuana leaves materialized and the stoners began to light it up.

"Hey homies," one of them called, "Remember that bush we were growing in the nuns' front yard. Well, it's time to savor the harvest!"

Oree, Jimmy and Chester looked at each other as some of the other kids took hits from the bong. It was passed around by the group and when it came to the three of them, Oree inhaled deeply and coughed immediately. The stoners began laughing. "Oree dude, you gotta inhale lighter, you're not smoking a Marlboro."

Oree took another hit and held it deeply in his lungs. He released it and took a sip of his beer. He envisioned that this was his true graduation – from sheltered put upon to being a man of the world who partook in all its many pleasures. After a second hit, everything seemed to grow calm and mellow. The leaves swayed gently as if suspended by the warm air which circulated through the branches. The group broke off into smaller cliques as some of the kids went to play frisbee, others went to sit on a park bench to smoke cigarettes, and some sat on the grass laughing and reminiscing about the tortures they had endured at the hands of the gestapo nuns.

The rest of the afternoon, Oree remained fixated on how he felt, and trying to ascertain if it was the result of the beer or pot. Was his head buzzing? Were his fingers tingling? Was he dizzy from the pot or the beer? Was he hearing voices in his head? He thought, "Boy getting high takes a lot of work" and he decided he didn't like it very much. He couldn't drink more than half of the beer, so that was given to Chester who had already finished his and seemed to have an aptitude for the stuff.

As the group sat there chatting, he looked over at Sandra Lopez. He wondered if she had been impressed by his beer chugging and pot smoking abilities. He had just enough beer and buzz to gather the courage to sit down next to her.

"Hey Sandra," he said.

"Hi Oree," she replied.

"Glad the year's over? What are you going to do this summer?" he suddenly began to stammer and lose his confidence.

"Yeah, I can't believe we're graduating," Sandra said twirling her hair which was now shoulder length and no longer the long flowing mass which it was during her early years of school. "I am going to Guadalajara for a month to stay with my aunt and her family. My mom says it's to help me better appreciate what we have in this country, or some nonsense like that. I would rather spend it at the beach."

"I know what you mean," Oree continued. "I am going to be working with my dad a day or two a week to sweep the floors and do bottle returns at the Hollywood Ranch Market."

"Bottle returns?" Sandra asked.

"Yeah, you know when you take your coke and 7-Up bottles back to the store, they have to be put in crates to be sent back to the manufacturers for re-use. Someone has to sort the bottles and I will get a buck for each full crate," Oree continued. "Plus, a lot of celebrities buy their groceries there so I might get to see some movie stars."

"Well that sounds like you'll be busy," Sandra said. "You know I'm going to an all girl's school in fall?"

"Yeah, I heard. That sounds fun," Oree said suddenly somewhat sarcastically. Then he decided now was as good as any time to make his move. He did not want to enter high school without having his first kiss – that would be worse than being a virgin.

"Hey, Sandra, can I kiss you?" he said whispering in her ear.

Sandra smiled and let him, and with that Aurelio tasted his first pair of lips. At first, he felt slightly embarrassed, yet strangely warm and squishy inside. He wasn't quite sure, but he thought for a brief moment her tongue may have brushed against his upper lip, which got him excited in ways he had never imagined.

The other kids tried to behave like they hadn't seen the brief but fiery interlude. And then, it was over.

"Well, maybe I can see you over the summer sometime?" Oree said looking in her eyes and still feeling the buzz from Sandra's kiss.

"Sure," Sandra replied with the unspoken knowledge that she would likely never see Oree again following their graduation.

"Summer" by War started playing on the 8-track and Oree vowed to make it his theme for the next three months as summer was truly his "time of year." He enjoyed the cool, unrushed rhythm of the song and the lyrics made him feel, well groovy. He knew this was how all teenagers must feel.

The afternoon seemed to drift by and Oree and his friends sat as classmates for the final time. By 4:30 in the afternoon, Oree knew it was time to call his mom to pick him up. He wasn't sure if he was stoned or drunk, but he'd been warned that he needed to "maintain" when he called his mother – no signs of buzz from anything. He called home and quietly said he was ready for his mom to come. He was sure he had "maintained" and that he didn't have to worry about his mom coming up in his face to smell his breath like some of his friends had shared their mothers did. Walking back from the pay phone by the restrooms, he looked out across the sky which for some reason seemed unusually vast and clear. He saw the sun slowly slipping down against a cloud-feathered yellow, red and orange backdrop which canvassed the west. He felt a warm breeze brush against his cheeks and through his now wavy hair. He heard the song "Summer" floating in his mind which had suddenly grown calm and quiet, kind of like when the class would meditate with Sister Judith. In contemplating his grade school years, it felt like a lifetime had already passed.

Grade school had not been that bad. Sure, it had its trials and tribulations, but it also held many good memories. He remembered the excitement of discovering books, the pain of friendships, the rewards that came with maintaining good grades (even if no one recognized it), the embracing of his faith as a member of God's church, and the changes that he had seen within his family. He made a pledge that high school would be better and that he would do more to fit in. He smiled as he remembered a phrase his grandfather Jesus had once told him: "Sometimes your life can end up being so much more than you hoped for."

He vowed to make that his mantra for high school.

CHAPTER 12

HIGH SCHOOL

A few weeks before he was to start high school, Oree's mother took him to San Fernando Mall to buy new clothes. Now that Anthony had moved out, there were less things to hand down, and as her oldest son had such a big appetite, his absence and Anita's endless activities away from home, made Maria's shopping trips and food budget easier to maintain. This left room for items such as new clothes for Aurelio. The open air San Fernando Mall had everything you could want to furnish a wardrobe – J.C. Penney's, People's Store for Men and Boys, Kinneys Shoes and the Sears Roebuck Outlet Store. With Anthony, Luz and their new baby Eva settling in with Albert's parents, Maria was glad to have a break from all the changes. Shopping with her "normal" son would be a welcome treat, and her sister would be joining them. As lately Cathy had seemed to retreat further and further away from her sister, Maria was surprised when she accepted her invitation to join them in shopping.

"Your aunt is going to meet us in Penney's," Maria said to Oree who was eyeing a pair of earth shoes in the window of Kinneys.

"Hey ma, can I get a pair of earth shoes? They are really cool and everyone has a pair," Oree said pointing to the wallabie-like brushed leather shoes in the window. Earth shoes were told to have numerous health benefits and they featured a sole that was thicker at the front of the shoe and thinner toward the heel, so the wearer was forced to walk more uprightly. "They'll last me the whole year, I promise."

"They look weird, but let's go try them on," Maria smiled, surprising herself at the buoyancy she was feeling. She generally tended to avoid buying "trendy" things for the children. She recalled the time that Annie wanted a pair of monster bell bottoms which flared out 12 inches at the legs. After Annie kept tripping and falling over them, Maria took them back to Sears. The shoes didn't look like they could cause too much damage, so she relented and Oree made his first purchase of the day. She looked at her son and had a moment of pride in thinking that he was growing up to be a fine, young man. As he grew over the years, she had hoped that his dark, brown skin would lighten up much like blond haired babies often end up with brown hair as they mature, but alas, as Aurelio continued to grow, much to her disappointment, he remained dark as ever.

The next stop was People's. The men and boys' store had all sorts of clothing, from Dickies work wear to the latest silky, polyester slacks which were quickly becoming the thing to wear. People's also catered to "low riders," meaning they had a wide selection of Pendleton plaid shirts, Levi's® with special lengths that could be easily cuffed, sleeveless undershirts typically called "wife beaters" and black canvas shoes with rubber crepe soles called "chinos." Suddenly, Oree felt pressured. There were so many possible looks he could pursue, and he had heard there were four primary groups in high school – low riders, surfers, stoners and nerds – he wasn't sure which group he would end up in so he decided to keep his fashion choices safe. He got a pair of tan khakis and a plaid short sleeve shirt (although he suspected the last choice might lean him more closely toward the nerd group than what he was comfortable with).

"So Oree, have you given much thought of what you want to do in high school?" Maria said breaking his thought.

"Uh, study, learn, go to football games, you know do high school stuff," Oree responded.

"That's not what I mean," Maria said. "Everyone knows you're smart. What are you going to do with that?"

"Finally!" Oree thought to himself. "It practically took an act of God for someone in my family to recognize that I am not your average beaner – that I don't have to get someone pregnant or to wave a protest flag to get attention." He suddenly felt self-righteous and thought "I'm going to like being an only child in this house."

To his mother he responded, "Well, they are putting me in college prep classes, that is something I need to consider. I think I might want to go to college."

Maria sighed and almost felt herself tear up as they walked toward Penney's. "Finally, one of my children might graduate from college. I should have always known it would be Oree." She thought of a statistic she had heard on the news which came from the United States Census – only 5% of Hispanics finished four or more years of college in 1974. Although it was too late for Anthony and possibly Anita, who was skipping classes with greater regularity than registering for them, it wasn't too late for Aurelio. "I just hope he doesn't get a girl pregnant," she thought as they spotted Cathy in J.C. Penney's dress section.

"Hey Cath," Maria said hugging her sister. As she embraced her, she felt Cathy's body grow rigid, but knowing that her life with Raymond was one big pressure cooker, Maria had long ago gotten used to her sister's inability to relax. She also knew that Cathy's children were a sore spot that was better left undiscussed – Lupita remained in Albuquerque where she was raising her daughter on her own; Raymond Jr. had gone into the army following graduation; Cynthia always seemed to have a dazed look, oily straight hair and unkept clothes; and Narciso, who was closest to Oree's age, was in a juvenile hall "camp" for slapping a teacher.

Instead of planning for activities for the families to develop closer bonds, over the years Maria had increasingly kept her children away from their cousins in the hopes that their behaviors wouldn't rub off (Raymond Jr. being the exception). Maria prayed nightly for her sister, and she continually asked God for guidance on ways to speak with her. She had given up on the "Why don't you leave him?" pleas which were always greeted defensively and fraught with excuses. When she saw her sister, she instead chose to make their visits pleasant so Cathy knew she had someone to come to if she needed help or advice.

"Hi Maria," Cathy responded. "How are you Oree? You all ready for high school?"

"I'm getting there Aunt Cathy," He responded kissing his aunt on the cheek, a touch of thick red rouge rubbing off on his lips. "Mom, I'm going to go to the sporting goods section downstairs."

"O.k. I'll be here in the ladies section with your aunt," she responded as he bounded down the nearby stairs.

"So, what's new?" Maria asked Cathy, surveying her body for any possible signs of bruising or scratches which were sometimes covered up with long sleeve shirts worn during heat waves or the like.

"Not much, I'm getting Cynthia ready for school and they're supposed to send Narciso home from 'camp' in a few weeks so he can go back to regular school," Cathy responded, understanding that her use of the term "camp" was synonymous with the Juvenile Camp Joseph Scott youth correctional facility in nearby Saugus. "Then, when they let him out I have to take him to a counselor to learn about anger management. With a father like his, what would they expect from the kid? Raymond Jr. sent me a letter from the Army. He's stationed in Missouri and there's talk about having to go overseas as the Middle East keeps screwing around with gas prices. Remember the oil crisis and how we had to line up to get gas? It could be like that again."

"I hope not," Maria responded. "Remember, we had to go on alternating days to get gas? That was ridiculous."

"I know," Cathy continued. "How are you enjoying being a grandma?"

Maria laughed, "I still am not used to hearing that name. When we're around the house, my husband is constantly calling me 'granny'. But still, things are so much quieter now that Anthony is gone and Annie isn't around as much. Oree's starting high school, so soon he'll be out more often too."

"I am thinking maybe once all my kids are out of the house, I might get out too," Cathy said seemingly out of the blue. "Nothing holding me back, and I certainly don't want to be a punching bag when I'm 65."

Maria grew quiet. This was the first time she had heard her sister bring up the idea of leaving and the mention of abuse. She decided to play it cool as the slightest agreement could easily send Cathy scurrying back into her shell.

"If there's anything I can do?" Maria asked. "You and the kids could come and live with us until you get on your feet."

"Thanks Maria, I appreciate that. I'm supposed to be the big sister, but you are always the one who knows the right thing to say and do," Cathy continued, tearing up.

"C'mon. Let's go get Oree and go have a Danny's Dog," Maria said changing the direction of the conversation. "I am in the mood to have one of those chili mustard dogs – and I might even have onions on it."

"Danny's Dogs it is then," Cathy said smiling slightly for what seemed to be the first in a long time.

It took a few weeks for Oree to grow accustomed to high school. He wasn't used to having to keep track of his own schedule and to moving from classroom to classroom across the expansive campus. St. Francis the Abbey High School was twice the size of his grade school and there were many more students. The school had separate buildings for practically every course – religious studies, math, social studies, English, foreign languages, etc. Plus, the sprawling campus had a large gymnasium, an auditorium, and both football and baseball fields. By the end of the first week, Oree was exhausted. He was not used to having to exert any amount of energy as far as it related to school. It just always came easy to him. Although the class work didn't seem too difficult, the amount of different courses, preparing for them and having to decipher what the student body of St. Francis was all about, was new and all-consuming.

As the other members of the United Nations had gone to different schools, Oree was at first at a loss with whom he should try to become friends with. When he went to the communal gathering area "the quad" every day for lunch, it seemed like everyone was already divided off into their respective groups – low riders, surfers, stoners, nerds – were the most obvious, and it was fairly evident to decipher who fit in with those groups. Additionally, there were the jocks, drama fags (it didn't matter if you were a boy or girl, if you were in school plays, you were classified accordingly), the music nerds, cheerleaders – whew, there were far too many groups. Things seemed more inclusive in high school, but Oree did not want to put himself into a situation where attention would be drawn to him as a result of his race. He had already learned his lesson the hard way. So, he avoided groups that seemed to have a high proliferation of Anglos.

In the end, he deferred to his own color and gravitated toward the low riders. He had been friends with a few of the guys in grade school, and there was little need for discussion of race as his dark skin made it evident that he could easily fit in. Each day at nutrition (there was no recess in high school – that was "too grade school") and at lunch, the group would hang out in front of the school gymnasium to talk all things low rider – who was thinking of joining a gang, who had a car that was lowered or had wire spoke rims, who was cruising The Mission or Van Nuys Boulevard, or who was "getting down" with whom. Basically, it was a lot of the talk based upon the fantasies the group projected – most of the youths came from families similar to Oree's, meaning they were lower or middle class, didn't really know any actual gang members and were all looking to get to first or second base.

Oree understood the thing most important to the existence of the group was that they all looked very cool in their Pendleton® shirts over their "wife beaters," creased corduroys and chino shoes. Oree kept to his dress code taking care to avoid the wife beaters which reminded him of something farm laborers would wear, but he did adopt a few of the group behaviors such as creasing and cuffing his pants and having a metal rope keychain which extended from his belt loop to inside his pant pocket. He smiled when he thought up this fashion accessory as his was attached to a pocket watch his grandfather gave him, so it was both stylish and functional. He may have spent nutrition and lunch socializing with the group, but when it came for studies, he kept quiet. He couldn't let them know that he was being reviewed for inclusion in college prep classes and following his most recent testing, learned he had the reading comprehension of a second year college student. The group didn't spend much time talking about school, it was just the place where they had to go to every day, so Oree avoided any conversations that might be construed as "intellectual." He had gotten smart enough at this point to understand that high school was just a transition to something else.

What that "something else" was, wasn't entirely as clear. He saw his brother Anthony adapt to working life and to becoming a father. His brother seemed to enjoy his life with his new wife and baby, but Oree didn't want that kind of existence. His parents chose it as did his parent's parents. There had to be something more to life than simply ensuring the next in lineage had a more comfortable existence than its predecessor. He saw Annie's angry vigilance continue to grow, and at times he feared for her. She was like a 10-speed bike without brakes – that troubled him because at times it seemed she was fighting for something that wasn't there, at least this was how he saw it. How would she ever become something if she was always fighting for somebody else? Based upon these alternatives, none of which seemed very attractive, Oree decided to use high school as his "laboratory" for exploring different potential avenues for his future existence.

After a few weeks, he had settled comfortably into high school life and was considering joining a club or two to help widen his circle of friends. School at times came as a relief as things at home between Annie and their parents were becoming increasingly tense. It seemed like any time the three of them were in the house, there would be a fight. Even asking Annie to do a simple chore like washing dishes, could result in an explosion. Annie had dropped out of school entirely and had taken a job at Fotomat in the Rincon Plaza which freed up her time to participate in Chicano rights' activities. Oree was impressed by Fotomat's one-day photo service guarantee, but he was not impressed that his intelligent sister was wasting her talents at a film store kiosk while she spent her free time at incessant rallies, sit-ins and pickets. In any case, it seemed whenever Annie was around there was constant bickering and yelling.

One afternoon, Oree dropped by the Fotomat to have film from a school project developed. Annie was on duty and he was hoping to get to talk with his sister away from his parents. He walked up to the kiosk.

"So sis, do I get a family discount?" he said to Anita. "You know I'm a starving student."

"We'll see what I can do," Annie said, handing him an envelope to deposit the film. "Here, fill this out and put the film roll in there. Maybe when it comes back I can say that the film was damaged or something and the customer complained and then you don't have to pay for it. Use a different last name."

Oree began filling out the envelope. "You know, you don't have to fight with mom and dad every time you see them. You should let them get a win every now and then."

"Is that what you came for? You don't understand Oree," Annie said. "It's not about winning anything. Mom and dad push this crap down our throats about how we should be grateful for every little scrap of food we get. That's not how the world works. We are Americans like anyone else and deserve everything that every other person born in this country gets. Because we're Mexican, it means sometimes we have to work harder for that. But, it shouldn't be that way."

"I want to make sure that I pave the way for my children and for yours – so that they don't have to eat humble pie every five minutes and take whatever is given to them without question. I want them to get everything they are entitled to – regardless of the color of their skin," she continued. "If we accept everything like mom and dad do, how are we to evolve? How are we as Chicanos to gain the same rights as everyone else? The status quo is just not that easily willing to give them up."

"Well, I don't know about the status quo…." Oree began before his sister interrupted him.

"Don't kid yourself. You know if you walk into certain stores or behave a certain way, people are still saying 'those beaners' under their breaths. I don't want to live in a world where that's tolerated," Annie continued. "That's why my work is so important."

"But Annie, you're working at a Fotomat instead of going to school," Oree said. "Don't you think you'd make more progress if you had a college education?"

"Perhaps, but right now the movement needs me," Annie said. "So, I have to see it through. Here, give me the envelope."

Oree handed his sister the envelope and said, "Well, I sure hope you know what you're doing. You don't want to piss dad off so much that he kicks you out of the house."

"Don't worry. I know what I'm doing," Annie finished. "I'm an adult and take responsibility for everything I do."

Despite the talk she and her brother had, Annie continued to spar with her parents. Their battles were becoming a daily affair, and everyone in the household was continuously feeling the tension when Annie was present. During what would become the final fight, one afternoon during their regular Sunday dinner, Annie took her self-righteousness to a place from which she could not return.

"The Chicano Liberation Party is going to take down the establishment and ensure all Chicanos know of their rights. This will make it easier to rise through the ranks of the proletariat," Annie said loudly in response to her father's suggestion that perhaps she should find a better job than Fotomat. "Don't be surprised when one day you see on TV a massive pushback by the Chicano movement. This will be bigger than the Black Panthers and even the Civil Rights Movement. We will go to any lengths to ensure our people are heard as Chicano rights are seminal to the future of our people. Plus, we are going to continue fighting for immigrant rights."

Her father looked at her in disbelief and was more concerned than angry. Who was this angry, young woman glaring and sitting defiantly before him? Surely it could not be the sweet, little Anita who used to like ballet. He envisioned Patty Hearst and how her captors had brainwashed her into believing they were right. He knew this Joaquin person held great influence over her, but he reasoned she was smart enough not to do something illegal in the interests of furthering any perceived cause. Albert thought back to the day he took his family to the cardboard city in Tijuana and wondered if his daughter would be the angry person she was today if they had skipped the visit? Plus, her mention of the Black Panthers, a militant group known for its violent activities, alarmed him.

"Seminal? Proletariat? What the hell do those words mean?" her father pushed back. "I don't know where you're getting these big words from as they just make you sound stupid. How are Chicano rights gonna pay your bills? You need to think of your future – not that of the entire race."

"I think you're full of crap Annie and you don't know what you're talking about. There is nothing you're going to do that is going to change any immigrant's life. I know how tough it is to make it, and if they don't speak English or have papers, it will be impossible for them to succeed in this society. The only way you can truly change anything is by changing things within the system, not in the gullies of a farm worker ditch," her father continued. "You're wasting your time, and that boyfriend of yours, that Joaquin. He's nothing but a big loser. He probably takes any money that shitty clique of yours collects and spends it on hair conditioner. He's a faker, an imposter, and he's using you because you have a brain. Once you talk to him the way you talk to us, he's gonna kick you to the curb and move on to another bubblehead who can be brainwashed by his looks."

At this point, Anita had been insulted beyond her tolerance, and her pride would no longer allow her to listen. It did not matter that the person confronting her was her father. He was shallow, ignorant and a nemesis to all she believed in.

"What has the middle class gotten you?" she said digging her heals in. "You work at a grocery store. You're still brown, people still look at you as a second class citizen. You'll never be welcomed at the places where you should be. You should see that I'm fighting for you if you weren't too stupid to understand!"

"I should beat the crap out of you for talking to me like that. You're not fighting for shit," her father snapped back. "I don't need you to defend me or my life or any goddamn thing I have done with it. And, that grocery store paid for your education, your dance classes and all those pretty things you have sitting in your pretty, little bedroom."

"Well, I don't need them. I don't need any of it. I can get plenty of bread if I need it," Annie screeched.

"Annie, you may want to calm down," Maria jumped in understanding what the next part of the conversation would entail if her daughter did not back down.

"I am not gonna calm down, MARIA," Annie called out as if she was her mother's equal. "I am going to get the hell out of here. I can no longer live with you. You don't appreciate who I am and what I believe in. Joaquin has been asking me to move in with him and I think it's time I did so. It is time for me to start living my life as I see fit and not under your shadow. You have brainwashed me enough with this weak acceptance of whatever pittance coming your way as being enough. I am making a difference in people's lives and I am going to have a good future. Screw this false humility. It's people like you who are responsible for Chicanos being stuck in the rut we are. I'll just get some of my stuff and be out of here."

"Well, don't take any of the shit, this low life grocer paid for," her father yelled.

"Don't worry, the movement will provide me with everything I need. You two make me sick with your stupid ass, middle class lifestyle, acting like you're white people, when you're nothing more than some poor man's version of the American dream. I don't ever want to see you again. I hate you – and everything you represent makes me sick," Annie said sharply as she went off to her room and slammed the door.

The table was silent and Albert and Maria looked at each other. Maria began to sob and was muttering something about "I've lost my daughter. Albert do something, our daughter says she hates us and is leaving." Albert sat in shock. He could not believe the words his daughter screamed. He also could not forgive the fact that everything he fought to create for his family was something that his daughter now perceived with disdain. He kept hearing the words "I hate you" over and over in his head. He could not let it pass, would not let it pass. He got up out of his seat and walked to Annie's door.

He knocked and as he did so, he spoke, "Anita. I want you out now, and don't come back. I am sorry your family is a disappointment to you."

Albert then walked on to his and Maria's bedroom and quietly shut the door.

The house was totally silent except for the sobs of Maria in the kitchen and the sounds of drawers opening and closing, slamming rather, in Annie's bedroom. Oree sat at the table in disbelief as his mother cried. First, his brother was gone, now his sister would be leaving as well. He wondered if he should go to Annie's room and try to talk some sense into her, but decided that he, like his parent's, needed a break from hurricane Anita. They had all grown tired of the constant fighting, and as they heard Anita's car squeal back out of the driveway, inside they felt a sense of relief, although no one would admit it. Albert sat quietly in his bedroom on the edge of his bed, crying into his hands, "My God, why have you done this to my family? What did I do to deserve this?"

CHAPTER 13

SUSAN VALDEZ

By November, the Rodrigo household had calmed down. At times, it was as if Oree could sense the sadness within the walls which once resounded with the sounds of laughter. His mother seemed to spend her afternoons watching a litany of soap operas, and with two less people in the house, she wasn't as attentive to maintaining the care of the home as she had been in the past. It was as if the ghosts of his siblings still resided there, silently walking the hallways and leaving footprints of emptiness where life used to be. Other times, Oree would reflect upon the fun his family would have at dinner time when they were children – the evening he threw a plate of spaghetti at Anthony which ended up with strands of the yellow pasta hanging like jelly fish tentacles from the ceiling. Or the time a young Annie tried to drink a full glass of milk in one gulp which ended with the white liquid spewn across the table, floor and walls. With the amount of Spic and Span used in the Rodrigo household, his family should have bought stock in the powdery stuff.

Now, when Anthony and his family would join them for Sunday dinner, everything seemed much quieter – even with the boisterousness of their baby Eva. Everyone could feel the absence of Annie at these meals, but her name was rarely mentioned. Her parents had not heard from her since she left the house, but Anthony confessed that she called him every now and then. She and Joaquin were living out of a hotel in

Bakersfield where they were trying to organize farm workers in efforts to demand better living conditions for their families while they were working in the fields. During these Sunday dinner conversations when Albert discussed Annie, there was no mention made of her parents. He never said, "Annie said to say hi or ask about you." Albert would sit there quietly during these times and not encourage the conversation. The lack of communication with her daughter cast a dark shadow over Maria. How could Annie have turned on her? What had she done as a parent to make her daughter so rebellious to the point of non-communication? Albert relied upon his job to preoccupy his mind and fill in the spaces where he would be left to question his "failure" with regard to his daughter.

Family had always been most important to them, and at times Albert wondered how far his had strayed from what he had envisioned. In his dreams, he imagined Sunday dinners with Anthony, his wife and two or three children hovering around grandma and grandpa. Annie, who was now a successful teacher, would bring her lawyer husband who liked to discuss football. They would be planning to start a family once her husband made partner which would be soon as there was a need for bilingual lawyers (which he would be). Oree would be in school getting some sort of degree, but one that would lead him into a high paying profession.

Now, it seemed that none of that would ever happen and it made him sad. He understood how his wife must feel, not having two of her three children to tend over. Plus, as both of her parents were deceased, she did not have her mother to offer advice or provide comfort. Maria was not very close to Albert's parents, although they would take Oree to visit them sometimes on Sunday. Her closest relative, her sister Cathy, had enough of her own problems, so Maria tried not to burden her. Albert was growing older and was beginning to feel the effects of all of his many years of physical labor, so he considered quitting the Alpine Haus wait job, which he only worked at a few nights a week. Plus, as he was no longer financially responsible for Anthony or Anita, the family didn't need as much to live on. If he did keep working both jobs perhaps they could spend the money on something nice like a brick barbecue or a fresh coat of paint and new furniture. That might cheer things up. He noticed the change in his wife's behavior and he reasoned it might be a good idea for him to spend more time at home – in three years Oree would be graduating from high school and then there would be no more children. He wondered how Maria would react to that. These were things he thought about and felt, but could not bring himself to discuss with his wife.

During the first semester of school, Oree and the other students were tested to gain a better sense of their educational strengths and weaknesses. As was expected, he scored high on the test, so it was decided in the second half of the year he would enter college preparedness classes. These classes would better prime him for a college education, and the credits could also be applied as college units, meaning he would get a head start on his college courses. If all worked out, by his high school senior year, he would be taking on-campus classes provided by the local community college, so he would already have transferrable units when he graduated. Oree was pleased with himself and came home and told his parents. As they had not been to college, they didn't really understand what units were or how their son could be attending college while he was still in high school, but they said they were proud of him which made him happy.

One morning during his home room period, the teacher welcomed a new student. Her name was Susan Valdez and she would be joining the class for the remainder of the year. Her father was a diplomat from Mexico who had been appointed to a short term project working with the local government in Los Angeles. It had something to do with the flow of immigrants coming from Mexico.

"Susan comes from Mexico, but she has also lived in Germany, England and now America," Oree's teacher said in introducing her.

When she stood and waved, Oree experienced one of those moments where time stood still. To him, this Susan Valdez looked like a Latina Brooke Shields. She wore a cream-colored blouse which buttoned at the wrists, a pair of tan, wool slacks with a thin gold belt and a pair of white Candies slip-ons. Her hair was pulled back to one side with some sort of pearl beret. She had clear, brown eyes and a slight set of dimples when she smiled. She was tall, thin and her light skin was slightly tanned.

"As Susan has joined us a few months into studies, I am going to need someone to get her up to speed. Oree, Susan has a few classes with you, so if I may ask you to get her up to the present on what she's missed, as well as introduce her to life here on campus."

"Sure thing," Oree said. When the first class bell rang, he walked up to Susan. "Hi, I'm Aurelio Rodrigo, but most people call me Oree."

"Hi Aurelio," she said using the proper pronunciation of his name and extending her hand in a firm handshake. "I'm Susan, but I guess you heard that. When do you want to meet?"

"How about lunch in the quad?" he said, thinking this girl has quite a strong grip for, well a girl. Perhaps her parents taught her that as part of their diplomatic work. "You'll recognize it by all the different cliques that hang out there."

"Oh, o.k.," I'll see you at lunch then," Susan said, and then pointing at her syllabus, added, "Can you tell me where this class is?"

"Sure, it's the next building up," he said. "See you at lunch."

During the nutrition break, Oree was the center of attention amongst the low rider boys.

"Ese, you gotta chance to make it with a diplomat's daughter." "She is way out of your league brown boy." "That girl lived in Germany and England? She's gonna want nothing to do with a poor, brown boy from Sylmar." Pretty much every person in the group had something to say, but to Oree it all came down to one thing – the homies were jealous. He took it all in stride, understanding that for once he was the center of attention in a good way, and only replied, "Yeah, she's pretty bitchin'."

When lunch time arrived, Oree took special pains to make sure he picked a bench in the center of what would typically be all the action. As gossip at the school traveled faster than cold germs, he knew by now it was likely that the freshman class was aware it had some sort of Mexican royalty in their midst. He wanted to make the best of it. Susan showed up with a lunch tray loaded with Saran-wrapped food containers and a carton of milk. His family couldn't afford daily cafeteria lunches (he was allowed one a month on Friday as a treat), so he pulled a bologna sandwich and a bag of Cheetos out of his brown paper bag and began eating.

"Hi Oree – not Aurelio – right?" Susan asked smiling and sitting down.

"Yup," Oree said in the midst of a big, chewy bite of his sandwich. "What do you think so far?"

"Well, the studies don't seem like they're going to be too much of a thing," she said speaking in perfect, non-accented English. "But, the religion stuff is another story. My family doesn't really practice, so it's kind of like sitting in a history class."

"You guys don't go to church? Wow," Oree exclaimed. He had been in Catholic School since kindergarten, and hadn't been exposed to those of other or little faith.

"Yeah, my dad is a science kind of guy, and if you can't see or measure it, he doesn't think it's really worth getting involved with," she continued.

Oree sat there, amazed in thought that this Susan person seemed smart – perhaps even smarter than him. "So, are you from Mexico originally?" he asked.

"Yes, born in Mexico City and we lived there until I was about six. Then, we went to Germany until I was nine and then England for two years, then back to Mexico. My dad is involved in the government, so we have been all over the place. And now, here I am in the U.S. Are you from Mexico?"

Oree paused, never before had he been asked if he was from Mexico. He wasn't sure if he should be honored or offended as at this point in his life, he took great pains to ensure his façade was that of a cultivated American. Still, he had asked her first, so he needed to respond. "Nope, born in San Fernando, California, and I've lived in the Valley all of my life."

"*¿Hablas Espanol?*" Susan asked.

"My parents do but never taught us, but they speak it, sort of, to each other. Usually when they don't want us to know something," Oree said looking down at his sandwich as though all of a sudden he was sorry he didn't speak Spanish. "It's funny, I am about as American as they come, however because of the color of my skin, people always assume I speak Spanish. My family was all born here, none of them know too much about Mexico or being Mexican in that way. Being American, why should anyone in America assume I speak anything other than English?

"Why didn't your parents teach you? I mean Spanish is a very useful language," Susan said unwrapping a green colored Jell-O dish.

"I'm not quite sure, but it has to do with the way this country is," he went on. "We don't really do too much Mexican stuff, mainly because we weren't exposed to it. Like, we eat spam more often than menudo and we're football fans, not soccer."

"So, you're a coconut?" Susan said somewhat flippantly. "Brown on the outside, white on the inside."

"Geez, you know that phrase? I thought it was an American thing," he said feeling his blood pressure beginning to rise. Over the years, he had heard that term a few times, mostly from Mexicans who were originally from Mexico or were second generation and still speaking Spanish primarily. Each time he heard it, he had the same reaction – *"How dare you pigeonhole me because of the color of my skin!"* Before responding, he took a breath to calm himself.

"My parents work very hard for us to live an American life. It's not that they're ashamed of being Mexican, it's just that, well, like I said, we're Americans," he said to Susan. "I'm not sure if you've lived in the states before, but speaking Spanish is frowned upon here. If someone hears you speaking in Spanish on the street, they'll call you a wetback or beaner. I even got hit in grade school when I said something in Spanish, so it's a sensitive subject with me. It's different here than in Mexico. You're lucky because you don't have an accent and you look kind of *international*. So, you could pass for any number of races."

"I'm sorry. I didn't mean to offend you, really," Susan said looking at her Jell-O.

"I mean, people expect because I have brown skin that I am supposed to be a certain way," Oree said, now realizing he was on a roll. "Like they used to call me names and beat me up because I was either too brown or too white. I realized that I would always be too white for those from Mexico and too dark for those from America. So, I stopped trying to be one way or the other."

"Again sorry. I didn't know that was such a sore subject in the states," Susan said. "Other countries I've been to have been more embracing of other cultures. I'm just surprised that America in all its many facets isn't more, *como se dice*, progressive."

"I wouldn't expect that in my lifetime. America has always been prejudice. Look at the slaves and stuff. Like did you know, in 1964 we still had segregated water fountains and bathrooms? Blacks couldn't use the same facilities as white people. I think it will continue as long as there are the haves and have nots," Oree said. "That, however, is why I am planning to go to college. If they see a dark skinned person in a good paying job, they have no other choice than to overlook the 'lazy Mexican' stereotype."

"Got it. Not to change the subject, but what do I need to know about school here?" Susan said, sensing the conversation could lead into a disagreement.

"Well, as you can see, we serve the finest in gourmet food," he said lightening up with a smile as he pointed at the food globs in her foam dishes. "And, I'm sure the plentitude of social activities and clubs you can partake in will rival that of all the places you've lived."

"I've already learned one," Susan said. Then, she took to mimicking a trend that had recently surfaced in the San Fernando Valley. "Like I live in Encino, so that like makes me totally a Val, and it is a totally, bitchin', totally rad place to live, fer sure."

The two both broke out in laughter and it quickly became apparent that they would be simpatico. Within a few weeks they had become close friends – Oree worked to help Susan catch up on the coursework she had missed, and Susan taught him about life in other countries.

When it came time to discuss families, Susan was surprised that Annie, an unmarried young woman, wasn't still living at home as was the custom in Mexico, and Oree learned that Susan had two brothers, Mario, who was already in college in England, and, Alejandro, who was a senior at their school. Even though they shared the same Latino blood, their lives couldn't have been more different, but they both took delight in learning about each other's cultures. Susan shared that she didn't have many friends as their family had moved around so much; Oree downplayed his role in being part of the low rider clique and instead focused his efforts on sharing that he was part of the National Honors Society club in which membership was extended to only those who met the stringent academic criteria.

A few weeks into their friendship, Susan bumped into Oree on her way to religious studies.

"Hey Oree. Glad I ran into you. We have an extra ticket for the Hollywood Bowl this Saturday night. My dad has another function he has to go to, so the rest of the family will be going. Do you want to go?" Susan asked. "You just have to get there, but our cook is going to make food. I guess we are supposed to have a picnic there. It will be you, me, my mom and Alejandro."

Oree had never been to the Hollywood Bowl, but had heard a lot about it. He was excited, however he wasn't sure if this was a date, or just a friend asking a friend. Over the weeks, he had become so immersed in their relationship that he hadn't had time to categorize it. He knew his mother wouldn't be too happy about driving him to the Bowl, but perhaps his dad could change a work shift and pick him up on the way home from the market.

"I'm sure it won't be a problem. Thanks for the invite," Oree said excitedly. "What time should I get there?"

"Great. I'll give you the ticket tomorrow. I think we're getting there at 6:30," Susan said. "The Philharmonic is doing some fundraiser and I heard it can get cool there this time of year, so you may want to bring a jacket."

"That is like totally awesome! I will wear some totally cool Val clothes," Oree said, mimicking the Valley speak that they sometimes sarcastically used with each other. It was now pretty common that all the cool kids at St. Francis were now mimicking the quirky "Val-speak."

"Mom, I gotta go to the Hollywood Bowl Saturday night for a class project," Oree said when Maria picked him up from school that afternoon.

"What is this class project? You know going into Hollywood on a Saturday night will be a pain in the neck," Maria said thinking back to the times when as a youth she, Cathy and their friends would venture into Hollywood via the Cahuenga Pass. All that changed with the addition of the Hollywood Freeway, so the traffic would not be that bad.

"It's for Humanities," Oree said making up the lie as it left his lips. "We have to study this piece of music and the teacher thought it would be a good idea for us to experience it together. She already got the tickets – for free – so you just have to get me there. Can we ask Dad if he can work another shift so he can pick me up at 11?"

"Well, sounds like you've already got this all planned," Maria said. "When did you find out about this?"

"Oh, a few weeks ago, but I forgot to tell you, and I have to go or I'll get a crappy grade, and I need this grade so I can get into the college prep classes," Oree said amazed at the proficiency of his deceit. The school had already decided he would go into college prep classes months ago, a fact his parents would have known had they listened to him or gone to the school's parent/teacher conferences they always skipped.

Oree took extra care in ironing his clothes for the Hollywood Bowl. He chose a pair of brown corduroys and a blue flannel checked shirt. He brushed and hair-sprayed his suede earth shoes, and even pressed his blue Dickies workman's jacket. He carefully combed his collar-length hair which he had "feathered," following the latest hair trend. He had always wanted to visit the Bowl, but it was something his family never got around to. The Rodrigos did not really have an understanding of "culture," and the arts were something foreign to them, so they never seemed to get around to exposing their children to classical music, museums or the like. Now, Aurelio had the opportunity of going to a classical music event with a beautiful Latina Brooke Shields and her bound-to-be loving family. He had his mother drop him off at 6 so he could be sure to meet Susan's family on time.

When he stepped out of the family's blue station wagon, he was awed by the images of the three muses on the pillared fountain which fronts the Hollywood Bowl. He had seen them from the car before but up close they looked even more magnificent. The setting looked like something out of a twenties movie and he felt his heart begin to pound as he walked up the tree-lined promenade to the Bowl, which had strands of incandescent lights strewn across the trees and walkways. He heard whispered laughter and a steady hum of conversation, but couldn't quite decipher where it was emanating from. It was like it was bouncing off the hills and trees which smelled of cool, fresh eucalyptus. Once inside the entry gates, ushers in white shirts and black pants with red bow ties chimed: "Programs, 25 cents. Get your program for 25 cents." He saw guests dressed in khakis and button down shirts, long flowing skirts and espadrilles; eating, drinking and laughing on picnic tables and on blankets strewn out over the walk ways. The picnic settings were very elaborate. Oree couldn't believe the displays of linen tablecloths, crystal wine glasses, china plates and silverware – even candelabras with glowing candles. Oree tried his best to look like he fit in and figured he should walk up the hill to where their seats likely were as Susan hadn't specified. He looked down at his ticket which read "Garden Box." He wasn't sure where that was, so he asked an usher who directed him to the Garden Boxes.

As he walked through the curtained entry, Oree's heart began to race. He opened his eyes on the expansive outdoor amphitheater which stretched back almost farther then he could see. He thought it was the most beautiful setting ever, with perfectly aligned green benches forming the Bowl, and trees dotting the surrounding hillsides. He looked up to see attendees laughing and enjoying themselves. He then looked to his right and looming seemingly above him was a massive concrete shell with seats and music stands on the raised stage. The shell was delicately lit in bands with a warm yellow glow, and Oree was so excited he felt his breath stop. He had never seen anything so beautiful in his life and decided when he was older he would be a regular visitor to this Hollywood Bowl. He had driven by the amphitheater numerous times when he accompanied his father to work, but he never imagined what it was or how beautiful it would look. He looked below which was an area dotted with private boxes which had a much more intimate feel than the bleachers above. He felt his palms get sweaty as an usher walked him to the box seats where the Valdez family sat. Susan looked up and waved.

"Hi Oree," she said motioning him to the four-seated box. "This is my brother Alejandro and my mother Sophia."

Oree extended his arm to first shake Alejandro's hand, then Sophia's.

"*Muy contentos de conocerte Aurelio,*" Sophia began as she extended her long, light-skinned hand on which a rather large, pear-shaped diamond sat plumb on her ring finger. They both had the same firm handshake that Susan had, so Oree reasoned it must be a family thing.

"Aye Mommy, Oree doesn't speak Spanish," Susan interjected.

"*Lo siento*, I'm sorry," Sophia said smiling. "You're just so dark, I assumed you were from Mexico as well."

"No ma'am," Oree smiled back with his whitest grin. "Born and bred in the USA!"

"Well, please join us Aurelio," Sophia continued. "Our cook has made us a nice picnic supper. We have lamb with mint jelly, curry potatoes and lemon asparagus. Susan, pour Aurelio some Perrier."

Aurelio was in awe. He sat down and put his cloth napkin on his lap. He could see his reflection in the silverware which of course was real silver. He had never before seen such a feast and he was a bit daunted by the menu selections, but didn't want to let on to his lack of international dining epicure. He had never seen so many forks and spoons, and wasn't sure which to use and when. Susan politely gave him a lesson on silverware protocol. Then, using the correct fork and knife, he took his first taste of lamb which he thought kind of had the consistency of birria. The curry potatoes didn't taste like any he had ever eaten before, but he liked their spiciness. At first, the bubbly water tasted a bit bitter, but he surmised that perhaps it was stale and he didn't want to embarrass his hostess by mentioning it, so he drank politely. Susan looked beautiful as always in a white cotton skirt and blue striped polo shirt topped by a white sweater. Alejandro, who was tall and slender, looked like he had just walked off the pages of a Lacoste ad, and Sophia, was full and regal, her hair swooned back in careful coifs of light blond with silver wisps. Her fingers and wrists were adorned with gold rings and trinkets, and she wore a single strand of cream colored pearls across her neck. She smelled like citrus and light musk, and Aurelio thought she resembled Spanish royalty.

"So, Aurelio, do your parents speak Spanish?" Sophia asked as she delicately cut her lamb. Aurelio could see that Susan was getting uncomfortable, but he didn't want her to be self-conscious, so he politely answered.

"Yes. Both of my parents were born here in America. Although their parents spoke Spanish, they didn't really encourage my parents to teach us," he said.

"*Que lastima*. It's so sad as Spanish is such a beautiful language," Sophia said. "The other day my daughter and I were in a dress store and we were talking in Spanish. The manager came up and asked us to speak in English as he said he was afraid the other customers might complain."

"What did you do?" Oree responded, secretly glad that they had an experience similar to the many he had been exposed to in his young years.

"I told the manager, 'I guess my money isn't good enough for your store, so we'll take our business elsewhere. *¡Qué vergüenza!*, What a shame," she continued. "We have never heard such rudeness in other countries. Take Switzerland for example, in some parts they speak German, others they speak French, some even Italian. It's much more continental."

"Well, I kinda wish my parents had taught me Spanish as it would make getting good grades in Spanish class much easier," Oree laughed.

The dinner continued with light conversation and Oree learned more about what Susan's father did for a living. He envisioned what his family would be like if his father had some sort of diplomat job or even just a government one, but he cut the fantasy short understanding that it would take a lot of advanced education and a few lucky breaks for him to have any sort of life such as that of the Valdez's. Occasionally, Oree would look out of the corner of his eye at the other diners in the surrounding boxes. He noticed the entire box section was comprised of Anglos who looked wealthy and somewhat bored. Every now and then, one of the bored faces would glance over at the Valdez table looking at the spread of food and the people sitting at it. With glances that resembled disdain, perhaps they thought someone with a long-standing box (it often took years for a family to be deigned a box at the Hollywood Bowl as the waiting list was so lengthy), gave their maid and her family the night off as a special treat. What a spectacle.

Approximately 15 minutes before the show, an array of ushers descended upon the boxes, folding up the small picnic tables and helping to arrange seats in preparation for the performance. Oree thought it was all very stately and well organized. He imagined this happened at each performance when you sat in a box seat. He profusely thanked Susan and Mrs. Valdez for the invitation, and considered that he should perhaps add a polo shirt to his closet.

As the lights dimmed and the orchestra took to the stage, Oree felt like he was part of a magical adventure, and even somewhat like Cinderella attending the ball. He had dreamt but never really understood that people lived this way. It was like there was a secret language which wasn't spoken, but was very much understood. Everyone seemed placidly content and had a distinct look and behavior. It was clear that this group knew which fork to use and when.

He could tell by the way that Mrs. Valdez spoke to Susan and Alejandro that there was a distinct protocol to their behavior, much like the unspoken language of the Bowl. He could tell that it was expected they were to behave like the others in box seats, even though their skin was a different color. As the music played, he thought more about the Valdez family. He understood that none of their children would be part of any picketing or have any unwanted children. They would attend a university, follow a profession that would place them in good social standing, and at the appropriate time, they would marry and have a bunch of little Susan's and Alejandro's – all to carry on the carefully cultivated lineage. He wondered why his family wasn't more like Susan's family. After all, his parents had been born here and his grandparents were established. He thought, "Why hasn't my family been blessed with wealth and manners?" Mrs. Valdez spoke quite highly of her other son who was at school in London. She said his education, combined with her husband's friends in the business world, would land him a very good position when he graduated from school.

Oree began to see that education seemed to have something to do with the whole of this affair – even Susan's mother, Sophia, had a degree in political science. It was obvious by looking at the Bowl crowd that they had been well taught, they knew when to applaud and when not to (Oree caught on quickly after he broke out in applause following the first movement), and they knew what a good life *felt* like. He envisioned what his life would be like if he had box seats and he thought more about the education he would need to get him there.

It was at that moment that Oree decided that he wanted more from his life than the sound of crying babies, picnics at El Cariso Park or Sunday mass and treks to the panaderia. He wanted a life like that of those who sat complacently in the boxes. He said to himself: "I will do whatever is needed to be in a position where I feel at ease in grand places such as this."

The evening continued nicely and at the 9:45 p.m. intermission, Oree had to excuse himself. His father got out of work at 10 and said he would pick up Oree on Highland Avenue outside of the Bowl shortly thereafter. He again thanked Susan and Mrs. Valdez and said good night. He could tell they were a formal family, so he gave a firm handshake to each as he left.

As he walked out toward the street, he could hear the music still echoing from the Bowl and the sound of crickets replaced the quiet laughter that was earlier. He looked up through the lights and branches of the trees into the sky where he saw a few stars twinkling. Even though he knew it was corny, he heard himself whisper, "Star light, Star bright...."

CHAPTER 14

CHANGES

As he stood out in the cool evening air on Highland Avenue awaiting his father, Oree's feet were still floating 10 feet above the ground. He had never before been to a classical music concert, and although he realized he probably needed some practice on when it was appropriate to clap, he felt the music to be quite beautiful and moving. His father pulled up in his Chevrolet truck and ushered Oree in.

"How was the show?" his father asked.

"It was good. Classical music is actually pretty good. I always thought it was something people listened to when they wanted to go to sleep, but it isn't. It was actually kind of exciting," Oree responded animatedly. "Plus, the Hollywood Bowl is really cool, and people have picnics with candles and wine. Why haven't we ever gone there? It's not that far from the house."

"Well, I guess I never thought about it. I figured since they played high-end music, it would be too expensive to get tickets," his father said with a sense of embarrassment. "Plus, I don't really know anything about that kind of music, so I figured you kids would be bored. That music isn't really for our kind of people."

Rather than respond out loud, Oree quietly thought: "But I wouldn't have been bored and that music is for everyone! If I was exposed to things such as the Bowl, I could be so much further along! There are things we should have been exposed to. Those people at the Bowl didn't look all that rich, they just seemed to enjoy things more than watching football on TV on weekends. We could be more like the Valdez family!"

"Ah dad, it wasn't really THAT boring," Oree said understating his reaction to the concert, while understanding how hard his father worked just to sustain his family, let alone entertain any thoughts of culture. He sat quietly for a moment as he realized something he had never before considered. His father, his family, was a certain type of family. They were simple, proud and humble. Those were virtues in themselves, although Oree thought there had to be more to life than simplicity. He knew he was not destined to work at a supermarket, but he wasn't sure how to get to where he needed to be. And, what would happen when he got there.

Worse yet, he had no role models. No one in their family had ever graduated from college, let alone held a professional job. It made him sad as he realized that anything he accomplished, had to be on his own accord. Then, thinking upon what Mrs. Valdez had mentioned, he slipped back into reality and switched gears to the subject which had embarrassed him with her. "Hey dad, why didn't you and mom teach us Spanish?"

"We've talked about this Oree," his father answered, wondering why his son had so suddenly taken an interest in learning his native language. "You have great grades and are doing well in school. What if we had been teaching you to speak Spanish at home and then you had to speak English in school. It would have been confusing, your grades might have not been as good, and we would be subjecting you to ridicule if someone thought you were a Mexican from the other side of the border because you had an accent."

"But what if all that is untrue?" Oree asked looking out the front windshield at the blur of white lights streaming along the other side of the Hollywood Freeway. "What if I could speak Spanish and do well in school?"

"Well, I'll tell you what," his father responded. "When you get married and have children, you can teach them Spanish, although I think by then, even less people will be speaking Spanish in this country."

Oree reasoned that his father was probably right. If any of the kids going into grade schools had teachers like the nuns at his elementary school, they wouldn't dare speak any language but English.

"Oh, before I forget, your mother asked me to ask you if you've heard from your cousin Narciso. Apparently, he ran away last week and your Aunt Cathy hasn't heard from him since," his father said. "She's been looking all over and is afraid he's going to have to go back to that juvenile camp."

"Nope, Narciso and I have different interests, so I doubt he'd be calling me to help him out," Oree said as he played with the roll up window knob. "Is Uncle Raymond drinking a lot?"

"Is the pope Catholic?" his father responded plainly.

By the end of his freshman year, Oree had begun to change his perception on the purpose of school and what it was that he sought to gain from St. Francis. He began to see it more as a stepping stone to his future life, and the college prep classes he was enrolled in made it more challenging. Much of this change in his attitude was based upon the influence of Susan and her family. He visited the Encino estate the Valdez's were renting on a few occasions, and he wondered how different it was from his home. Everything had a place and it was clean and modern looking. There were no stains on the walls or ceilings and strangely, the living room had no television. He knew they could afford it, but didn't want to ask why it was overlooked. He began to wonder how his life might be different if he had born into an educated family, meaning one in which the parents both had professional careers and the children were being groomed for a certain type of life. His family was messy. There was little plan given to the children's educational paths and his parents didn't emphasize the importance of anything with regard to Oree or his siblings' futures. Perhaps this was the reason his dad was destined to what to be what Susan's father referred to as "unskilled labor." And, as for Annie's behavior, it would never be tolerated in a household like the Valdez's. It simply wouldn't have happened as in their household, there little was concern paid to Hispanics who worked for them or who came from the working classes. They were something to be represented or dealt with, not something to advocate for.

Oree was thankful for his relationship with Susan, and although they kissed one night after a sock hop, their bond never seemed to blossom into the romance he had thought was possible when he first met her. As he got to know her better, he realized that for better or worse, she was being groomed for a life that he did not have access to. She had a unique air of confidence far different from other girls at school, which was likely the result of how her parents had raised her. She never looked down at him or treated him any differently, it was just an unstated fact that she was destined to one day have her elaborate wedding covered in a four-color, double spread in one of the Spanish language newspapers in Mexico, *"Daughter of Diplomat Marries…,"* and that he was not to be the groom. The homies were right, she wasn't in his league.

As Susan's family was slated to return to Mexico at the end of the semester, she and Oree took great pains to assure each other that they would remain in touch, for Susan had learned from Oree as well. In their relationship, she discovered the great sense of freedom, optimism and opportunity which underscored so much of the lives that the American people led. She was secretly jealous that Oree could come and go as he pleased. His parents never gave him a curfew as their philosophy was, "You can stay out as late as you want – understanding you WILL get up at 6:30 the next day to go to school." His family didn't have all the rules and customs which were carefully woven into the fabric of her family's life. She could tell that Oree's parents took great pains to ensure he was a well-behaved young man, but there didn't seem to be any expectations beyond that. This was quite different than the continuous drills she encountered at home.

Her mother was always making statements like: "Susan, if you want to have the right kind of future, you have to study hard so you can get in the best university possible. Your father has a great many connections, however you have to do all the hard work to ensure those connections aren't wasted. Your father and I are confident you will make the correct choices." Susan wanted to stay another semester in America as she was really opening up to its sense of freedom, but her family had to return to Mexico to await his father's next assignment, which could come in a matter of weeks, months or years.

On the last day of school, both Oree and Susan were sorry that it had arrived. He told her: "We won't say good bye, only 'I'll see you later.' I heard it in a movie once and I think it's very appropriate." She thought it was a bit silly and embarrassedly answered with a "fer sure, like totally." Her awkward farewell was less painful than stating the obvious; she knew she would never again see this quirky, dark-skinned, funny young man who had become such a dear friend.

As they stood at the curb waiting for their mothers to pick them up, Susan's mother pulled up to the curb in a beige Mercedes Benz with oversized sunglasses and a white turban. Oree kissed Susan's cheek, they hugged and then she got into the passenger side, waving to him like she was the queen of the Rose Bowl court. Then, Mrs. Valdez who was also waving at Oree through the front windshield, drove off.

Far away, in a dusty American Legion Hall in Bakersfield, Annie, Joaquin and members of the Chicano Liberation Party, sat discussing what actions would need to be taken to provide the farmworkers with the housing, pay and support they needed to sustain a better life in America. Members of the group had gone to the Central Valley to try to establish an alliance with the UFW – United Farm Workers – a labor union group responsible for implementing significant changes within the farm worker community. The UFW was held in high regard with all civil rights groups based upon their efforts to improve the lives of Latinos. Understanding the important role UFW held, the Liberation Party had tried to develop a relationship and arrange meetings with its leader, Cesar Chavez, but were turned down as the understanding within the labor community was that groups of this nature were perhaps a bit too radical for their own good. The Liberation Party in fact had garnered a reputation of being quick to act – without putting too much forethought into its actions.

Under Joaquin's leadership, the group continued to push forward, at times staging pickets outside of ranches that were known to mistreat their workers, or at agricultural packing houses which offered below minimum wages. It was clear that they were trying to make a name and forge an identity for themselves – even if it was based upon the efforts and work of the UFW. Annie, who at the time considered herself to be in love with Joaquin, supported him and the group's actions blindly.

"We need to move forward, to take a stance and make the voices of these workers heard," Joaquin said. "The beef processing plant is one of the worst offenders of labor rights and we need to make them the example…"

Annie had heard this type of rhetoric before and Joaquin's voice seemed to drone on. The hot, airless confines of the hall made her head hurt and her mind began to drift. At times she missed her comfortable life, but she reasoned that if the group was successful with its work, they would all eventually lead better lives. Plus, she was pleased that she was mastering the Spanish language by having regular interactions with the field workers and their families.

Despite this, she considered that she was at times increasingly finding herself at odds with Joaquin. When she would question his or the group's actions, Joaquin would in turn, belittle her. "What do you know of life, when you grew up as a privileged middle class wanna-be," Joaquin would tell her. "My parents were farm workers and immigrants and I know how hard a life these people lead."

Annie could not argue with him on that point, however she had heard from other members in the group that Joaquin's father was an alcoholic who had deserted his family when he was child. His mother was forced to become a waitress at a ranchero bar, and he grew up with a string of "uncles" coming and going in and out of his life -- and the apartment his family resided in. In a few tender moments, Annie would try to get Joaquin to open up and share the real story of his life, but he would always shut down, cross his arms and refuse to speak.

Now 20-years-old, Annie liked the excitement of blood coursing through her veins as the group set out upon its pickets or confronted what she perceived as being crooked employers. It gave her life meaning to think that she was serving as Joan of Arc for all those who could not speak. Still, at other times, she began to wonder what her life would be like in five years. Although she was wasn't ready for marriage, she did see that her parents had a decent life together and she wondered if Joaquin would ever be ready to trade in the picket posters for a marriage license. She still wanted to be part of *El Movimiento*, but she began to wonder if there could be some sort of compromise so she could one day have a family of her own. She envisioned this future life, especially late at night when she found herself alone while Joaquin was at this meeting or out with friends from The Liberation Party.

In the silence of night, alone by herself, she would mull over her harsh actions toward her parents. It gnawed at her and she regretted all the fights she had put them through. Having had some time and distance from them, she now realized they were only doing what they thought best as being her parents. Still, *El Movimiento* and Joaquin needed her. She couldn't take back what happened --and the past was in the past.

She was jarred awake from her heat-induced day-dreaming by Joaquin's sharp words.

"We need to do something radical at that beef processing plant," Joaquin said interrupting her thoughts. "The management is not responding to our demands and their mistreatment of workers has got to stop. I have got a plan to make them stand up and pay attention..."

CHAPTER 15

CATHY

It was an early spring morning in the second half of Oree's sophomore year when there was a loud knock at the front door of the Rodrigo house. Through the haze of his slumber, Oree, heard his father say "It's 2 a.m. What the hell?" as he lumbered out of bed and banged his half-asleep body into a hallway wall. "Coming!"

He heard muted whispers in the living room and then he heard his father speak: "Maria, come here please."

Oree heard his mother walking down the hallway and then utter, "Yes, I am she... No. I don't want to sit down... What is it?"

"Maria, sit down with me." Oree heard strain in his father's voice, as one of two police officers began to speak softly. He couldn't make out anything other than it sounded almost like a whisper.

The next sound Oree heard was once he would never forget. His mother loudly choked on her breath, then wailed, "Oh God no, not Cathy. Oh my God. Albert, tell me they're lying. Albert they're lying right? Oh God, not Cathy." Oree had never before heard such a guttural wail of pain come out of any human, let alone his mother, and she gasped for air as she struggled to get words out. He wanted to climb out of bed to run and comfort her, but he was paralyzed by her sounds and words.

"Maria. We have to listen to the officers," Albert said pleadingly through her hysteria. Oree climbed out of bed and quietly crawled into the hallway and sat along the wall. He could see the bottom of the legs and feet of one of the two police officers who were sitting in chairs in the living room. He saw dark blue pants and boots that were a shiny black. He listened to the officer speak.

"Yes, her husband has confessed to the stabbing," the officer said. "The daughter, Cynthia, was home and I guess there's another child, a Narciso. We are trying to locate him, but our understanding is that he ran away from home some time ago, and the family hasn't heard from him. Do you know anything about the son?"

"No. We know he ran away and we haven't heard from him," Albert said. "They have two other children, Raymond Jr., who is in the military, and Lupita. She's an adult and lives in New Mexico with her two children."

"What else can you tell me about the family?" the officer continued.

Albert spoke as Maria was still sobbing uncontrollably. "Raymond, the father, has a long history of alcoholism, and from what I know, he liked to use his wife as a punching bag. We tried to get her and the kids out of the house, but she would never accept our assistance."

"I tried, God I tried. Oh my God, he stabbed Cathy. He killed my Cathy," Maria cried. "She was so close to leaving. She was so close. I tried and tried."

"Of course you did. You tried everything you could," Albert said, comforting his wife as he slowly rubbed her back. "My wife did all she could to help her sister. Raymond has always had a problem, but he has been getting and losing a lot of jobs lately as a result of his boozing, so that probably put him over the edge. The only ones living in the house were my sister-in-law, their daughter Cynthia and Raymond."

"Raymond could get violent, but I didn't think he was capable of killing anyone. If I'd known this, I'd….." Albert said, his voice trailing off.

"We handle domestic violence cases all the time, and it's common for the person being abused to avoid any assistance offered. In most cases, they defend the abuser until something close to this bad happens, or it gets so out of control that they have no other choice but to go into a shelter," the officer stated. "For what it's worth, apparently this incident was caused when the husband arrived home early from work and came upon his wife packing a suitcase. Her daughter said she was planning to leave."

"Where is Cynthia?" Albert asked. At this point, Cynthia was 19-years-old, taking classes at a junior college and still managing to stay home, perhaps out of fear something like this could happen to her mother. "Why that girl stayed in the house is beyond me?" Albert thought.

"The young lady is in the hospital being x-rayed as my understanding is she tried to intervene and the husband threw her against a wall and knocked her out. They are running x-rays as she may have broken an arm in the fall," the other officer spoke. "That is the extent of her injuries as I understand it."

Oree sat in the hall and slouched back against the wall. He really didn't know what he should feel. It was understandable when his grandparents passed. They were older and it seemed to make sense that someone who had lived a long time was ready to move on to heaven or wherever it was that people went when they died. The fact that his aunt, who was much younger, was murdered at the hands of her husband, confused him. He wasn't sure if he should feel sad or angry. He simply felt numb. So, he just sat in the hallway, breathing quietly and trying to absorb the words being spoken in the living room.

"How did Cathy get stabbed?" Maria asked through her sobs. "I need to know how this son-of-a-bitch killed her."

"Ma'am, right now we're still collecting evidence at their house. Plus, it's probably not the best time to go into detail," the first officer spoke looking at Albert and motioning a "no" with his finger which indicated that it was likely a grim crime scene. "When the trial happens, you'll hear more about this than you probably wish to, but know your sister put up a fight, as the husband has scratches all over his face and arms. He's already being processed downtown. Can I get your phone numbers so we can contact you in future days?"

Albert gave them their home number and his work number. Oree heard the officers say: "We are sorry for your loss," get up off their chairs, and then Albert walked them to the door. He heard the front door quietly close. For a moment there was a deafening silence except for a creak in the floor as his father walked back toward the couch. Then, the silence was broken with a hard thud as Oree's mother fainted onto the floor.

Within a day of Cathy's death, Albert joined Maria and her remaining siblings, Dominic and Robert, in the funeral preparations. Everyone tried their best to behave like her death was more akin to natural causes, rather than at the hands of her husband. The fact that Cathy had suffered abuse for years and did nothing to get herself out of the situation was beyond the reason of the siblings. They asked themselves over and over again, "Why didn't she say anything to us? Why didn't she leave?" While in the funeral home pouring over caskets, each shared stories of the bruises, scratches and other marks they had individually seen on their sister at various times. If only they had spoken with each other earlier, perhaps. Well, they reasoned there was no way for them to determine if anything they said could have made any difference.

In planning for the funeral, as a family courtesy, the police conducted a search in their databases for Narciso, who was nowhere to be found. Raymond Jr. came back for the funeral. His intention was to take his sister Cynthia, who had been staying with Albert and Maria in Anita's room, back to the base at which he was stationed. Lupita came with her children and she also offered to have her sister move in with her. When Cynthia saw how ill-behaved her children were, she reasoned Lupita would likely use her stay as an opportunity to secure a free babysitter, so she declined her sister's offer. Albert's parents, who were now very old, attended the funeral with Anthony and his family. In consoling Maria, her mother-in-law shared, "The day at Annie's graduation party, I wish I had said something, but I didn't want to meddle." Missing from the funeral was Annie, who Anthony had shared was somewhere in Mexico with Joaquin. She could not be found.

In the weeks following the funeral, Oree's parents continually met with police and prosecutors as they tried to piece the case together against Raymond. They said there was a good chance that Raymond would spend the rest of his life in jail, based upon the ongoing abuse that had transpired in the household. Oree's father quit his restaurant job. Since Cathy's murder, something had changed in Maria and he felt it best to keep a close eye on her.

Although it was expected she would suffer from a fair amount of grieving, after a month had passed, she continued to spend most of her days "fumbling," for lack of a better term. She couldn't seem to get herself out of bed and frequently spent the day either there or on the couch, crying. Albert told Oree that it would pass, that his mother was merely grieving, but Oree wasn't convinced. His mother seemed to have lost all interest in living and he worried that one day she would simply disappear into the fabric of the sofa cushions. Oree had become master of Eggo's, and it had gotten to the point where even he was tired of eating Lucky Charms. He had grown accustomed to his mother's inability to cook breakfast, so at this point he was old enough and fine with preparing food and doing dishes for himself. Getting to school was always hit or miss, and fortunately a nearby neighbor had a daughter attending Oree's school, so he frequently caught rides with them.

When school let out for the summer, Oree took part in driver's education classes as he was approaching the age where he could get his driver's permit and license. The first two weeks of the class were spent studying the various laws that governed the roads and then taking tests. Oree was happy that this course was far easier than his college prep classes. The next few weeks were spent in a trailer, where they sat at mock car interiors with steering wheels, brake and accelerator pedals, basically everything you would have on the driver's side of a vehicle. They sat in the hot, stuffy trailers twice a week watching grainy 8mm films of roadways and scenes of pedestrians walking in front of cars and the like, with the goal being to show the students how to maneuver a vehicle in various driving situations. The final week was spent in the school parking lot, where the students got to actually drive a vehicle.

Once he obtained his permit, Albert would let Oree drive him on Saturdays to his job at the market. Oree had been saving the money he earned from working there, and when he saw an ad in The Recycler for a 1962 Chevy Bel Air for $350, he snapped it up. His father said he would pay for the insurance since he realized with Maria's present state, Oree would likely have to be driving himself to school and everywhere else.

Oree returned to eleventh grade in September. Similar to the time in his freshmen year, he was happy to go back to a place which kept his mind off all the drama at home. He had gotten his conditional driver's license after passing with a score of 95. He started most days making breakfast for himself and packing a lunch with whatever he could find in the refrigerator. Occasionally, his father would be getting ready for work at the same time and he would slip him a $5 bill "for lunch or whatever." Every morning, he would walk past his parent's bedroom door which was always shut, and tap lightly, "Bye mom. I'm going to school now." He would at times hear a stir or the noise of a bed spring popping, but mornings were not a good time for his mother. On many afternoons when he returned from school, Oree would walk into the house and it was clear that afternoons were not good for his mother either. She would often be found lying on the couch in her bath robe, and from her unkempt appearance and that of the house, it was obvious that her day's activities were highlighted by a move from the bed to the couch.

Some days, Oree would walk past her on the couch and pick up half full cups of coffee and plates with bread crumbs from the living room coffee table. Maria would respond a weak smile and softly say, "You're my good boy. I know I can always rely on you to be here." Sometimes, her eyes would brim over with tears.

Oree had hoped that his return to school might mark some improvement in his mother's state of mind. However, things had not improved. Trips to the grocery store were made usually when the refrigerator began to look like an empty box. The Sunday meals the family always shared were on hiatus. Whatever cleaning within the house took place was at the hands of Oree. He was proud that he had mastered clothes washing and he would maneuver the vacuum around the house like a professional maid. Maria would sometimes make attempts to clean the kitchen, often without much success. Oree could always tell when his mother had been in the kitchen as there would be opened jars of mayonnaise or jelly sitting on the counter, or a sink full of dissipating bubbles half covering plates and glasses and covered with debris. It reminded him of the time he cleaned the poor family's house for "Service Saturday." He now understood why the woman sat in her living room crying on the shoulder of the nun. It was likely depression brought on by the deportation of her husband. His mother had now been caught in the same grips of depression, only hers was brought on by the loss of her best friend and sister.

Finally, after months of continued malaise, Albert insisted on taking Maria to the doctor. She fought back saying, "*Yo tiene nervios*/I just have nerves." Albert responded that they were going anyway. Then he slipped and said, "I want my wife back," which sent Maria into a deeper state of despair. It took days for him to recover from that statement as Maria would cover her ears or turn her head whenever he spoke. Inside, she grew increasingly fearful that he would leave her, so she finally gave in.

The doctor said Maria was suffering from depression based upon the weight of her many losses. Albert thought for a moment, "She lost her parents, then her son, her daughter and her sister." Of course depression would be the devil which had been draining the life out of his wife. The doctor recommended that Maria begin taking Prozac, an anti-depressant medication which could help take the edge off of her suffering. They fought over the decision to take psychiatric medication for weeks. During these arguments, she would tell her husband, "Taking these pills is a sign of weakness and I may be sad, but I'm not weak." Maria had always been taught that those who suffered from mental illness were either "weak," "fakers" or "crazy." Her parents had raised her to believe that: "Only white people have the luxury of suffering these types of things. They pop pills for everything. Mexicans have to go on with life whether they're sad or not." She was always taught that mental illness was a sign of weakness, so it was no surprise to find her highly resistant to the thought of taking medication to make her whole again.

Finally, Maria reluctantly agreed to take the medication after her doctor used the analogy: "When you have strep throat you take penicillin, when you have high blood pressure, you take water pills. This is the same sort of thing; the chemicals in your brain are out of sync, so this medication will help put them back in balance." This somehow made sense to her; that the fact that she had been so sad was not the result of her weakness, but rather the imbalance in her brain was the result of her many losses. Albert was relieved that something was finally being done to help his wife as lately he had begun to have fears that one day he would walk into his house and find Maria hanging from a closet pole or something like that. The prescription was filled and Maria reluctantly began to take the pills.

Once the new pill regime was established, at the time when he normally would have said his good byes in the morning, Oree had a new routine. Instead of feebly whispering, "Have a nice day" through the door of his parent's bedroom, he would now walk into their room with one of the green and white pills and a glass of water, and say "breakfast time" which always roused Maria. At first the medication seemed to make her even worse. Sometimes she would be extremely anxious, wringing her hands like they were dripping with water, or she would slur her words like a drunk. Sometimes, Oree would walk into a room to find his mother simply staring blankly into space. When he would ask, "What are you doing?" it was though he had broken Maria's trance and she would respond, "Oh, uh, nothing," like she herself was surprised and had somehow returned from an out of body experience.

At times Oree felt like he was the parent, but slowly, ever so slowly, Maria began to improve. The first concrete sign of improvement was one morning when Oree went into the refrigerator to make his lunch sandwich and he was greeted by a brown paper bag with a smiley face written on it feebly with a black marker pen. He opened the bag and found a peanut butter and jam sandwich, a Hostess ding dong and a banana. "This I can live with," he thought. It would take a long time before his mother resumed the making of eggs, bacon and the like for breakfast. And, when she did, there was a sort of hollowness to her activity. It was like she knew this was what she was supposed to do, rather than something she enjoyed, as if anyone ever enjoyed cooking breakfast every day.

Oree spoke with his collegiate advisor early in the semester who suggested that scholastically he was in "tip top shape" for college, however he needed to round out his program with some extracurricular activities, so Oree joined the Speech Club, started attending California Scholarship Federation meetings and became a member of the Spanish Club. He thought the last sign-up to be rather ironic as at this point, his Spanish was far weaker than that of any non-native speaker. He reasoned that the abuse Sister Anastasia had inflicted upon him in kindergarten was a trauma so severe that he had been psychologically damaged for life. No matter how many Spanish classes he took, he would never feel comfortable speaking the language. These activities kept him after school many a day. When he would return home in the evening, his mother acted like he had abandoned him.

He would often walk into the kitchen while she sat at the breakfast table watching a small TV on the kitchen counter. Rather than ask how his day was, she would issue statements such as, "You're not going to leave are you?" "You are spending too much time at that school, you should be home with your mother." "In my family, the children always came home from school directly. We had chores so we were not allowed to run wild in the streets."

It was the last statement that would make Oree bite the inside of his lip. What did she think he was doing, hanging out in a street gang? He understood that her lack of education made her unsympathetic to the fact that THIS son was studying to make something of his life. But, the guilt mongering was something that was difficult for him to accept – regardless of his mother's present capacities or state of wellness. There would be no unplanned pregnancies or picketing of corporations for employee rights with this son – he wanted to be working for the corporations (although he wasn't sure in which capacity). He waited for her condition to improve further, but it would be a long time before

Maria would utter, "How was your day at school?" rather than assigning guilt as he walked in the door.

When Albert's father Eduardo passed away in early winter, the family pulled together for the funeral. They joined at the church and then at the San Fernando Mission for the burial. Albert noticed that his wife, who was always a great crier, did not shed a single tear and she seemed rather emotionless considering the situation. He found it odd, but realized it might be a side effect of the medication as Maria was taking a high dose of Prozac. (The doctor was slowly ratcheting down her dosage as she showed signs of improvement.) Albert, who had made great strides in being a caretaker of his sick wife, made a mental note to ask her doctor about Maria's lack of tears and emotion.

As they joined at his father's grave, Albert stood with his arm wrapped around the shoulder of his mother Elizabeth who quietly wept. Anthony, Luz and their children, Eva and a recent addition, their second child Eduardo II, "Eddie," sat closely to Elizabeth as they had become an integral part of their lives as the seniors aged. Baby Eddie cried incessantly as it was near to his feeding time and young Eva, held the hand of "Gran Beth" as she called her based upon her inability to pronounce her full name. As the priest sprinkled holy water on the casket, Albert looked up, in the far distance, he thought he saw a young woman wearing a white blouse and a brown skirt. She looked like Anita. He wasn't sure as she appeared older and her hair was shorter, but there was something familiar about her. He blinked his eyes and when he opened them, the image had disappeared. "Must be *nervios*" he thought.

During the course of his junior year, a new phenomenon began which helped to free Oree from the worries of his home life and the monotony of his studies – it was called disco. Oree's initiation began first with the film, "Saturday Night Fever," followed by a visit to a teen night club on Van Nuys Boulevard called "My Uncle's." A sub-group of the low riders had heard about the new music and club from their girlfriends, so Oree drove a few of his friends to the disco one Saturday night. They paid a $3 cover charge and entered through a long hallway to a room filled with sound which seemed to make the room pulsate. Glittering disco balls, strobe lights and flashing neon tubes cascaded light into unison with sound.

"Native New Yorker," by Odyssey began to play over the booming speakers and suddenly Oree was transformed to a whole new world. Although he wasn't a New Yorker, he quickly identified with lyrics: *"Where did all those yesterdays go?"* This was the place, this disco, was where he could be free of everything going on in his crazy, somewhat sad life (he didn't like the taste of alcohol, so that outlet was not an option). He danced with one girl who was wearing an emerald green dress and matching heels, but after she twirled around him a few times and came in for a back bend which nearly put them both on the dance floor, it was obvious that his dance game needed improvement.

When Oree returned to school Monday, he asked his friends if they knew of other people who liked to go to discos with the hope that they might be able to connect him with someone who could teach him a step or two. He was told of another Junior, Patty Ochoa, who was known for her expertise at disco dancing. When he first met Patty, she was dressed like all the other girls in school and looked kind of plain. He had trouble picturing her as being some sort of disco diva. As they negotiated why she should accompany him to My Uncle's, she let on that she knew six different versions of The Hustle. He was impressed. Patty told Oree that she would meet him at the club that Saturday night, but that he needed to get new clothes if she wanted to be seen with her.

Oree took her comments to heart and using the money he had saved and received from his most recent birthday ("Thank you grandma Beth"), off he went to People's at the mall. Oree found a pair of black Angel's Flight pants which at first made him uncomfortable as they were so tight and form fitting, and a gauzy tan and brown polyester shirt which had a print of little Asian bridges and birds flying. His favorite part of the outfit was the black platform shoes he found. They added an extra two inches to his height which was fine by him, as one of the areas he was lacking in, physically speaking, was height. For once he understood how tall people felt – and he loved it.

When he walked through the living room of his house to go out that Saturday night, his father looked up from his *Life* magazine, "What the…?" His mother peered up from the Mary Tyler Moore Show and smiled weakly. Oree looked like a freshly washed car. He had used a blow dryer to slick back his thick black hair and he uncomfortably adjusted his Angel's flight pants while teetering on his platform shoes. "Did the circus come to town?" his father jibed.

"This is what everyone is wearing at discos," Oree defended. "If you would go to a movie every now and then, you could have seen *Saturday Night Fever* and then you'd understand. It is the style and it's gonna get me lots of babes."

"Babes?" his father laughed. "O.k., well you better not put a lighter near those pants or they'll melt on you. Maria, will you look at what your son is wearing?"

Maria looked up and said, "He goes out too much and you let him. Oree, you better be home early."

Oree looked past her comment, as he went to My Uncle's where he met Patty. He barely recognized her. She bore little resemblance to the plain girl he met at school as her face with shiny with deep blue eye shadow, thick black eyelashes (likely fake), heavy rouge cheeks and glistening red lipstick. Her hair was teased up and she wore a gold rope head band. Glitter sparkled in her thick brown hair. She wore a short gold lamé dress and a pair of glittery open toed shoes. Oree gave her a hug and was amazed at her transformation. She gave his outfit a thumb's up and then she proceeded to show him a few versions of the hustle, as well as a few partner dances. He quickly discovered that Patty was one of those young women who were light years ahead of most of the girls in high school.

She coolly sauntered around the disco like she was its owner, or at least spent a great deal of time there. As she encountered people she obviously knew, she would greet them with a kiss on the right, then left cheek, like Oree had seen in foreign movies. Oree was thankful that she had agreed to meet him to "show me the ropes." They danced until the club closed at 1 a.m. and then he treated her to pancakes at the International House of Pancakes, a few doors down. In talking, Patty shared that although My Uncle's was a racially mixed night club, there were several other teen discos in the Valley – not all were so welcoming of Latinos. Oree took her words with a grain of salt and continued eating his syrupy pancakes.

Over the next months, Oree made friends with a few of the young people at the disco and he occasionally met Patty there. When he started becoming attracted to her, she confessed she was secretly seeing a freshman in college and didn't want the word to get out as he was over 18. His low rider friends had told him about a new teen night club that had opened in Northridge – "The Ozone." Looking to expand their circle of potential dating opportunities, a few of them, including Oree, ventured to Northridge, a primarily Anglo community, one Saturday evening.

The club was in a mini mall by a movie theater and you could hear the music pounding through the walls into the parking lot. Oree and his friends paid the $5 cover and walked inside (things were more expensive in Northridge – even the cokes were $3). While "Le Freak" by Chic played over the booming speakers, they surveyed the auditorium. It looked like the room had been converted from something like a Knights of Columbus hall, but the lighting and music were fine, so they paid for the expensive cokes. From the looks of it, the room was filled mostly with preppy types, but Oree didn't really pay attention. He danced with one girl and then he went to approach a blond who was wearing a white tank top, blue gym shorts and striped ankle warmers. As he was approaching her, a red haired jock stopped in front of him.

"What do you think you're doing wetback?" the jock said.

"I was going to ask that girl to dance." Oree responded, "And, I'm not a wetback. I was born here."

"Well, there's two reasons why you aren't going to dance with that girl. First, she's my girlfriend, and second, she doesn't want anything to do with stinking, smelly beaners," the jock laughed.

Oree saw black and then he punched the jock who stumbled back. The jock rebounded and was quickly all over him, punching his arms, ribs and shoulders. Oree covered his stomach area and face and got a few good jabs in before they were pulled apart by a security guard.

"Take it outside assholes," the guard who was much bigger than both, said.

"That beaner was hitting on my girl," the jock said. "I was defending her."

"Look, I don't give a shit, you're both out of the club – now," the guard said grabbing Oree by the back of the neck and holding the jock at bay.

Oree said, "We're getting out of this white-ass shithole, so don't worry about us leaving." He was surprised at his tone, but he noticed the words that once used to tear him apart no longer hurt him, embarrassed him or made him feel sad or feel anything, other than anger. He wasn't sure if this feeling of anger was a step forward or back – but it felt good not to let someone put him down because of his race.

For future disco outings, he decided to remain close to home and went to My Uncle's.

CHAPTER 16

SENIOR YEAR

Over the long days of summer leading into his senior year, Oree spent time at his familiar haunt – the public library. This time, however, he wasn't pouring over the new and classic book shelves, he was reviewing college catalogs. Having had time to think about all that had transpired over the years of his childhood, he came to a conclusion about his future – he wanted to study political science. He wasn't entirely sure what a career in political science might exactly look like, but as he had matured, he took into account all that had happened in his youth – his sister's activism, the treatment of minorities, the murder of his aunt, the family in despair over the deportation of their father. All these things had one thing in common – they required change, political change. He thought back to what his parents once said – the only way to effect change was from within the system. In reviewing schools, he considered local ones, but was drawn to Columbia University. He heard it was a good school for his major – and it was smack in in the epicenter of the universe – New York City!

From his many book adventures, Oree wanted to know what a winter with snow felt like. What it was like to take a subway. What it was like to be part of the hustle and bustle of a vibrant city. What it was like to be around people who were as smart as he. He certainly had the grades and related involvements. Only one question remained. How would he pay for it? For books? For housing? For food? Further, what would his parents think? His mother had been making progress in getting her strength back, but would she be strong enough to deal with yet another child leaving the roost after all the loss she had already endured?

Oree thought long and hard on the last point. His parents had always emphasized the importance of family and of loyalty. Sometimes he really hated all the talk of the importance of *la familia*. It was such a deterrent to achieving anything.

Oree reasoned that if Mexico was not directly south of the United States, it would make his life much easier. Those with Northern European roots were not called upon to make examples of their loyalty to the United States and they all looked relatively the same. There was no dark skin or foreign accents. No one knew were they came from, so of course it was assumed they were nothing but American.

By the time he returned to his senior year at St. Francis, Oree was resolute that he would attend either Columbia University, or a similar school back east. Within weeks of the new semester, he arranged an appointment with his guidance counselor. As it was his senior year, he was assigned to a new counselor. Mr. Salazar, who had attended UCLA, was in his twenties, taught social studies and was new to St. Francis.

"Good to meet you Mr. Rodrigo," said the counselor as he welcomed Oree into his office. Oree sat down as Mr. Salazar opened a manila folder. He glanced quickly at it and then closed it. "So, what can I do for you today, Aurelio?"

"You can call me Oree. I want to find out what I need to do this year to ensure I am accepted at Columbia University in New York. I've already got 16 college units and have participated in numerous extra-curricular activities," Oree said matter-of-factly.

The thought of the Ivy League school permeated his brain. Each time he uttered "Columbia University" out loud, he grew more and more confident that it was the best solution for his college education. Now, if he could tell his parents and figure out the tuition part, all would be well.

"I want to study political science," he continued.

"Well, aren't you ambitious?" Mr. Salazar retorted with a tinge a sarcasm. "Well, Oree my friend, you got nothing to worry about."

"Why is that?" Oree asked

Mr. Salazar pointed toward Oree's arm. "That my friend. The color of your skin. Universities are dying to get a few minorities on their books, makes them look progressive. It worked for me. Figure, less than 10 percent of Hispanics graduate from college. That's gotta look bad for all those universities that pride themselves on being inclusive – colleges love that term, inclusivity. Plus, all these bleeding heart, liberal foundations and others want to make examples of us cast down upon minorities. That's the easiest ticket in, and in glancing, I see your grades are at least passing, so that will make it a walk in the park."

Oree felt his ears turns red with anger and he took a deep breath in. "Did you even look at my folder – at my grades? See all those A's? I didn't get those because of the color of my skin. Did you see all the scholastic awards I have won? Did you see all the clubs I participate in? The fact that I have a job while I study? That is not the color of my skin and you're just as racist as everyone else."

"Whoa, settle down Sparky. For one, I'm not a racist, I merely understand that we should take advantage of every possible opportunity we can. White people have had the cards played in their favor for years. I'm not opposed to using my race to benefit me, and you shouldn't be as well. I was merely explaining what the realities are," he said as he picked up Oree's folder and began to look more intently at it. Looking up, he added, "Of course your grades are important and I see you understand that from looking at them. *Hablas Español?*"

"You too!" The red from Oree's ears now moved down to manifest itself as bulging veins in his neck. "No, I don't speak Spanish and my parents are not farm workers and they did not come from Mexico. They were born here and I don't speak Spanish. I get so tired of everyone asking me if I speak Spanish. I am American, so why should I speak any language other than English? Got it? Do you ask French students: *Parlez-vous Francais?* Germans if they *Sprechen sie Deutsch?* I didn't think so. Look, I don't think you're a good counselor for me. I need someone who sees value in who I am and what I am doing with my life. Not trying to pass me off as some token brown boy."

Mr. Salazar put his hands together and then brought them to his lips. He smiled and took a breath. "There you go again, getting all excited! You're like my grandma's chihuahua, Mickey. He gets agitated so easily. I apologize. You're right. I did not consider your credentials and I did not mean to peg you as any sort of stereotype. You certainly have a strong sense of who you are which will come in handy when you get to college."

"I have learned this much in life. That you have to defend who you are, whatever that is," Oree returned, realizing that all he had gone through in his young life had gotten him to this point of resolve.

He thought back to that time many years ago on a park playground. He saw the very young Oree crying and hurt by names that were unfurled upon him because of the color of his skin. He now understood that it was on that day that he first learned the importance of being strong in who you are, regardless of your race, your intelligence or your lot in life. He had always wondered why his mother hadn't defended him that day. He now understood what she was trying to prepare him for.

He realized that every incident when he had to defend himself, fight back or use reason to get through a situation, had led him to this point in his life – to preparing to leave for college and ultimately become the first college graduate in his family. He gave thanks to that little straw-haired, dark-skinned boy he once was for being strong and for making him who he was.

"O.k., so you want to Columbia University in New York, let's see how we can get you there Sparky," Mr. Salazar said as he turned to a credenza behind his desk and pulled out a copy of the Scholarship Handbook.

"Can you do me one favor?" Oree asked as he began to relax.

"What?" Salazar responded.

"Don't call me Sparky," Oree smiled as he sat back in his seat, calmed his breath and then listened as Mr. Salazar began to read from the book's pages.

∽⬧∼   ∽⬧∼

In the weeks that followed his conversation with Mr. Salazar, Oree began to get nervous. He had started sending out college applications and he would race home after school to get the mail before anyone else as he did not want to have to deal with his mother asking why he was getting letters or oversized envelopes from places like Massachusetts or New York. He hadn't yet told his parents he wanted to go to a school out of state. He was constantly worried about his mother having a breakdown or something when he shared the news.

He had seen positive improvements in her health and lately she was beginning to feel like his old mother. However, when talk came about regarding any sort of change, she would push back or go into her room, which would make Oree grow anxious. She had become closer to Anthony's wife Luz, who brought the children over more frequently so they could play with "grammy." Maria loved spending time with the children and Luz tolerated her constant references: "When my daughter, Annie, was young…" or "Eddie Jr. looks just like Anthony did when he was a baby…"

When Eddie was 11-months-old, Albert said to Maria that it would be a great idea to have a family dinner celebrating his birthday. Maria, at first paused. She hadn't participated in or planned any sort of celebration since Cathy's death, but the Prozac had made her feel much better about life. She finally agreed that, yes, they should have a first birthday party for her grandson. She told Albert she didn't want it to be like the Sunday dinners the family had shared in the past, she wanted a Saturday afternoon party instead. She would make chicken and cheese enchiladas, beans and rice – a real traditional Mexican dinner. Albert agreed that would be a great menu.

On the day before the party, Maria took a $10 bill out of her wallet and gave it to Oree. "Go to the party store and get some streamers and balloons to decorate the back yard. Also, get a small piñata, Eddie won't be able to do it, but little Eva will have fun hitting it."

Oree was surprised and happy. He began to feel like maybe his impending news might be met with favor. The trick was to pre-occupy his mother's mind. Keep her thoughts off of grief and replace them with grandbabies. He went to the party store and got a small burro piñata, balloons and blue and white streamers. He spent Saturday morning blowing up balloons and hanging them and the streamers in the back yard. While he was setting things up for the party, he began wondering if it might be the ideal time to share the news of his plans with his family. He had already received one letter of acceptance and was hopeful he would get one from New York shortly.

Anthony, Luz and their children arrived Saturday afternoon. They brought a very old and fragile Elizabeth with them and Albert went out to the porch to help his mother make it up the short steps to their house. Eva gave Maria a big kiss and hug, and Oree picked her up and said "I want to show you something in the back yard. C'mon!"

The family went to the back yard and Elizabeth softly remarked, "*Es muy bonita*, it's so beautiful. Just like the parties we used to have."

"Yes, just like the parties we used to have Elizabeth," Maria said grasping her hand as she helped her to sit down at the big redwood picnic table which Albert had recently constructed. (He had lately taken up the hobby of building things to help pre-occupy his time now that he no longer had a second job.)

Little Eva was jubilant when her Uncle Oree lifted her up in the air to grab a blue balloon. He gently put her down and she excitedly ran around in circles flailing the balloon by a string, giggling the whole time. As the rest of the family took their places around the table, Maria smiled and looked out across the yard. For a moment it was like the ghosts of her children, sister and her family breezed past her eyes as they danced and laughed in front of her – and then disappeared. Maria was thankful they had shared those times, even if they were all now in the past.

When it came time for dinner, Maria had Luz help her bring out the food, and the family enjoyed each other's company as in years past. Baby Eddie shook his head and started crying when Eva put her finger which had enchilada sauce on it up to his lips. This solicited a hearty laugh amongst the group, except for Eva who got a light tap on her hand from her mother.

Halfway through the meal, Albert lifted his Dixie cup in a toast, "I want to thank you for joining us in celebrating my grandson Eddie's birthday. I am very happy to have my family here today, and although we're not all here in person, we are all together in spirit. I wish my father were here to see this. That we are all still a family."

"I have my family with me. It has helped comfort me through times of difficulty," Maria added as Elizabeth sat by and wiped her eyes. "Now, seeing my grandchildren reminds me of how life goes on, despite everything, and it gives me hope for the future. I also know my own son, Aurelio, is planning to go to college, and I am so happy he will be going to college close by, so he can stay with his mother and father while he learns; so he can help to keep our family whole."

Oree couldn't believe what he was hearing. Earlier, he had told his parents that he was planning to go to a university and that he was "keeping my options open" as far as where that school may be. He couldn't believe that they had interpreted that as, "I am going to stay at home and take care of my depressed mother while I go to a community college down the street." He had far greater plans for his future and they did not include staying in Sylmar.

"Uh, I didn't say that," Oree spoke out. "I told you I was planning to go to a university and that I was keeping my options open."

The table suddenly grew quiet. At some point, Anthony, looking down at little Eddie who was smiling up at him, said, "Having your family around you ain't that bad."

"Oree, we'll talk about this later," his father finally spoke. "Let's have Eva break the piñata for Eddie."

Oree led Eva over to the tree and as she was so young, he didn't blindfold her. He let her swing and swing with a wooden rod as he raised and lowered the piñata. His family laughed as she gently tapped at the burro and giggled. After she began to tire, Oree said "Let me take over short stuff. Stand back."

He tied the rope that suspended the piñata to the tree and with one hard, long swing he sent the piñata and candy flying out toward his family. Eva scrambled under the benches for candy. "Ouch, that hurt," his mother who had been sprayed with candy, yelled out.

Oree held the wood rod tautly and simply glared.

That night after everyone left, he was too tired to go out and he had lately heard that disco was on its way to a slow and painful death, so he stayed home with his parents and helped his mother clean up the kitchen in silence. When they were finished, they went to join Albert who was reading a *Reader's Digest* on his recliner in the living room. The TV was blaring some documentary on migrants planning to come from Central America as a result of wars going on in their country. Oree said he was going to go to his room. His father stopped him.

"So, what's this about a university and it sounds like you're planning to move out?" his father said looking up from the magazine.

"Oh no, he can't move out. Who will help me? I need Oree here with me," Maria pleaded. "He has to stay with his family."

"Says who?" Oree said plainly. "Look, it's awful that Aunt Cathy died and grandma and grandpa are gone, and that you don't speak with Annie, but this isn't my life. It's your life."

"We're not asking you to not go to school, only that it might be better for you to go to school closer to home. The city college is right down the street. Is it too much that we ask that you make one, small sacrifice after all this family has been through?" his father said, putting the magazine down.

"One, small sacrifice? Is that what you said? We're talking about the future of my life. Given the color of my skin, if I don't have the best education possible, I don't stand a chance of ever becoming anything," Oree said. "I want people to look at my resume, my credentials, what I have in my brain. If they can't see past my skin, they certainly can't negate an Ivy League education."

"Ivy League, huh? All I'm saying is maybe wait a year or two," his father continued. "That's all we're asking. Your mother is getting stronger every day, and today she was talking with Luz about her watching the kids during the day, so Luz can work part time. My mom won't be here forever and some day they'll have to get a place of their own. They need to start saving money."

"Great. So, I can stay here and go to a local college, so mom can watch the children of my brother whose key contribution to this world is providing it with two kids. There's something you need to know,"

Oree said, calmly taking a breath. "I've applied for universities outside of California and I especially want to go to Columbia University in New York to study political science."

"What the heck is political science, and tell me how are you going to pay for that education and make a living doing political whatever it is?" Albert said. "Do you have any idea how expensive New York is?"

"Oree, you can take political science here. You can go to the community college. It won't cost us or you anything," his mother said as she began to wring her hands.

"I thought the whole point of having kids was that they could grow up and be something really big, really important. Now, you're pushing all this *familia* crap on me like somehow I'm responsible for helping to keep this family together," Oree said, as he began to raise his voice. "It's not fair. I am the kid remember? I didn't create my brother's life and I certainly didn't make my sister decide on the choices she has. I've already been lining up financial aid so I can afford to go to Columbia."

"You're ungrateful," his father said angrily. "We did not raise you to desert your family. You're just selfish. How can you even think of leaving your mother with the state that she's in?"

"I'm not selfish, I only want my life, and I am not responsible for my mother's well-being. My whole life, I've heard 'Be humble. You're brown, take what you can get and be content'. And, then there's the my family, *mi familia*. You have to maintain the well-being of the *familia*, feed it like it's all some kind of poisonous, rotting plant that you have to nourish to keep alive. Well, all of this is just a bunch of crap and I don't buy it. I've seen how the family restricts you. I've seen how hard you have to work and what you get in return because you don't have a college education."

"Where are you getting all this from? You sound exactly like your sister," Albert yelled. "And, for your information, my lack of education has kept a roof over your head and your food in your stomach."

"Dad, there has got to be more to life," Oree said. "You had your life and now it's time for me to have mine. Political science can open up a number of careers to me."

"Careers? I don't even know what political science means," his father continued. "I wish I could have had a career, but I was too busy trying to keep my family fed to think of such nonsense."

"Well, that was your choice," Oree said. "You chose that life and you can't blame me because you had me."

His father grew increasingly angry and got up out of his recliner. He was standing over his son who sat on the couch. "I had no goddamn choice, Oree. I was Mexican at a time when we could barely get anything. Hell, our own government was trying to ship us back to a place we never had roots in. We didn't have the luxury of thinking of a college education. So, don't be so goddamn smart about it."

"Well, you were stupid about it," Oree yelled up to his father. "You could'a fought back. I'm fighting back. I'm not gonna be a beaner my whole life. I am going to be a person who does something with his life. You and mom raised us to believe we could have more in our lives and now you want to take that back? Well, guess what, you can't."

"Maria, I am going to smack this kid, so help me God. Stupid, my kid is calling me stupid?" Albert stammered. At this point, Maria began fearing that a break like the one they had suffered with Anita was approaching.

"Don't say something you'll regret Albert," she said as she began to cry. "Remember Annie. Remember Annie."

"Ma, don't worry, I am not turning my back on my family. I only want more than a house in Sylmar and a bunch of brats running around my feet," Oree said. "Don't cry. I'm not deserting you or dad, and dad I didn't mean you're stupid, it's only this is my time to choose my life. You have to understand that. If I get that letter from Columbia and can swing it financially, I'm going."

"I'll be fine *mijo*," Maria said dabbing her eyes as she began to settle down. "I'll be fine. It will all be fine."

"Well, I don't think it is fine," his father continued. "Your son owes us that much. I don't think it's asking too much for him to go to a community college for a few years, so this family can get back on its feet."

Oree felt his blood pressure rise to the point of seeing stars in front of his eyes. He got his house keys off a table in the home's entry and said, "I'm going out for a walk," as he slammed the front door shut.

It was a warm evening and Oree felt himself walking for blocks. He ended up at El Cariso, the same park where he had his eighth grade picnic, and sat on a bench.

He began to feel his ears burn and hot tears streamed down his cheeks as he tried to process everything that was slamming into his brain. "I have worked so hard to make my education pay off for something. I have a chance to go to a university in New York. I can't just throw it all away. But, even a good education is no guarantee I will make anything of my life. I'm still a beaner, no matter how much education I get. My dad is right. What if my mom goes downhill? What if she's too frail? What if she tries to kill herself, I won't be around to help. My dad is right. I owe them that. They made me, paid for my schools and they're getting older. Someone with a brain needs to be around to help them. Someone needs to be around if she takes another turn for the worse, and my leaving could cause that. Still, it is not my fault that she had a breakdown. I can't be responsible, I just can't."

"I can't believe my parents are guilting me. My whole life I have not had one role model to encourage me to do anything with my life. To say, 'Oree, you're a smart guy and if you make these choices, you can have a future you're proud of. You can do whatever you want in this life!' I've never had anyone I could talk to about all the books I've read, to help me understand what some of them meant when I couldn't figure them out, to tell me of ones I should have read. None of my uncles or aunts went to college. If they did, maybe our family would be different now and Aunt Cathy would have been smarter to leave before... How in the hell am I to succeed in college without anybody helping me? I will be the first one to graduate from college. Doesn't that mean anything? Don't my parents see the importance of that? What do they want me to be – the same as they are and never achieve anything with my life other than getting a pay check in a dead end job. My brain will die if I do that. I can't believe what I am being asked to do. My brain will suffocate.

"My dad sacrificed everything for his family and what has that gotten him in return? A son who knocks up some girl and a daughter who says she hates him. Community college would be a lot cheaper and I could transfer to UCLA in a year or so. But, I don't want UCLA, I want Columbia," he continued. "Do white people need to make these choices? My friends in the Scholarship Federation all say their parents are so proud they are being accepted to these wonderful universities and how they will do anything in their power to help their children succeed. And, here my dad is trying to guilt me out to take care of my mother? Will there ever be a time in my life where things work out the way they should? Where I don't have to make choices because of family or my skin color? Where I can just be who I am?"

Oree calmed himself as he again reminded himself, "You will be the first in your entire family to graduate from college. That will count for something. You will know what you accomplished and that's all you can ask for. Your family might not ever understand, but that's not important. It's important that you understand that this is right for you." He blew his nose and then wiped off his face. The coolness of the evening air helped calm him as it brushed against his flushed cheeks. He took a few more deep breaths as he felt a sense of resolve. He now understood what he needed to do, and henceforth that would not change. He walked back to his house and when he got home, noticed all the lights were off. He opened the front door and walked in. Through the darkness, he saw the outline of his father sitting upright in his recliner.

"Are you better now?" his father asked calmly, and through the darkness Oree could faintly make out the whites of his father's eyes which appeared to be glassy.

"Yes and I plan to go to Columbia if they accept me. I'm going to bed now," Oree said walking to his bedroom.

Two days later, a packet from Columbia University arrived. Aurelio Rodrigo had been accepted as a first year political science student.

CHAPTER 17

GRADUATION

It took two long weeks of conversation upon conversation, endless arguments with no resolve and bouts of stone, cold silence, before Oree was able to persuade his parents to understand the opportunity and importance of his attendance at Columbia University. That, by getting a university education, Oree would not only be positioning himself for the best possible outcome, but he would also be positioning his family and their families for whatever the future might hold. Imagine the example he would set for Eva and little Eddie, to have an uncle working in a professional career. Plus, to have a college educated son would put him in an even stronger position to assist his family should a need arise. At times, Maria would vacillate and seem to be within the grasp of the depression that once held her captive, but Oree would help to nudge her back to center and reassure her that she wasn't losing a son, she was gaining a college graduate. That would make her smile. When that didn't work, he would reassure her that if they needed to adjust her medication, they always could.

Following his acceptance at Columbia, things began to move very quickly. His guidance counselor Mr. Salazar turned out to be a true ally, and he helped Oree to uncover no less than six scholarship opportunities – most of them proved successful – except for one from the Minority Council on Growth (The reason for the denial? His father made too much money!). He had secured enough financing to pay for his schooling, as well as housing on campus, and he planned to take a part time job when he got to New York to further supplement his schooling needs. Oree took his mother with him when he went to accept the Knights of Columbus scholarship. In accepting the award, he shared, "It is through the strength and support of my parents, my mother especially, that I am able to humbly accept this honor…" Maria sat and quietly wept as he spoke. She recalled the popsicle stick house which once sat on top of the refrigerator and remembered how it once made her feel. That gave her strength.

In addition to the scholarships and a few awards he was to be presented with at graduation for his scholastic achievements, Oree learned that he would be school valedictorian. Although he occasionally felt bad that he was would be leaving home, he was proud of the work he had completed to earn him the awards, honors and recognition.

He thought back upon his friendship with Susan Valdez, and he realized that now, he too, had the opportunity of attaining a life like she and her family. At least now it was within his reach. He thought back upon the past when things were not so good – of the times he felt shame, embarrassment and sadness over who he was based upon the color of his skin. He remembered the names he was called and how they made him feel, the times he was bullied because of who he was. He vowed to ensure that one day he would set the example for other brown-skinned children to dare and believe that they could be anything they wanted to be.

Over the years, his friendships with the low rider group had ebbed and flowed, but as the end of the school year approached, he noticed a change. That group now was divided into two subgroups – those who were going to get jobs directly out of school and those who were planning to go to college. Of those continuing with their education, some were going to junior colleges, but a few, which surprised Oree, were going to UCLA and USC. He was surprised that others were like him, and that they too held secrets of aspirations for their futures.

In the end, he was glad that he had at least been friends with that group. They helped provide a cultural tie to his "Mexican-ness," whatever that could be defined as. There was a sort of comfort in knowing that many of them had shared the same experiences at home that he did. The group also helped to guard him from some of the isolation he sometimes felt in taking honors classes where he was often the sole minority. Oree may have been smart, but he couldn't hide the insecurity he felt at times when thrown in with a group of high achievers who were being groomed by their parents in a manner similar to what Susan was. They had advantages he simply did not have, but in the end, he realized those were not deterrents.

As graduation approached, Oree thought about his family and all they had been through. Anthony was doing o.k. with his life. He seemed to have a happy marriage and his children were well-behaved and loving. Anita, well Annie was a story that had yet to be finished. Oree would fantasize that one day she would simply walk in the front door of their home and pick up with her life where it once was. His father had grown more quiet as he aged, and at times he still smarted from his son's assessment of him being "stupid." He would brush the thought away as he still had much to do for his family.

Oree's father was also sobered by the realization that Maria might not ever be the wife and mother she was as the children grew, but she was a survivor and would be by his side as they aged. Maria started going to a grief counselor on Wednesday afternoons to discuss her feelings. Although it did little to placate the sadness which at times threatened to overtake her, it did make her stronger in the resolve that as a parent her job was to help her children succeed, even if it meant them leaving the comfortable confines of the family home.

As the days to graduation grew closer, Oree's parents took pride in what remained of their family and at times, Oree would hear his father brag at work: "Son number two is off to New York to study at Columbia University. Yes, that's right, that is my son!" His mother's conversations with the counselor additionally helped. Oree was thankful that she no longer pressured him to remain close to home, and that her definition of *la familia* was slowly expanding with the realization that as time changes things, families must change as well.

Oree felt better that his mother had found someone to discuss her feelings with, and he realized his fights with his parents were the result of "growing pains." He truly did love his family and understood that the changes his family experienced were changes that all families likely go through as children leave their "roosts and roots." His friends had shared with him that they had similar experiences with their parents when they told them they planned to do things other than what their parents had envisioned.

In preparation for his graduation, his mother took him to Orbach's in Panorama City to buy a suit. The store was what one would consider to be a "high end establishment" and this would be his first adult suit, so he wanted to get something that marked the change in his transition from boy to man. His mother said they should get something made of a quality fabric, so he could take it to New York for whatever things might come up. When they got to the store, his mother went off to women's wear as Oree perused the racks of black, blue and tweed suits and sports coats. He daydreamed about how they might look on him and how appropriate they would appear when he attended his first scholar's mixer at Columbia, or perhaps a cocktail party of a professor who had become enamored with his superlative intellect and had to introduce his prize student to peers.

He thought about all these things as he brushed his hands along the fabric sleeves to see which felt best.

"May I help you young man?" his daydreaming was interrupted by a sales lady.

"Uh, I'm looking for a suit for graduation and for college," Oree replied.

"Well, the one you have your hands on is wool and is $400. If you'll allow me, I will take you to some more reasonable ones made out of polyester," she said coldly.

"How do you know how much I can afford? What gives you the right? Why... well never mind," Oree said angrily, although on the inside he knew he could not ask his parents to buy him a $400 suit. "You know, I don't need your help. I'm fine looking by myself."

"Have it your way," the clerk said as she walked away.

Oree wondered if there would ever be a time, now or in the future, where his race wasn't somehow used as a marker against him. He dreamt of a time in the future where all races lived peacefully together and were appreciative of the gifts each culture brought to the melting pot known as America. He mused how wonderful it would be if words like "beaner" or "wetback" failed to exist. If people perhaps first noticed the color of someone's eyes or the smile on their lips rather than the color of their skin, or the nappy folds of their hair, or the accent with which they uttered their words. He laughed to himself. "I know I can help build an America where all people are treated equally – whether they're from New Hampshire or Nairobi."

In the end, he and his mother found a black wool blend suit on a sale rack which would do just fine for his graduation and for Columbia. As they walked toward the exit door with the suit wrapped in a plastic suit carrier, he carried it over his shoulder and seeing the sales lady who insulted him earlier folding sweaters, he turned, smiled and thought, "When I'm your age, I won't be folding sweaters in a department store, that's for damn sure."

In the weeks leading up to his graduation, Oree had his final meeting with his guidance counselor.

"Now, when you get up there to make your valedictorian speech Mr. Rodrigo, don't wet your pants and don't cuss, other than that, anything goes," said Mr. Salazar laughing. "I mean, you should say something inspirational and non-controversial. You want the audience to cheer with you, not jeer at you."

"I think I have some ideas," Oree smiled. "Don't worry, I'll make everyone proud – at least everyone who's important to me."

"I have to tell you, you taught me some things," Salazar continued.

"How do you mean?" Oree asked.

"I learned you can't make assumptions about young people – that they are likely to surprise you when you least expect it. You kind of remind me of me when I was your age," he said. "I learned that you can't judge a book by its cover, or the color of its binding or the look of its stitching. Sometimes you have to delve deep into the book to understand what it holds. And, like any good book, there are surprises, plot twists and turns, and maybe an ending you didn't see coming. Mr. Rodrigo, I want you to have an ending I didn't see coming."

"Dang, that was good. Did you just make that up?" Oree smiled. "Don't worry, I will have an ending that's blazing. Don't be surprised when you see me coming back to Speaker's Day in a government-owned vehicle with flags on the hood."

"I wouldn't be surprised at all," Salazar finished.

On the day of his graduation, Oree was up before dawn. His father had already left for work at 5 a.m. so he could get off early to attend Oree's afternoon ceremony. He sat at the breakfast table in his family's kitchen and he reviewed his note cards. He had prepared his Valedictorian Speech about the importance of being different, a topic the school administration had approved.

Somehow, today his house felt different. It was as though this was the last time he would be some one's child sitting at a breakfast table. After this afternoon he would be a graduate of high school and four years from this, he would be a graduate of a university, and beyond that, well that was anyone's guess. He imagined he would return to this table many times in the future, but that it would be different. At first it would be on college breaks, then perhaps with the woman who was destined to be his wife, and then even later on, with his own children. He could envision it all – he sitting at the kitchen table feeding Gerber to baby Oree, while grandma Maria stood over the stove turning bacon and making fried eggs. They would likely have long conversations about his latest project and how cold the weather was back east.

His thoughts were interrupted when his mother shuffled into the kitchen to pour a cup of coffee (Oree had started drinking coffee in his senior year, it seemed like the mature thing to do).

"Who's gonna give me my happy pills when you go?" she smiled, sitting down with a yawn.

"I think you got this under control ma," Oree said looking out the kitchen window.

"You know, I was talking with your dad. Perhaps we can come and visit you in spring. I don't think I want to know what a cold, snowy New York feels like, so we'll wait 'til you're settled. If Cathy were here…," his mother's voice trailed, then resumed. "I want to see the Rockettes at Radio City Music Hall. I've always wanted to do that and I think your father would enjoy it – all those pretty legs."

"That would be great mom," Oree continued, smiling. "By then, I'll know some things about the city and we can go to places like that, the Statue of Liberty and World Trade Center. I heard the view from the towers is incredible."

"You know *mijo*, I love you," his mother said quietly with a shaky voice as she patted her robe down on her knees and looked at the floor as if she was sort of embarrassed. She paused and then spoke again. "My counselor says that I need to learn to vocalize things I feel. You are very important to your father and me."

Oree sat stunned. In all his life, he had never heard either parent say, "I love you." He had been told it was a Mexican thing. That parents wouldn't utter the words to their children – especially boys – out of fear that they might become "soft," or something like that. Physical displays of affection also fell into this category, so it was for that reason, that Oree's parents rarely hugged him. He knew when the time came and he had his own family, he would make it a point to always say "I love you" to his spouse and children. Hugs would be given out on a daily basis, and he would always ensure his children understood their importance in his life and as part of his family.

Oree felt himself bend inside and he was also humbled that his mother – that she who had been through so much and lost so many dear to her – could say those simple, yet powerful words to him.

"I love you too ma," he said as he got up, kissed her on the forehead and went to prepare his clothes for graduation.

It was a hot spring afternoon as families filled the seats set upon the football field of the stadium of St. Francis. Oree's attendees included his parents, as well as his brother and his family. His Uncle Dominic came with Elizabeth, who now needed a wheel chair to go distances. The family had already made reservations to dine at the El Presidente restaurant after the ceremony as Oree didn't see the point in having a big party.

The ceremony began and proceeded as graduations typically do. Oree felt his stomach churn as time for his Valedictorian speech drew near. Finally, he heard the principal mention his name as he began to introduce the Valedictorian. To Oree, it was weird to hear someone else talk about things you had done in school, but it was even weirder when they were talking to a stadium filled with people. Just seemed too much like bragging.

"I would now ask our class Valedictorian Aurelio Rodrigo to join us on the dais for his speech," the principal said in calling him up.

Oree rose out of his seat and walked up to the stage. He climbed up the few stairs and made his way to the lectern. He stood behind it and put his note cards upon it. Looking up and out at the crowd he was surprised there were so many in attendance. He got a few "woo hoos" from the students which surprised him as he didn't think most people in school even knew who he was. He looked down at his note cards.

Suddenly the speech he had prepared seemed all wrong and he froze. After all that had happened his short life – the happiness, the sadness, the losses and the riches he had gained – he could not simply give some pat explanation on the importance of being different. What happened to him was important, and he suddenly felt that it was equally important that he shared his experiences in the hopes that others in the audience might somehow become a bit more tolerant, understanding and accepting of people's differences.

He realized he needed to speak from the heart – from his heart. He recalled all the hundreds of books he had read over the years and reasoned, "This is just like reading from a book, only it's my life." He began slowly and his voice was quivering.

"When I was a child, someone called me a beaner. I didn't know what a beaner was, but I knew it wasn't a good thing.

Being a beaner made me feel ashamed. It made me feel I was bad. It made me embarrassed and it made me feel sad. Being a beaner meant I was less than everyone else and that they were in turn better than me. Knowing I was a beaner meant I couldn't succeed like everyone else. I didn't have as much, wasn't smart enough, didn't have a good enough house or the right kind of family, and worse, there was no chance that I would ever amount to much.

Being a beaner was something that I always knew I was. I knew it every day I walked into the classroom, when I joined the Cub Scouts, when I went to stores to buy things and when I applied for scholarship applications for college. When I went to church I used to pray to God to make me anything but a beaner – to take that mark away from me.

My grandparents were beaners when they came to this country and tried to make a better future for my parents. My dad, who is the most hard working man I have ever met, is nothing more than a beaner. My mom – who raised her children to take responsibility, to be proud of who they are and what they have, and to stand up for things that are right – is a beaner. My brother, who values the importance of family, is a beaner. And, my sister, who is somewhere battling for the rights of those who are taken advantage of because of their surnames or skin color is a beaner.

I'm thinking, we will never be anything but beaners for the rest of our lives."

He could feel those in the audience begin to shift, some uncomfortably, but he also looked out and saw the wave of minority students who sat alongside each other. Some smiled and nodded in approval, a few dabbed tears in their eyes. He decided he needed to continue.

"And, you know what? This beaner stuff? I'm o.k. with that. I'm o.k. with being a beaner.

I look out across our student body here today and I realize we're all beaners. Whether your skin is white or brown, yellow or black. Every time someone makes you feel bad because you aren't pretty enough, aren't smart enough or maybe don't wear the right clothes or have the right haircut, you're a beaner.

We Americans are too clever to limit ourselves to just a few words like the one I mentioned. We've created some winners like 'chinks,' 'Pocahontas' and the 'N' word, which I refuse to use (the audience gasped on that one). As if single utterances were not enough, we've come up with a whole vocabulary to define our prejudices: 'Go back to where you came from' or 'Laziness is a trait of blacks' or 'Illegals are all a bunch of criminals.'

These are ways we use to demean people because of their race or characteristics they may have.

There's more to it. Every time someone says you're too fat, too skinny, too ugly or too stupid; maybe your family doesn't have enough money; or your dad is a janitor. When people laugh at you because they think they're better than you. These are all insults made to hurt. Using these terms and words makes us feel better about ourselves, but they don't really. They do just the opposite and make us less than the human beings we are.

See. We've all been beaners at some point."

Oree looked back over the audience. They had grown silent, Was he taking it too far? Did he need to soften his tone? In his quick thinking mind, he paused and took a breath. Then, he saw something he hadn't anticipated.

He looked toward the back of the seats that lined the football field. He looked hard as he saw his sister – Annie was standing behind the last row of seats, nodding her head in agreement. She was wearing a dark blue dress and was dabbing her eyes with a Kleenex. She quietly raised her closed fist in support. Oree quickly looked down at his father and caught his eyes in an effort to get his attention. He then looked back toward his sister as his father turned in his seat and got up, moving slowly toward the back of the seats. Oree felt a lump form in his throat as he continued.

"Uh, excuse me. Being a beaner is o.k. It makes you stronger, trust me.

Being a beaner helps you to have a tough skin. It helps you to fight for things you believe in…"

He looked out and saw his father hugging his sister who was crying as she buried her head into his chest. Oree's voice began to get stronger as he realized that everything that made him strong was in front of him today – his family.

"And, sometimes those things take you far from home. But these things all make us grow. I now understand that names can't hurt me. Ignorance can't hurt me. The only thing that can hurt me is if I don't take action. A beaner is now something I call myself with pride. I take the word back. You can't hurt me by calling me that name, and you can't be hurt by names people call you. When people use these terms it shows how small they truly are.

So today, I look out at you all and welcome the future we embrace. I look forward to a time when the words and phrases people use to hurt us are put in a time capsule, as a reminder that we can never let ignorance come full forward again. That we as human beings are better than these words.

I am standing in front of you today because of my grades; because of the things I have done here in school. I have accomplished these things while still being a beaner, so I guess we can't be all that bad. I am an American and I am going to college and I am going to help to create a future where people can succeed – whether they're black or brown, white or yellow, rich or poor, smart or ignorant. That is our inherent right as Americans, as U.S. citizens and as human beings.

My name is Aurelio Rodrigo and I am proud to be a beaner."

The audience was at first quiet, then some of the students started cheering and a few parents too – parents of all colors. They all clapped, although a few may not have understood why. They did understand that the young man on the stage spoke with passion about things that had affected his life and the ways he planned to address them. Oree looked out and saw his father leading Annie back to the family seats. He shook hands with the principal and walked off of the stage.

At the end of the ceremony, rather than shake hands or hug his classmates, Oree ran back to be with his family.

They stood in an aisle by their seats and he rushed to hug Annie.

"You sure know how to make an entrance," Oree said to his sister as they embraced.

"Oree, you are so big now and I am so proud of you," Annie cried.

"Where have you been?" Oree asked.

"Oh that's not important," Annie said through her tears. "I need to apologize to you; to mom, dad and to Anthony. Dad, I am so sorry I hurt you. Anthony, I am sorry I missed your wedding and your family. Mommy, I wanted to come home, but I was so ashamed. I was so ashamed that I couldn't come back. I couldn't come home until I had fixed some of the mess I made."

"Aye, *mija*, what are you saying," Maria said. "What mess?"

"I spent so much of my youth being self-righteous – being prideful. I joined that group as I believed we were going to change things, like those people we saw in Tijuana when we were kids. Joaquin got me to believe that we were going to give everyone equality. Soon, it started to get complicated and Lupita saw it. She saw it and she broke away from the group. Like I said, it started to get messy and when it was decided we needed to do something radical, like torch a beef processing plant, I wanted to leave and come back home, but I knew it was too late. I knew I had no home to go back to. I had messed up everything here and I was in too deep where I was. So, some bad things happened and I had to go live in Mexico. I didn't do anything, but I was there when it happened, so I had to disappear. I stayed in Mexico with the family of one of the workers for a while. Since then, I came back and live in Palmdale. I am going to college out there and if you can believe this, I work in an insurance office."

Albert was quiet. "*Mija*, did you do anything illegal?"

"No dad, but I was close enough to it, that I had to get separated from it. I needed some time and distance, and believe me, after living in Mexico for a few years, I see how good we have it in America, how you and mom made us such a comfortable home. And, I took it all for granted," Annie said as she stopped crying. "I know I have done some wrong, but I am going to make it better. I miss my family, *mi familia*, and I need you. Mommy, I need you."

"Aye Anita," Maria said breaking down and pulling her daughter to her breast.

Within minutes they were both sobbing loudly, just as they had done in the past, which at this point made everyone laugh. The sun had set high in the afternoon sky and was bathing everyone in a golden light as Anita was introduced as "Tia Annie" to her niece and nephew for the first time. Albert asked if she had been at his father's funeral which of course brought more tears when she nodded yes and she further apologized for not joining her family in mourning – and for missing Cathy's funeral as well. Finally, she looked upon her mother who seemed somewhat withered, hollowed and suddenly aged. She asked her why she looked so different. Maria simply responded, "*Mija*, we have all been through so much, but with you here now, I know it will be fine. *Mi familia* will all be fine."

Oree laughed as he mused over the term *mi familia*, which in the past had generally made him bristle. This time the use of the Spanish term didn't seem foreign. It felt like the appropriate phrase to use and it gave him comfort.

"*Mi familia*, my family. This is who we are," he thought, smiling as he looked out toward the sun which was beginning to crest over the hills. "Sometimes your life can end up being so much more than you hoped for."

ACKNOWLEDGEMENTS

This novel was a 25-year journey and there are a number of people to thank for their support and the nourishment of my writing career. First, I thank my parents Manuel and Mary Padilla for being the role models represented in "Coconut." It was they who forged the path for their family, and for Oree and his family, to succeed. To my brothers Vincent, Michael and Mark, thank you for being part of a childhood where we were free to roam, explore and share in some pretty amazing adventures! They provided much of the inspiration for Oree and his siblings. To my nieces, nephews and grand-niece, the world is all yours to have!

Professionally, I wish to thank Fran Krimston for seeing something in a scraggly wanna-be writer, and for developing him into a professional who not only sought to use his head and writing tool, but his heart, in building a career. To The California Endowment, thank you for teaching me the importance of the equality of the human spirit. To my old team at LAPFCU – you always inspired and encouraged me to pursue this dream, and well, now here it is! To my other "family" in alphabetical order -- Diane Block, Dianne Contreras, Tim Griffin, Alan Maletzke, Ruben Moreno, Joanne Peressini, Tom Simi, Deborah Staunton, Jose Thometz and Chester my writing buddy – thank you for suffering this fool gladly as I forced you to sit through countless fables which probably bored the tears out of you. Finally, to Orestes Cardero, you warm and nourish my soul every time it starts to grow cold or faint.

Your simple words of encouragement and support carry more weight in my heart than any ingot of gold.

Lastly, this book is for all the little and not so little people out there who don't fit into any mold, whose skin might be a different color, who may think or act differently, who fear they'll never find their rightful place, or who've been told they're not good enough. Your presence and spirit are very much needed on this planet. History has shown that it is the ones we couldn't possibly perceive as having any worth – it is they who provide this world with its greatest gifts. Keep up the fight. Oree needs you!

REFERENCES

McGuire Sisters. "Sincerely." "Chris, Philly, Dottie." Decca Coral, 1956. Record.

Martha & the Vandellas. "Dancing in the Streets." "Dance Party." Gordy Records, 1965. Record.

King, Ben E. "Stand by Me." "Don't Play That Song." Atco Records. 1961. Record

The Supremes. "Baby Love." "Where Did Our Love Go." Motown. 1964. Record.

Danny & the Juniors. "At the Hop." ABC. 1957. Record.

Earth, Wind & Fire. "Shining Star." "That's The Way of the World." Columbia. 1975. Record.

Deep Purple. "Hush." "Shades of Deep Purple." Parlophone. 1968. Record.

Gaye, Marvin. "Got to Give it Up." "Live at the London Palace." Motown. 1977. Record.

War. "Summer". "Greatest Hits." Rhino. 1976. Record.

Davis, Mac. "It's Hard to Be Humble." "Baby Don't Get Hooked on Me." 1980. Casablanca. Record.

Odyssey. "Native New Yorker." "Odyssey." RCA. 1977. Record.

Chic. "Le Freak." "C'est Chic." Atlantic. 1978. Record.

Frank, Anne. "Diary of a Young Girl." Contact Publishing. 1947. Book.

Leonard, Sheldon. "Andy Griffith Show." CBS. 1960. Television Show.

Sid and Marty Kroftt. "H.R. Pufnstuff." ABC. 1972. Television Show.

Schwartz, Sherwood. "Brady Bunch." ABC. 1969. Television Show.

George Lucas Dir. "American Graffiti." Universal Pictures. 1973. Film.

Steven Spielberg Dir. "Jaws." Universal Pictures. 1975. Film.

William Peter Blatty. "The Exorcist." Harper & Row. 1971. Novel.

Made in the USA
Las Vegas, NV
19 January 2021